MERCY RING  BOOK THREE

# COLE

## NYSSA KATHRYN

COLE
Copyright © 2023 Nyssa Kathryn Sitarenos

All rights reserved.

An NW Partners Book
Cover by Deranged Doctor Design
Developmentally and Copy Edited by Kelli Collins
Line Edited by Jessica Snyder
Proofread by Amanda Cuff and Jen Katemi

❀ Created with Vellum

**She's a single mom with a secret. He's a former Delta who doesn't let people too close.**

Aria Callas understands struggle and sacrifice. Getting pregnant at sixteen, she's spent more than a decade and a half ensuring her and her son's safety the only way she knows how—by staying on the move. Too long in one place and Zac's father bursts back into their lives, bringing nothing but chaos and pain in his wake.

During those same sixteen years, Cole Turner's career as a Delta has taught him just how ugly and unforgiving the world can be. Now retired from the military and running a boxing club, Mercy Ring, with his ex-teammates, life is simple—until he notices the woman living across the street. He vowed years ago to never entrust his heart to another...but he can't get his enigmatic neighbor out of his head.

When familiar danger inevitably finds Aria, Cole can't keep his distance any longer. He'll do whatever it takes to save her, even if that means putting his life—and his heart—on the line once more.

# ACKNOWLEDGMENTS

Thank you, Kelli, you're my book doctor. Thank you for making everything make sense. Jessica, thank you for checking my sentences read the way they're supposed to. Amanda and Jen, thank you for finding all those mistakes that I read over a hundred times and miss.

Thank you to my ARC team, my release wouldn't be what it is without you. Thank you to my beautiful readers. You guys are amazing and push me to write the next book. And thank you to my husband for your patience and support, and my daughter Sophia, for giving me reason.

# CHAPTER 1

$\mathcal{W}$hy on earth Aria Callas had thought coming out to a bar tonight was a good idea, she had no clue. It couldn't be because the brown slatted walls and strong stench of beer and male cologne had drawn her in. And it certainly couldn't be that she'd wanted to pull on these skin-tight jeans and heels that made her feet ache.

She sipped her drink. It was a Brown Derby, one of the only cocktails on the menu here at Lenny's Bar and Grill.

She shot a look at the empty barstool beside her. You'd think by now, she'd have made at least a couple of friends here in Lindeman, Washington. Even one. She'd been here for a whole freaking year. But running an online fitness business, creating exercise routines for women, didn't exactly get her out, about and mingling with the locals.

Gah. She took another sip, watching Lenny hand a beer to a woman down at the other end of the bar. Could she consider Lenny a friend? It would definitely help her feel less pathetic. They chatted whenever she was here. Sure, it was probably out of pity because she was always alone, but hey, she'd take what she could get.

The man stroked his long, bushy beard, which hit his belly. He had a sleeve of tattoos and an ear piercing. In his younger years, he'd probably been really good-looking. That edgy, dangerous kind of good-looking.

As if he felt her eyes on him, he looked her way. His smile lifted her mood a notch.

He moved down the bar toward her. "What's on your mind, girly?"

That was a loaded question. "Oh, you know, just contemplating my life decisions. As you do at a bar." Not all her life decisions. God, that would give her a complex.

He slung a towel over his shoulder. "How's that going for you?"

Her lips quirked. "Does it ever go well for anyone?"

"Nope."

"Didn't think so." Her gaze caught on the wood-slatted walls again. "Hey, you ever thought about bringing some color into this place? Adding some color, or maybe a nice modern stone?"

"Not once."

Fair enough. "Well, if you change your mind, I know a fabulous design—"

"No." He leaned over the bar. "I've owned and run this bar for forty years. Haven't had a single complaint till you waltzed your skinny butt in here."

Aria grinned. "So you waited forty years for your design angel?"

He huffed, but she saw the hint of a smile on his face. What the hell, she was gonna call it. The guy was officially on her friends list.

When his gaze landed on something over her shoulder, she turned her head.

The smile slipped from her lips. *Oh God.* What was he doing here?

Cole stepped into the bar, closely followed by two other men who looked just as dark, handsome and dangerous. The guy had recently moved in across the street from her. She was pretty sure one of the men with him lived there, too.

Memories from that very afternoon whipped through her mind. Of her sixteen-year-old son pushing her out of the way so he could get to his car. Of Cole storming across the road and reprimanding Zac.

Zac would never hurt her. Sure, he got angry, but he was sixteen. The same age she'd been when she'd had him. Cole's intervention hadn't been necessary...but at the same time, his attempt to protect her had a little trill of awareness rushing through her body. Or maybe that was his chiseled jaw and deep, smooth voice.

Tonight, his thick biceps stretched the fabric of his charcoal shirt. He wore jeans that did nothing to hide his powerful legs. And God, he was tall. Well over six feet and built like a gladiator.

The guy was sexy, but a smile once in a while wouldn't hurt.

She turned back to Lenny. "Do you know them?"

Lenny nodded, lifting a glass from the sink and drying it with his bar towel. "Cole and Ryker work at Mercy Ring, the new boxing club."

Her heated blood turned cold, and she had to force herself not to flinch at the word "boxing".

"The third guy," Lenny continued, not seeming to notice her minor internal breakdown, "Erik, comes in every so often but lives a bit out of town from what I hear. They're all former military."

They definitely looked it.

"But not all boxers?" Aria asked, trying to keep her voice steady.

"Erik supposedly spent a bit of time in the professional boxing world. But not the other two. I wouldn't discount them though. They're former Deltas. I'm sure they could take down the meanest opponent."

3

She gave Lenny a tight smile before he moved down the bar.

Boxing club. She lived across the road from people who ran a *boxing club*. Great. If that wasn't a glaring sign from the universe telling her to stay the heck away from the man, nothing would be. She couldn't get close to a boxer.

Not again.

A shudder coursed down her spine at the thought.

She took a sip of her cocktail. The cool liquid tingled on her tongue. Maybe she shouldn't have come out tonight. Maybe she should have stayed safely within the walls of her home and...and what? Drank a cocktail alone and watched reruns of *Dream Home Makeover* on Netflix?

Pfft. No. She'd needed to get out of the house. The work she did was remote, meaning she spent all day, every day, at home—alone—a lot of it on her laptop. Sure, she was active. She couldn't live without her morning runs and daily workouts, but neither helped her interact with real people. She'd volunteered at Zac's previous schools, but every other parent was at least ten years her senior and looked at her like she was in the wrong place.

Nope. Definitely not the wrong place. The second the stick turned pink, she'd been thrust into adulthood. Into a world of diapers and little sleep and being responsible for another human. Her parents had been no help. Instead of supporting their teenage daughter, they'd kicked her out of her family home because no way were Mr. and Mrs. Callas raising a baby along-side their teen daughter.

Her jaw tightened at the memory. She hadn't seen her parents in a long time, and she didn't intend to.

A familiar guilt swam in her chest that Zac didn't have more family. That she was it. But she'd spent her life making sure he had everything he needed and that he was safe.

With a small exhale, she gave into temptation and turned her head. Immediately, she spotted her neighbor standing at a high bar table with his friends. Her heart clenched at the sight of two women with them, both tall and beautiful. Were they models? And where were their clothes? They wore dresses that showed a lot of skin.

One of the women, a redhead, touched Cole's shoulder.

Suddenly, his gaze hit Aria's. She sucked in a sharp breath and looked away.

Dang it. He'd caught her staring.

"Hey."

She turned to face a man beside her. Or really, less of a man, more of a boy. He had short, light brown hair and straight white teeth but a young face. God, he didn't look much older than Zac. Was he old enough to be in here?

"Hey." She gave him a tight smile and looked away.

The stool scraped against the floor beside her, then she felt his heat against her shoulder. He wasn't quite touching her, but he was close. Too close.

She frowned at him. "What are you doing?"

One side of his mouth lifted. "Thought I could buy you another drink."

The smile on his face wasn't the charming look she was sure he was going for. Creepy? Sure. Unsettling? Definitely.

She lifted her glass. "I have a drink."

Instead of standing and moving away, he leaned closer. "Come on, babe. One drink. Maybe a dance."

She almost laughed. Or maybe she actually did, because his eyes narrowed. "Babe? Kid, I'm probably old enough to be your mother. You need to go home before Lenny IDs you."

She rose, but the guy quickly stood with her, stepping into her space. "What, I'm not good enough for you?"

Okay, now he was pissing her off. She gave him one big shove and he stumbled back. "You're not *old* enough for me. I already have a kid I take care of. I don't need another." She lifted her drink from the bar and moved away from him before he could say anything else.

Really? She was being hit on by kids now? Could the man not see she was in her thirties?

She was weaving through the crowd when her gaze once more caught on a very dark set of eyes. Cole was looking directly at her. For a moment, she paused. There was something hard and intense in his expression. His muscles were bunched, and he looked a stone's throw away from...what? She wasn't sure.

His gaze shifted to the kid at the bar. Had Cole been about to come over and step in like he'd stepped in earlier today when she and Zac had been arguing outside her house?

She took a breath and moved over to a tall bar table before taking a big gulp of her drink. Maybe she looked like she needed saving. Which probably wasn't far from the truth.

God, she needed to finish her cocktail and go home, because that man's eyes were doing things to her that they should not be doing.

She sent a quick text to Zac as she took another sip.

*Are you okay?*

Their relationship had been so strained these last few months. Actually, not just these last few months. The last few *years*. What happened to her sweet little boy who'd looked at her like she was his world? Around fourteen, that kid had gone *poof* and disappeared, only to be replaced by a tall, moody teenager. A teenager who was looking more like his father every day. He had his dad's eyes and black hair.

She took another gulp of her drink. *Don't think about him, Aria.*

Zac was *not* like his father. Not even close.

Anytime she *did* think about that man, she practically broke out into hives. He was scary. He was also the reason they moved around a lot. Why make it easy for him to find them? Whenever he did, he brought trouble in his wake.

Her phone dinged from the table.

*I'm fine, Mom. You don't need to worry. I just needed to get out of the house.*

Out of the house and away from *her*? Argh. She hated arguing with him. The memory of their argument this afternoon replayed in her mind. Of her reminding Zac they might have to move again. Of the anger and frustration that washed over his face.

And she got it. She did. He was a kid. He wanted stability. He wanted to finish his final years of high school in the same place. He also hated his father and didn't want the guy to dictate their lives. She understood *all* of that.

But she also understood that her ex was damn good at finding her when she stayed still for too long, and when he did, it never ended well for them.

It was her job to protect her son, just like she'd been doing for the last sixteen years.

God, she'd been so dumb to get mixed up with her ex. But to be fair, he hadn't turned into the scumbag he was until a few years later. At least, she was pretty sure he hadn't. The warning signs had probably always been there. The only good thing to come out of their relationship was Zac. She loved that kid more than she loved anything else in the world. Exactly why she would do whatever was needed to keep him safe.

She quickly typed back a response.

*Stay safe. I love you. X*

She watched her phone for a couple of minutes, hoping for a response, but none came through. With a sigh, her gaze moved across the room again. Her insides rolled. The redhead was now all over Cole. Hanging off his shoulder. Pressing her breasts into his side.

Well, if that was what he was into, it was none of her business.

Another big gulp of her cocktail.

When her phone vibrated again, she looked down. She frowned when the words blurred a bit. She lifted the cell and pulled it closer to her eyes. Zac.

*Love you too, Mom. And I'm sorry about pushing you today. I was frustrated. I'll see you tomorrow. Xox*

She wanted to smile at the response, but she was too busy trying to figure out why the words were so fuzzy. No, not just the words—the phone itself. Her *hand*.

Why the hell did she have to blink three times and squint before the words made sense? This was her first drink.

Frowning, she slid her phone into her pocket and when she tried to take a step away from the table, her legs shook. She stopped and grabbed the table to stay steady. What the heck was going on? Was she sick?

Aria blew out a breath and tried to take another step. Suddenly, she was exhausted. For a moment, she closed her eyes to breathe.

When she opened them, men's shoes stood in front of her.

# CHAPTER 2

*S*omeone was watching him. Cole felt eyes on them the second he stepped into the bar. He was careful to keep his features neutral as he turned his head left and glanced around the large room. The bar was busy, and the combination of music and voices made it loud.

Ryker and Erik walked closely behind. Could they feel it too? Or were the eyes only on him?

When he didn't see anyone, he covertly swept his gaze around the right side of the room. That's when he saw her. She was just turning her head back to the bar, so their gazes never met, but he knew who it was.

Aria.

His muscles twitched, and there was a kick in his gut. Fuck. He'd come here to get the woman out of his damn head. Because going over there this afternoon and having a single conversation with her had made unfamiliar emotions invade his body. Which emotions, exactly, he wasn't sure. Something that drew him in. Something that made him want to go to her now. Talk to her.

He shut his emotions down and moved to the furthest free table from the bar.

Ryker joined him, and Erik went to the bar to grab some beers. Cole refused to look over there, in case his gaze darted back to her.

Ryker frowned. "What's got you tense all of a sudden?"

Shit. Was he that damn obvious?

"I'm not tense." Lie. And his friend no doubt heard it. But Cole sure as hell wouldn't be admitting to anything.

Ryker was silent, which was worse than words.

When Erik returned to the table, he set down three beers. "Is that your neighbor at the bar?"

*Shit.*

Ryker shot a glance over his shoulder, and when he looked back, he had a huge fucking grin on his face. "Yes, it is. Funny, I was just telling Cole he looked tense. Wonder if the two are related."

One side of Erik's mouth lifted. "You *do* look tense."

He took a swig of his beer and remained silent.

"She's pretty." Ryker turned to Erik. "Is she wearing those tight jeans she always has on that hug her ass?"

Cole's jaw clenched.

"Yep." Erik nodded. "And she's matched them with some sexy heels."

The guys were trying to get a rise out of him. And fuck, it was working. Ryker had caught him staring at her through the window too many times in recent weeks. And Erik was around often enough that he'd probably seen it too. They'd *both* watched him go across the street this afternoon when that kid of hers had shoved her.

Anger pulsed through his veins at the memory. He hated seeing men getting rough with women. Didn't matter that he was a teenager or her kid. He shouldn't have touched her like that. Not that she'd seemed grateful for the intervention. Actually, she'd almost seemed annoyed. He wasn't sorry, though, and he'd do it again.

"Well, her kid brother's obviously not here," Ryker said. "This could be your chance to get her alone, Cole."

"Son."

Both guys frowned, but it was Ryker who answered. "What?"

"The kid's her son."

Ryker shot a surprised look over his shoulder. "He looks around sixteen. That would either make her a hell of a lot older than she looks, or she must have had him when she was—"

"Sixteen herself," Cole finished. Yeah, he'd been surprised by that little fact too.

Erik whistled. "Sounds like there's a story there."

He was sure there was. One that he wanted to learn. Not that he'd be admitting that to his friends, because then he wouldn't hear the end of it. And it didn't matter that he wanted to know her story. He wasn't a relationship kind of person, and something told him *she* was.

That didn't mean he avoided women. He didn't. But he was careful to only involve himself with those who understood he wasn't looking for anything long-term. Hell, he didn't even do *short* relationships. He didn't date.

He heard the click of heels before he saw them. Two women stopped at their table—a redhead, who stood between him and Erik, and a brunette, who leaned on the table between Erik and Ryker. Both wore short, tight dresses and heels that brought them up to Cole's shoulder.

The redhead smiled, her eyes only for him. "Hi. We couldn't help but notice you boys were alone."

The brunette shot her gaze between Erik and Ryker. "I'm Janice, and this is Violet. Want some company?"

Violet touched his shoulder, but he barely noticed. Not when he felt it again—the heat of someone's eyes on him. He told himself not to look. Fuck, he shouted it in his head. But it was like he had no damn control. His gaze lifted and collided with

Aria's bright aqua stare. Her chest rose, like she was sucking in a large breath. Surprised he was looking at her too?

Something kicked in his chest.

She swung her attention back to the bar. He was about to look away when he noticed a guy drop onto the stool beside hers. He sat close. Too close. The guy said something to her, and she responded.

*Look away, Cole. It's none of your business.*

Before he could turn his attention back to his friends, Aria rose. The guy stood with her. He leaned into her personal space.

Cole straightened. Violet said something, but it was like background noise, his entire focus on the bar. He was moments from moving over there when Aria pressed her hand to the guy's chest and shoved him away.

Good. The guy looked pissed, but Aria didn't seem to care. She grabbed her drink and walked away. As she moved across the bar, her gaze flicked to him again. For a moment, she stilled, and they just watched each other. Something passed between them. Something intense and unfamiliar. Something he had no fucking idea how to navigate.

Then his gaze switched to the asshole at the bar. The guy was watching her too, but when he didn't make a move to follow her, Cole relaxed slightly. The only thing he hated more than an asshole, was an asshole who couldn't take no for an answer.

The fingers on his shoulder tightened, pulling his attention back to the redhead.

She frowned. "Hey. You okay?"

He stepped out of her hold. "I'm fine."

He wasn't in the mood to be touched. Not by her. And damn if it wasn't taking everything inside him not to look over at his neighbor again.

The brunette, Janice, was talking to Erik and Ryker. He'd hoped Violet would get the message and do the same. Instead, she stepped closer to him again. She wasn't touching him anymore, but he could almost feel the heat of her body.

"What's your name?"

"Cole." He took another swig of his beer. Maybe coming out tonight hadn't been such a great idea. Maybe he should have gone to Mercy Ring and hit the shit out of a bag. They'd only opened the business a little over a month ago, but it had quickly become his second home. Only a year ago, he'd broken his back in his final mission as a Delta operator. It had taken months of rest then rehab to heal. Now, he'd finally regained his strength and fitness, and he didn't take that for granted for a second. He worked out often.

He was at Mercy Ring almost every day. He ran the place with his three former Delta teammates. Ryker and Jackson had grown up in this town. Cole, Jackson and Declan had come here for Ryker's funeral. Which was one hell of a long story, when you considered Ryker was standing in the bar with him at that very second.

When Jackson had asked him and Declan to stay and join him in opening the boxing gym, it had been a no-brainer. After the tumultuous last year, being active and with his team was what he lived for now.

Violet pressed her body into his side, interrupting his thoughts.

He was done with this. He stepped away from her again, ignoring her pout. "I'm not interested."

With a final swig of his beer, he left the table and headed for the bar. When the guy who'd been talking to Aria brushed passed him, Cole's eyes narrowed as he watched where he was headed.

Did the asshole not understand the word no? Cole may not have heard what was said between them, but he understood what a shove to the chest and her moving across the room meant. He watched the guy right up until he stopped in front of her. He waited for her to push him away again.

Instead, she swayed on her feet, and the guy grabbed her arm to steady her.

*Fuck.* How much had she had to drink tonight?

Cole moved through the crowd, keeping Aria and the asshole in his sights. When the guy slid an arm around her waist and began to lead her toward the door, Cole saw red.

He quickly moved in front of them, blocking the exit. "Get off her."

The guy frowned. "Who the hell are you?"

Cole ignored the question. "Don't make me ask again, kid."

"I'm just helping her get home."

He stepped forward, adrenaline pumping through him. "Last chance. Take your arm off her before I break it."

The guy's eyes widened. There was a beat of silence. Then, finally, he released her and stepped back. "Whatever," he muttered.

Aria swayed, and immediately Cole slid an arm around her waist to steady her. Shit, she really was wasted. He looked over at Ryker and Erik. Both guys were watching him. Had probably been watching the entire exchange in case they'd needed to step in. He signaled that he was leaving and got two quick nods in response.

He waited until they were outside to look at Aria. She was leaning heavily against his side.

"You okay?" he asked softly.

"I'm tired," she breathed. "And I feel really uncoordinated…"

"Yeah, alcohol does that," he muttered, not sure if she heard him or not. "Where's your car?"

She blinked a few times as she looked around. He followed the direction of her gaze and spotted her little red Beetle.

As he led her toward it, he carried almost all of her weight. His blood was still pounding in his ears from the altercation with the kid. What had he been planning? To get her into his car, then take her back to his place?

14

When she stumbled, he sighed quietly before sweeping her into his arms. "How much did you drink?" The woman didn't strike him as the kind of person to go to a bar alone and get wasted. But then, he didn't really know her.

When she lay her head on his shoulder, something flickered in his chest. She felt good in his arms. Too good.

"Only had one," she mumbled.

He stopped at her car and lowered her to her feet. "One?" This was not the work of a single drink. Before she could answer, he held out his hand. "Can I have your key, honey?"

The endearment slipped out unconsciously. He had no damn idea where it had come from.

He kept her steady with a hand on her shoulder while she slipped the key chain from her pocket. It held a single pair— probably car and house.

When the car door was open, he helped her into the passenger seat before reaching across her chest for the seat belt. He was careful to make sure he touched her body as little as possible. The woman clearly did something to him that others didn't. He wanted to avoid it at all costs.

Once she was belted in, he sucked down a quick breath, moved around the car and slid into the driver's side. God, this car was tiny. He was used to his big truck.

He pulled out of the parking lot and shot glances her way every few seconds. She scrubbed at her face, but her movements were slow and clumsy.

"You okay?" he asked quietly.

"I don't know what's wrong with me. Maybe..." She stopped. Whether she stopped from exhaustion or she just lost her train of thought, he wasn't sure.

She rested her head against the window. He frowned as he continued to drive. What if he hadn't been there tonight? She'd have been alone and vulnerable.

The thought had an uncomfortable feeling settling in his gut.

When he looked at her again, her eyes were closed. Thank God they lived close to the bar. He gingerly lifted her wrist to count her heartbeats. Normal. Everything about her looked normal. She'd just had too much to drink.

Maybe he needed to have a conversation with Lenny about him and his bartenders overserving.

When they reached her place, he got out and lifted her from the car. She barely stirred as he carried her to the house. When she nuzzled into his chest, his heart raced. God, he needed to get away from this woman.

Shifting Aria enough to hold her with one arm, he unlocked her front door and opened it.

"Bedroom?" he asked quietly.

She mumbled a response, but he had no damn clue what it was. Looked like it was up to him to find it.

A small living room opened into the kitchen on the right. Moving down a short hall, his gaze shot to a room immediately on the left. A bed centered the space, but it had dark, masculine sheets. He saw a guitar and noted men's clothing scattered around haphazardly. It was a mess. That was her son's room.

He continued, ignoring the way Aria nuzzled into his chest again. Her small moan that pierced the quiet. *Shut it down, Cole. The woman's drunk.*

The next room on the left had a desk on one side and workout equipment on the other. A treadmill, a bike, and some dumbbells.

He passed a bathroom on the right, then the last room was a pretty, feminine space. There was an earthy look to it, with beige sheets and a wooden bed and bedside tables. A couple of potted plants adorned the dresser, and there was a huge framed print on the wall of a younger Aria with her son. He looked maybe ten.

Cole moved to the bed and lay her down. Quickly, he removed her shoes. Once she was under the covers, he drew in a long breath. Why did touching the woman feel like torture?

He shook his head before once again lifting her wrist and checking her pulse. It was steady. Still, he didn't want to leave. He had no idea how many drinks she'd had, but she'd passed out almost immediately. She needed someone here to check on her throughout the night in case she got sick, and her son clearly wasn't home.

With a soft growl, he removed his own shoes, then sent a quick text to Ryker that he wasn't going to be returning home tonight. He'd sleep on the floor beside her bed. It wouldn't be the most comfortable night, but he'd had worse.

# CHAPTER 3

*A*ria scrunched her eyes closed. Man, she felt tired. It was a bone-deep, heavy-eyes-and-limbs kind of tired.

Was she sick? Did she have the flu?

She forced her eyes open. Not the flu. Her head felt fine, and she wasn't sniffly or coughing. So maybe a virus? Slowly, she pushed up to a sitting position, almost groaning at the effort it took. It was like gravity was pulling her back down with everything it had.

She swept her gaze around the room, pausing on the glass of water and pills beside her bed. Had Zac put them there? It was something he'd done in the past when she'd been ill.

Shoving the comforter off her legs, she realized she'd gone to bed fully dressed. Something she never did.

Next, her gaze caught on a pillow on the floor beside the bed, and she frowned. Then the shoes near the door...men's shoes.

Not Zac's.

Her lips separated. Someone had slept here.

What the heck was going on?

She frowned, trying to recall the previous day. Zac had

stormed out of the house, angry. She'd been trying to stop him from leaving when her neighbor had intervened. She'd gone to a bar that evening, still attempting to calm her nerves after the altercation with Zac and the neighbor. That's when everything got a little fuzzy.

She scrunched her eyes closed, concentrating. Fragmented parts of the night came back to her. Lenny. Cole stepping into the bar and grabbing a table with his friends. A kid hitting on her. Then…nothing.

Her skin was cold, even though the room was warm. Why couldn't she remember?

Carefully, she swung her legs over the bed, hating how fatigued she felt. She reached for the glass of water. The second the cool liquid hit her throat, she groaned in satisfaction. She was dehydrated. She was *never* dehydrated. As a personal trainer and fitness consultant, she made drinking water a priority.

She eyed the pills warily. Nope. Not gonna touch them without knowing what they were.

When she stood, she breathed a sigh of relief. Good. Her legs held. She swapped her jeans and shirt from the previous night for a pair of leggings, a sports bra and an oversized sweatshirt.

With a deep breath, she opened her door. Immediately, a savory smell hit her. Was that eggs and bacon? Cautiously, she stepped into the living room—where her feet slammed to a stop.

Because there, by the stove, was a man she barely knew. A man she tried like hell not to think about because he was too tall, dark and handsome.

"Cole?"

He turned his head. He didn't crack a smile, but then she'd never seen one on his face, so it wasn't a huge surprise. "You're up. How are you feeling?"

Slowly, she moved into the room, watching as he set eggs on top of a piece of bread that already had cheese and bacon on it.

Okay, she was still asleep, right? This was one big confusing dream.

"Are you making fried egg sandwiches?" she asked quietly. Her stomach growled loudly when she caught another whiff of the food, and her cheeks heated. Oh Lord.

Cole didn't comment on the embarrassing sound her stomach made, but the corners of his lips twitched. "I am. You had all the ingredients, and it's what I like to eat when I'm hungover. Not that I've been hungover for a while."

Hungover? She shook her head. He was wrong. She didn't have a headache...not even a little one. She just felt tired. "I'm not hungover."

His gaze flashed up to hers, and her breath caught in her throat. A little bit of Cole's attention made her skin tingle, but all of it? It made every single inch of her body tighten.

He tilted his head to the side. "You don't get hangovers after a big night of drinking?"

"Oh, I do...when I've *had* a big night of drinking. Not when I've had one cocktail." She was a mom who ran her own business. More than that, she had a dangerous ex. She couldn't afford to go out and get drunk. Had she even finished that single drink last night?

She expected surprise. Maybe confusion. So the humor that danced in Cole's eyes puzzled her. She straightened her spine. "You don't believe me?"

Finally, he dragged his gaze away, and the breaths moved in and out of her with a bit more ease. He topped both sandwiches with another piece of bread, then turned toward her.

God, the man was so broad and muscled. And standing here, in her small kitchen where he took up all the space, he looked even bigger.

"What I think," he said slowly, "is that I had to carry you across the parking lot last night at Lenny's Bar because you could barely walk."

Her skin chilled yet again. *No.* That wasn't right.

"Then," he continued, "when we got here, you barely opened your eyes when I lifted you from the car, took you inside, and tucked you into bed."

"You're lying," she whispered. He had to be.

The fine hairs on her arms stood on end, because something told her this man didn't lie...or joke...or make things up.

"I'm not. You were wasted." He turned around, all but dismissing her. The muscles in his back rippled through his shirt as he spoke. "I slept on the floor beside your bed and did hourly checks to make sure you didn't throw up in your sleep or anything."

If her current situation wasn't what it was, she might have felt her heart flutter for Cole's obvious care of her. But right now, all she could feel was cold and clammy. Something was wrong. *Very* wrong. The fact that Cole thought she'd been drunk when she knew it wasn't true. The fact that she couldn't remember the night before. The idea that she'd passed out.

Without hesitating, she spun around and returned to her bedroom.

"Aria?"

Ignoring Cole's call, she swiped her cell from her bedside table and searched for a number.

The bar owner answered on the fifth ring. "Lenny speaking."

Thank God he was there. "Hi, Lenny. This is Aria Callas. I was wondering if you keep video surveillance in your bar."

There was a beat of silence. "Uh, yeah, I do. Why?"

Her heart pounded. "I know you're not open right now, but could I come down and watch the footage? I think I was drugged last night."

EVERY MUSCLE in Cole's body tensed at Aria's words. He'd followed Aria to her room and caught those last two sentences.

Drugged?

When she hung up, she didn't even look at him. She donned socks, then grabbed her running shoes and pulled them on. Her fingers trembled, and that alone made his gut tighten.

"You think you were drugged?" he asked, dread and disbelief thick in his voice.

"Yes. Did you drive me here in my car?"

The sudden fury was like a tidal wave, washing through every part of him. "Yes."

"Good." She stood and left the room.

He grabbed his shoes and pulled them on before going after her. She'd made it a few steps from the front door when he grabbed her arm. "Hey."

A beat passed before she finally looked up at him. That's when he saw it—the fear in her eyes. The uncertainty. She didn't want it to be true any more than he did.

He took a small step closer. "Are you okay?" He kept his voice gentle, even though he wanted to rage. He wanted to go out there and find the asshole who'd done this and break every bone in his body.

She blinked, her eyes shooting between his. "I don't—"

The door to the house suddenly opened and Zac stepped inside. The kid was tall for his age, and where Aria had caramel-blonde hair and aqua eyes, Zac had black hair and dark eyes to match.

He stopped, his gaze shooting to the hand Cole still had on Aria's arm, then back up.

She tugged out of his hold. "Zac...you're home."

"I am." Zac stared at Cole. "What are you doing here?"

Aria spoke first. "He drove me home from the bar last night. I felt a bit sick, so he stayed the night to watch over me."

22

Zac frowned. "You were sick enough that he stayed? Are you okay?"

The same question Cole had just asked. But while he was pretty sure he'd been about to receive a truthful answer, he wasn't so certain she'd give the same to her son.

"Yes. All better. I'm just popping out for a bit."

There was another pause, where Zac looked at his mother with concern and questions, then he gave a quick nod. "Okay. Call if you need anything."

"You should eat something first," Cole said to Aria, the second Zac disappeared into his room and closed the door.

She shook her head. "No. I feel sick to my stomach at the possibility that someone—" She stopped, eyes flashing to Zac's door. "I'm not hungry."

He wasn't either. Not anymore. He pressed a hand to the small of her back and led her outside. He expected her to pull away from his touch. She didn't.

They'd just reached her car when he slid the keys from her hand.

Her brows twitched. "What are you—"

"I'm driving."

She shook her head. "You don't need to do that."

"If you *were* drugged last night, you shouldn't be driving. Not yet."

She nibbled her bottom lip, seeming to consider his words. His gaze shot down to that lip, and desire slammed into his gut.

"Okay," she finally said, moving around the car and sliding into the passenger seat.

He released a long breath and slid behind the wheel.

Neither of them spoke during the drive to the bar, but he could almost feel the tension bouncing off her. It matched his own. If she *had* been drugged, and he hadn't been there—

His fingers wrapped around the wheel so hard, his knuckles

were white. No. He couldn't think about that. He hardly knew the woman, but he still wanted her safe.

He'd barely stopped in the bar parking lot before Aria climbed out. She frowned when he joined her. "You don't have to come in."

He could have laughed, even though there was nothing funny about this situation. "I'm coming with you."

She almost looked confused. "But you don't need—"

"I'm coming in." That was nonnegotiable. If the woman had been drugged right under his nose, he needed to know.

She swallowed. Then, with a sigh, she nodded. Cole opened the door, not surprised to find it unlocked. Lenny lived upstairs, and even when the place wasn't open, the guy rarely locked it during the day. Seemed to be a small-town thing.

A grim-looking Lenny met them in the back hallway. Cole's insides clenched. Had he already watched the footage?

"Come with me, guys." He turned, and they followed him down the hall. "I've already called the police."

Aria stopped just inside the office. "Why?"

Cole ground his teeth, taking in the open laptop on the desk. She knew why. They both did.

Lenny dropped into a seat and pointed to the two on the other side of the desk. "Sit."

Aria started to shake her head, but Cole pressed a hand to the small of her back. Lenny spun the laptop around, and Cole urged Aria into a chair. By Lenny's dark mood, Cole knew she'd need to be sitting to watch this.

He sat beside her. He could almost hear Aria's breathing speed up as Lenny pressed play and the footage came to life.

Aria was sitting at the bar, her head turned. Toward him?

Cole's muscles tensed when he saw the kid drop onto the stool beside her. When she looked back toward the bar, then at the kid again, it was clear as day that Aria wasn't comfortable.

They exchanged words—but it wasn't until they both stood that Cole's skin iced.

When the kid stepped forward, crowding her, he slipped something into her drink.

Beside him, Aria sucked in a sharp breath.

It was subtle. So subtle, they only saw it because they were looking for it.

*Son of a bitch.*

He lifted his gaze to Lenny. "Who is he?"

"I don't know. I don't recall seeing him last night. I checked over the prior footage. He came in shortly before Aria, but he never ordered a drink. If he had, we would have ID'd him."

The little shit never ordered a drink? So he came in for the sole purpose of finding some unlucky victim and drugging her. It took everything inside Cole not to get up and punch his fist through a wall. He didn't know Aria at all, really...but for some unknown reason, he felt the need to protect her.

"He tried to walk out with her," Cole said quietly. "I told him to get lost and drove her home." But *damn*, he wished he'd known. He certainly wouldn't have let the kid just walk away.

When a visible shudder raced through Aria's body, he returned his hand to her back. She looked at him, and there was shock and fear in her eyes. But there was also anger. A lot of it.

"If you hadn't been there..."

"I was." Thank God for that.

She swallowed, her gaze never leaving his. Her lips separated to say something, but a knock came on the bar door. Lenny moved out of the room and reappeared a minute later with two uniformed officers, a man and a woman.

The man dipped his head. "Hi, I'm Officer Henry Hanon, and this is Officer Mandy Jenkins."

The woman also nodded.

"I'm Aria Callas," she said quietly.

"Cole Turner."

Hanon looked back to Lenny. "You said there was something we need to see?"

Lenny cleared his throat and moved back to the laptop. "Yes."

He played the same footage for the officers. But instead of watching the replay, Cole watched Aria, a sudden need to keep her close flooding his system.

# CHAPTER 4

*D*rugged. She'd been freaking *drugged*. An entire day had passed since she'd watched that video surveillance, and it still didn't feel real.

She moved her legs faster, pounding the concrete like she was being chased by a demon. Which she was. Only the demon was in her head. She needed to run like she needed air to breathe. Music blasted into her ears from the wireless earbuds. It did nothing to block out the world like she'd hoped it would.

After leaving Lenny's Bar and Grill yesterday, she'd gone to the hospital, and they'd run some tests to see exactly what she'd been drugged with. She'd expected the results to come back with some expensive street narcotic. She'd just assumed that was what assholes used for date-rape drugs.

A shudder rocked her spine at the thought. She ran faster.

But no, that wasn't what had been slipped into her drink. It was Klonopin. An anti-anxiety medication taken by millions of Americans every damn day. Apparently, when the drug was mixed with alcohol, it caused drowsiness and other symptoms, making it an effective date-rape drug.

She swallowed. She hadn't told Zac what happened, and she didn't plan to. The kid had enough going on.

Cole's dark eyes flashed in her mind. He'd stayed with her the entire morning yesterday, until she'd finally forced him to leave her at the hospital while she waited for the results. It hadn't been easy to get him to go. He'd wanted to stay. Hell, *she'd* wanted him to stay. The smallest touch had calmed so much of the storm inside her. But eventually, when she'd convinced him she was okay, he called a friend to pick him up.

She took measured breaths as she ran. She'd seen the emotions play out in his eyes before he left. Uncertainty. Anger. Guilt. The last one was ridiculous. The man had saved her. She owed him a debt she'd probably never be able to repay.

But that wasn't the only reason she couldn't get the guy out of her head. Man, why did she always have a thing for muscular, broody guys? Zac's father had been similar.

She swallowed at the thought of her ex. Nope. She was not going there today. And she certainly wasn't going to compare him to Cole. Cole had already proven with his every action—taking her home from Lenny's, watching over her throughout the night, staying by her side the next morning, all the comforting touches—that he was ten times the man Zac's father was.

She'd barely dated since leaving her ex eleven years ago, but on the rare occasion when she had, the guy always turned out to be an asshole. She'd been cheated on. Yelled at during fights, then made to feel like she was the bad guy. One time, a date had admitted to regularly taking illegal drugs like it was no big deal. Argh.

Apparently, she was great at choosing the bad ones.

She pumped her arms as she turned a corner onto her street. She was so deep in her head that when a hand touched her shoulder, her heart slammed into her ribs and she screamed.

She spun around so fast, she would have fallen on her ass if the hand hadn't suddenly clutched her arm to keep her upright.

A second later, the air whooshed from her chest in relief.

It was just Cole. A very unhappy-looking Cole.

She leaned over, trying hard to catch her breath. Holy crap, that had scared her to death. Once she could breathe again, she yanked out the earbuds. "What the heck, Cole? You scared the hell out of me."

"You shouldn't be running in the dark while listening to music. You need to be aware of your surroundings. What if I was a serial killer?"

Well, that was kind of like a "sorry for scaring you," except it wasn't.

"It's not dark. The sun's rising."

Well, it was a little bit dark, but hell, she was an early riser and liked to get her run in before the world woke up.

Cole stepped closer, and she almost stepped back. God, the guy was intimidating. In a very sexy way, of course. "It *is* dark, Aria. That, in combination with the earbuds, gives you impaired vision and hearing. That makes you an easy target."

She swallowed at his words. Okay, no easing of her heartbeat happening here. She lowered her voice in an attempt to calm him. "I run every morning. I've always been fine." Not the strongest argument, but it was all she had.

A small growl sounded, and it drew her attention to his chest. At the way his shirt pulled tightly over his muscled pecs.

*Do not look down at those powerful legs poking out of his running shorts, Aria.*

When her gaze returned to his, she almost felt like she deserved a pat on the back or a gold star.

"I'm not trying to scare you." His deep, smooth voice rolled over her tingly skin. "I called out, but you couldn't hear me."

Yeah, that was because of her pounding, block-out-the-world music.

"I appreciate the advice, Cole." That was really all she could give him. She couldn't promise the guy she wouldn't do it again.

She relied on her morning runs and her music to get through the day.

He sighed, as if he heard the words behind her words. Then his voice gentled. "How are you doing after yesterday?"

Yesterday. The terrible day that had been made a little bit better by this man. "I'm okay." If okay meant getting two hours of sleep because nightmares about what could have happened riddled her mind when she closed her eyes.

Something flashed in Cole's expression. Yeah, he saw right through her. "Any news on the guy?"

She swallowed. "Hanon called last night to tell me they don't know who he is yet, and they have no leads." So, he had a big fat nothing for her.

Cole cursed under his breath.

She stared at the earbuds between her fingers. "Everything was such a blur yesterday that I didn't actually get a chance to thank you." She looked up, studying him. "So...thank you."

"You don't need to thank me."

She felt like she did. He'd been her angel. Her very angry-looking angel.

"Do you have your phone?"

Her brows shot up at his question. "Uh, yes."

"I meant to give you my number yesterday, just in case."

In case she needed him to save her again? She swallowed. "Oh, sure." She pulled her cell from the pocket on her thigh and handed it to him. When their hands grazed, her skin tingled yet again. God, why did he have such an effect on her?

She nibbled her bottom lip as he typed in his number. When he handed it back, their fingers touched again, and yep, another sizzle of her skin.

"Call if you need anything," he said quietly.

He stepped away and looked like he was about to continue his run but then glanced at her once more. She breathed in his deep, masculine scent when he reached out and squeezed her arm. "No more running in the dark with music blaring."

She nodded because, well, she'd probably agree to give this man her left kidney right now if he asked. His hand had just dropped when her phone vibrated. She looked down.

The smile left her mouth. She felt the blood leave her face, and for a moment, she forgot how to breathe.

Her ex—Zac's father. He hadn't contacted them in over a year, but whenever he did, it was never good.

At the feel of warm fingers on her cheek, Aria's gaze shot up to see that instead of moving away, Cole had taken a step closer. Had he said something to her? His fingers were the only warmth on her body right now.

The phone stopped ringing, and she forced a smile to her lips. "Sorry, did you say something?"

His eyes flicked between hers, and they were so deep and intense, she could almost forget who had just called...almost.

"I asked if everything was okay."

Okay? No. She was never okay when it came to Zac's father.

"It's fine." As much as she wanted to share her deepest, darkest secrets with this beautiful stranger, they weren't close enough for that. He didn't need to know the truth about her complicated life.

He watched her for another beat before giving a quick nod. "All right."

Finally, his hand dropped, and the cold flowing through every other part of her body replaced the warmth in her cheek.

"Remember, call if you need anything."

She nodded, then watched as he jogged away.

The second he was gone, the panic tried to swamp her, but she pushed it down and walked the rest of the way to her house. The last time Zac's father had called, it was because he needed money. Not only that, but people had actually come to her house looking for him. Bad people.

If history was any indication, she had about a month before

he showed up in town. Two, tops. She swore he paid people to find her. Although he'd never admitted that.

Nausea swirled in her belly. She pushed through her front door and went straight to the kitchen to grab a bottle of water. She'd finished half of it when Zac stepped out of his bedroom. He wore only shorts, and his hair was mussed. He'd just woken up. When he looked at her, she forced a smile to her lips.

"Morning, sweetie. How'd you sleep?"

Had she sounded normal? She tried to protect Zac from his father as much as she could, but it was a futile effort. He knew exactly what they were running from.

He ran a hand through his hair. "Good. Did you just get back from a run?"

"Sure did."

He swung his gaze to the window, then back to her. "You should be careful when it's dark outside."

Her heart squeezed. They hadn't been getting along much lately, but every so often, her sweet boy returned to her. The one who tried to take care of her, even though it was her job to take care of him.

"I will. Thank you." She tilted her head. "Why are you up so early?"

"We have to get to school early today. My first period is visiting Mercy Ring."

A weight dropped in her belly. "Mercy Ring?" That was where Cole worked. The boxing gym he and his friends owned.

"It's for gym class." As if sensing her trepidation, he continued, his voice softer. "It'll be fine, Mom."

He was moving back toward the bathroom when she stopped him. "Hey...you haven't heard from your father, have you?"

The muscles in his back tensed. She almost regretted the question, but she had to know.

He turned his head. "No. Has he contacted you?"

32

She swallowed. "He called. I didn't answer." She almost never answered.

Zac's jaw clenched. "So we'll be leaving in the next month or two."

He knew the drill. And she hated that for him.

"I'm sorry, baby." Her gaze zeroed in on the small scar on his right brow. A scar his father had put there. Her insides rebelled just thinking about that day.

He nodded, his fists clenched, and moved down the hall.

Zac's father may have called, but it didn't mean he knew where they were. Not yet. It *did* mean she had to start looking into where they'd go next.

# CHAPTER 5

"*P*olice got any leads on the guy?"

Cole lifted the box of wraps and carried it to the front of the room before answering Jackson's question. "None. I called Hanon this morning and pressed him until he told me the CCTV footage didn't get a clear enough image of the guy's face to run it through the system." It was frustrating as hell. "If I ever see the asshole around here again…"

The kid would regret what he'd done.

Both Declan's and Jackson's eyes were narrowed like they were thinking the same thing. It was just the three of them this morning, running an early session for kids from the local high school, while Ryker had the morning off to spend time with his sister, River, who was also partnered with Jackson.

"Well, I'm glad she's okay," Declan said.

Yeah, he was too.

Running into her this morning had done nothing to get the woman out of his head. He hadn't missed the way she'd sucked in a breath when their hands grazed. She'd probably felt the same thing he did—awareness. And when he'd touched her cheek…

Fuck, he was getting hard just thinking about her.

He went back to the storage locker and grabbed a box of focus mitts.

"You know Anthony's in this morning's class," Cole said, eager to get off the topic of Aria.

Anthony was a sixteen-year-old kid who currently lived with him and Ryker, after running from his grandmother, who had guardianship. The story was long and complicated, but basically, he'd been chasing a man who turned out to be a serial killer's accomplice, something no one had known when they'd first met the troubled boy.

Declan nodded. "If the kid wasn't recovering from a bullet wound, he'd show the others how to hit. He's getting good in the ring."

Cole's brows tugged together at the memory of that dark day. Anthony had finally come face-to-face with the man who'd helped kill his sister...and been shot for his trouble. They were all hugely relieved and grateful it was a shot in the leg that missed his arteries, and he was recovering well.

"He'd better be using his crutches," Jackson said.

Cole scoffed. He was supposed to be using them full time, but he rarely did. "Michele still doing okay?" he asked Declan.

Anthony hadn't been the only person tangled up with the serial killer. Michele had been the main target. Luckily, she was okay, but it had been a *very* close call.

Declan smiled as he moved a chair to the side of the room. "She almost died twice, her apartment became uninhabitable after the fire, and yet all she can worry about is Anthony and her uncle Ottie. Oh, and she complained her ass off about potentially hiring a new person to take Anthony's place at the shop while he's recovering from his bullet wound. But when it comes to what happened to *her*? Nothing."

One side of Cole's mouth lifted. He was glad his friend had found Michele, and that Jackson had River. His friends were happier than he'd ever seen them, and that made him damn happy in turn.

Jackson's gaze swung to him. "Have you seen Aria today?"

He thought he'd gotten them off the topic. "Bumped into her on my run this morning." Less of a bump and more of him stopping her to chew her ass out about safety.

Declan frowned. "You run at the ass crack of dawn."

"Yep. She was up before me. And she had earbuds in with music blasting." Both guys gave him an incredulous look. Yeah, they knew how dangerous that could be. It made her an easy target for any predators. "Don't worry, I lectured her about it."

Whether she'd listen or not, he had no idea.

"Good," Jackson said firmly. Then his lips quirked. "So, you gonna ask her out?"

"No." There was no pause or hesitation.

Declan laughed. "Come on. She's pretty. She might even change your warped view on relationships."

"I don't have a warped view on relationships, I just know they're not for me." Never had been, never would be.

Jackson scoffed. "One day—"

"A woman's going to change my mind?" Cole finished. "Heard it before, buddy. And no, they won't." That was something he was absolutely certain of. Because he wouldn't let them.

He was just setting the last box of equipment beside the ring when the door to the gym opened. An older guy he assumed was the teacher stepped in, followed by a handful of teenagers.

When Anthony limped in at the end, Cole frowned. No crutches.

"Don't," Anthony said curtly, looking him, and then Jackson and Declan, straight in the eye as he grew closer.

Sure, he was barely limping...but was that for the benefit of his classmates?

Ignoring his order, Declan slung an arm around his shoulder. "Where are the crutches, kid?"

"They're annoying. I don't need them."

That was debatable. Cole scanned Anthony's workout clothes. "You're not participating today."

"I'll go easy."

"No."

Anthony groaned and shook his head, but as he walked over to the chairs, Cole didn't miss the hint of a smile on his lips as he sat beside Zac.

Interesting. Were they friends? Anthony hadn't spoken about any of the kids at school, but then, Cole didn't really ask. He and Anthony were similar that way. Kept their business to themselves.

Declan clapped his hands together. "All right. Welcome, everyone. Are you ready for the best gym class of your life?" He turned to the team and winked.

The next ten minutes were filled with introductions and explanations of what the sessions would involve. The kids listened well, all bar a couple of boys at the end of a row who whispered throughout the entire talk. Cole's eyes narrowed on them when he heard one of them snicker.

"Something funny?" Cole asked loudly.

"Nope." The kid's words contradicted the smile on his face.

Cole stepped forward. "What's your name?"

"Benny."

"Well, Benny, here at Mercy Ring, it pays to listen so you don't end up with a fist in your face."

He scoffed. "Okay."

*The little shit.* "Get up here. You can demonstrate the first move."

His smile widened. "Let's go."

Jackson moved over and wrapped his hands while Cole grabbed a pair of focus mitts. Once Jackson finished, Cole stepped forward. "Raise your fists."

Benny did as asked.

"Good. Put your nondominant foot forward, feet shoulder width apart and bend your knees. Bent knees give you more balance, mobility and power." He was talking to Benny, but also to the class.

"Power." Benny nodded. "I like it."

"When you punch, it's all about form. You don't want to just punch as hard as you can."

Another laugh from Benny. "My opponent probably couldn't handle that."

This kid's cockiness was grinding on Cole's nerves. He turned to the group, pointing to Benny's form. "This is called the orthodox stance. Imagine lines between your feet. You never want to have both feet on the same line."

He looked back to Benny. "Tuck your elbows in. Fists needs to be by your face." Benny followed the directions. "Now, let's practice the jab. By your foot placement, I can see you're right-handed, so you're going to jab with your left hand. You want to punch out, fully extending the arm, turn your knuckles at the end and aim straight in front of your head." Cole demonstrated before lifting the pads. "Go."

Something sparked in Benny's eyes. He jabbed, and it was fine. But when he returned his fist to his body, it wasn't covering his head. Neither was the other.

Cole swung his mitt and grazed the kid's head.

Benny's eyes darkened, and that annoying grin finally left his face. "Hey!"

"What did I say about covering your face?"

His jaw clenched and he lifted his fists. Benny did three more jabs, and twice more his fists lowered, and he got swiped by Cole's pad.

"Okay, nice first try. Next time, listen better. Could save you some head knocks."

Some of the kids snickered. Benny looked angry. Good. He needed to learn to pay attention.

ARIA STEPPED through the door of Mercy Ring. The sound of fists hitting mitts echoed throughout the room. There were heavy bags scattered around the space and hanging from the ceiling, though the suspended bags weren't being used at the moment. In the center of the room was a large ring that was also unoccupied.

She scanned the teenagers. They were paired up, one partner wearing focus mitts, the other with taped hands, performing a combination of hits.

Her gaze homed in on Zac, and a small chill raced up her spine. He had his back to her, so he hadn't spotted her yet, but she knew it was him. For a moment, she felt like she'd been transported back in time. Like she was a teenager again, watching his father practice.

"What are you doing here?"

She swung her gaze around at the sound of Cole's voice. Just like this morning, he was wearing a tight shirt, only this one had a little Mercy Ring logo on the left pec.

She wet her lips. "Sorry, I know I shouldn't be here. I just..."

Couldn't stay away? Felt an overwhelming urge to come down and watch her son at a boxing gym? Her gaze returned to Zac, and her stomach dipped. Yet again, the rest of the room faded and all she could think was *this is his dad all over again.* Zac hit with the same power and precision. Like he needed to hit hard enough that the man in front of him didn't get up.

Flashes of something else filled her head. Of his father's fists hitting walls in their home in his moments of rage. Of glass shattering. Raised voices—

"Hey."

She blinked, swinging her gaze back to Cole. God, for a moment, she'd been somewhere else entirely.

He stepped closer. "You okay?"

Did she look as pale as she felt? "Of course. I just...I don't love seeing Zac throw punches." When Cole remained silent and continued to watch her like he was waiting for her to tell him why, she scrambled to come up with something. "He had some trouble in our last town."

Which wasn't a lie. He *had* gotten into some fights. It just wasn't the whole truth.

Cole looked back at Zac. "From what I've seen of him this morning, he has a good head on his shoulders. Good at listening and then executing."

Yeah, he did. Until someone threatened him or her. She forced a smile to her lips. "I'm just an overprotective mother."

Another small nod from him. Man, he had to stop looking at her like he saw right through her phony lies.

"Cole!"

He turned his head toward the shout, but before moving away, he squeezed her shoulder. That small touch sent a familiar trill right through her body. She nibbled on her lip and tried to push thoughts of the sexy man out of her head before watching Zac again. She should leave before he caught her here. He'd be pissed. She shouldn't have come, but she literally hadn't been able to stay away.

She stepped to the side, behind a pair of kids.

"He says he's gonna try to get some Black Dust."

She frowned as she heard the conversation between the kids in front of her. They were talking in hushed voices while they took a water break.

"That new drug? I heard that shit's dangerous and some kids in Seattle died from it. What's in it, anyway?"

"Fuck if I know, but word is it makes you feel blissed as hell."

"Is it expensive?"

"Shit yeah. And hard to get your hands on."

"So, he's just talking shit and has no hope."

Her chest eased. Good. As far as she knew, Zac had never

been into drugs, but the further he was away from them, the better.

When Zac stopped hitting the mitts and started pulling the tape from his hands, she blew out a quick breath and turned toward the exit. Time to go.

She'd taken three steps when a kid stepped in front of her. "Hey there, babe. How you doin'?"

She raised a brow, just holding in a laugh. "Babe?" Did she have a big sign on her forehead this week welcoming kids to hit on her?

"I saw you watching Zac. You his sister?"

This time she *did* laugh. It was a common mistake. One she only corrected when she felt like it. With this Casanova, she didn't feel the need.

"Excuse me, I was just leaving." She stepped around him.

That's when she felt the hand on her ass.

She spun around. "Hey!"

The word had barely left her mouth when Zac was suddenly across the room. She gasped when he reared back his fist and threw a hard punch.

"Zac!"

She reached for him, just touching his shoulder before Cole's arm wrapped around her waist and he tugged her backward. Then two other guys wearing the same shirt as Cole were there, grabbing the kids and separating them.

The kid who'd touched her ass laughed, blood dripping from his split lip.

It just fueled Zac's anger, and he tried to fight his way out of his captor's arms. "Grabbing my mother's ass is fucking funny to you, Benny?"

*Oh God.* "Zac—"

"Mother?" Benny's brows rose. "What, was she a kid when she had you?"

Zac lunged again, but the huge man easily held him back. She tried to get out of Cole's arms, but he also held her firm, whispering into her ear, "Jackson's got him. And Declan won't let the other kid go, either. Just give Zac a second to cool down."

Some of the fight leached out of her at the feel of his warm breath on her skin. At his deep voice in her ear.

Zac's chest moved up and down with his quick breaths. "You ever touch her again, I'll kill you."

"Not if I kill you first—"

"Enough." Cole set her behind him and prowled over to the kid. The look he gave him would have scared the bravest man. "Apologize to her—*now*."

Benny's lips quirked. Then he looked at her. "Sorry I touched that fine ass of yours."

Cole lowered his head closer to the kid, still in his friend's hold. From her peripheral vision, she saw a short man wearing a name badge step forward.

"Mr. Turner—"

"You do it again," Cole said quietly, "and you'll have *me* to answer to. And I won't be as easy on you as Zac was." Without waiting for a response, he turned. His body stilled when his gaze caught on something across the room. "Are you recording this?"

Cole headed toward another kid, but the short man rushed over and stepped in front of him. There was a visible bead of sweat on his forehead. "I'll take care of it," the guy said quickly. He turned. "Ezra, if you filmed that, delete it now."

The kid gave the teacher a belligerent look. "Fine."

Finally, Declan and Jackson released the kids.

Aria took a small step toward her son. "Zac—"

"Just go home, Mom." His voice softened as he added, "Please."

# CHAPTER 6

ole reached the bottom of the stairs to see Anthony already at the table, a bowl of cereal and phone in front of him. "You're up early."

Anthony didn't raise his head. "Someone woke me at a ridiculous hour when they got up to run." A ghost of a smile was just visible on his face.

Cole moved to the kitchen counter and poured himself some cereal. "When your leg's better, you can join me."

"I don't run. Give me some sports tape and a bag any day. But running? Nah, there'd have to be something deadly chasing me."

Cole smirked as he topped his cereal with milk. "I could always chase you."

"I said deadly."

Cole smacked him lightly on the shoulder. The kid laughed. It was good to hear. He hadn't done a lot of laughing since arriving in Lindeman. Not that Cole blamed him. His mother had run off on him, his sister had been murdered by a serial killer, and his grandmother hadn't wanted him. It was a damn miracle the kid was still capable of smiling at all.

He dropped into the seat opposite him. "How are you doing?"

"I'm fine."

Fine. God, this kid reminded him so much of himself. "How's school?"

"It's also fine."

Was he doing this on purpose? "You got a favorite subject?"

Anthony lowered the spoon into his bowl and finally looked up. "You trying to bond with me or something?"

Cole's lips twitched. "I'm trying to check in on how you're doing."

Anthony seemed to consider his words for a moment. "Okay. I don't actually mind school. Benny and Ezra are dicks, but you get kids like them everywhere. Gym's my favorite subject, closely followed by math. I'm still working at Michele's shop after school, which you know I love. She's easy to work for and lets me sit and do food prep while my leg heals. And she just asked if I have any friends who'd like to work with me after school, and I'm thinking of suggesting Zac."

Cole's brows rose. "Zac across the street?"

"Yeah. I like him. He doesn't ask stupid questions or do stupid shit like some of the kids. And he's quiet like me, something Michele will appreciate." Anthony lifted another spoonful of cereal to his mouth. "Also...I would have jumped Benny for what he did, too."

Cole nodded. The incident had occurred three days ago. He kept telling himself he should check in on Aria, but he never did. Because he knew the second he talked to her, he'd get lost in her ridiculously vibrant aqua eyes. He'd want to touch that crazy-soft skin of hers.

He scrubbed a hand over his face. "I'm glad you've made a friend."

"I was actually thinking of inviting him over. Asking if he wanted to play some video games here or something."

When Anthony moved in, the kid had the spare bed that

was already in the guest room and the backpack he'd brought with him, but that was it. Since then, they'd bought him some drawers, a nightstand and lamp, a TV, and a video game console.

"If it's fine with Aria, it's fine with me."

Anthony nodded, turning back to his cereal and phone.

Cole cleared his throat. "I wanted to check in on how you're doing with the other stuff too."

The muscles in Anthony's neck visibly tensed. "Other stuff?"

Shit, he was bad at this. "You were close to your sister before you lost her. How are you doing with that?"

He lowered the spoon again and sat back. "You really want to know?"

"Wouldn't ask if I didn't."

Anthony glanced away briefly and swallowed hard. "Every day's a struggle. I literally wake up, remember why I'm here, and feel the pain all over again. The fucking guilt that tears at my insides. I've talked to Michele a bit. She lost both her parents, so she understands a little. That helps. She told me the pain will always be there, it just won't always dominate my life."

"That's true."

Anthony frowned at him but remained silent.

"I lost my dad when I was a kid," Cole said. "My parents separated, and I was living with him while my sister lived with my mom. Losing him was hard. He was my best friend."

It was the most difficult thing he'd ever gone through. He didn't tell Anthony that he'd lost his father a while *before* the guy had actually died. And he didn't share that he'd been the one to find his father's body. That was probably too much. Hell, it was still too much for him some days.

Anthony's throat bobbed. "I'm sorry. How did he die?"

"He took some pills."

There was a slight widening of Anthony's eyes.

No one knew if his father had done it intentionally, to kill himself, or if he'd just been so drunk he'd made a fatal mistake. He had been drinking a lot at the time.

"I was a teenager," Cole said quietly. "After he died, I was angry. I went back to live with my mom and sister, but that just made me angrier because I didn't want to be there. I kind of just existed for a while, biding my time until I was old enough to enlist and get out."

It had been less about getting away from his sister and more about getting away from his mother. The damage to their relationship after his father's passing was irreversible, in his opinion. He'd been forced to return to his hometown to heal from his back injury, after his last mission, and it had been the longest damn year of his life.

"I felt that when my sister died," Anthony said quietly. "The anger. I still feel it today sometimes."

"I know. I saw it in you. Losing someone you love is like losing a part of yourself, especially when the way you lose them doesn't make sense to you. It tears a part of your heart that'll never be whole again. But you learn to live with the scar."

A small nod of Anthony's head. "That's what Michele said."

"You ever need someone else to talk to, you can come to me. I don't always have the right words, but I'm a good listener. And an even better sparring partner."

There was a slight tilt to Anthony's lips. "Thanks. I appreciate it."

~

ARIA HUNG up the phone and dropped her chin to her chest. Great. This was the last thing she needed. Smack-dab, right-at-the-bottom last.

Zac had gotten into a fight at school. And not with just anyone. A fight with that kid who'd touched her ass at Mercy

Ring a few days ago. Benny. Christ. And the worst part, the principal said that Zac had started it.

She scrubbed a hand over her face. Was this why he hadn't come home after school? It was supposed to storm tonight, and she'd already sent him a few messages. Now his absence made sense. How long did he plan to avoid her?

She whipped out her phone and sent him another text.

*Hey! Where are you? A big storm's coming in and I'd like you home.*

She bit her nail and waited for a reply. He hadn't replied to her last couple, but maybe the third time was the charm?

When her phone dinged, her eyes widened. Wow, it really *was* the charm.

*I'm staying out tonight, Mom. I'll see you tomorrow.*

She blew out a frustrated breath. Her sixteen-year-old son was *telling* her that he was staying out for the night. Not asking. No. Because that would just be far too much to expect.

It wasn't just the storm or the fight she was worried about, though that was more than enough. Zac's father had called again. It made her skin crawl. It made her want to wrap her kid up and protect him from the world.

Her fingers moved quickly across her phone.

*I want you home, Zac.*

She watched her screen, waiting for a response. A full five minutes passed before it finally came.

*I'll be fine.*

Oh, man. If she could breathe fire right now, that's exactly what she'd be doing. She hadn't asked Zac if he'd be *fine*. She'd asked him to come home, period.

She was moments from calling the school and demanding every parent number they had when another text came through —but this time from a number she'd never used. Cole's number.

*In case he didn't tell you, Zac's here playing video games. He parked his car down the street, and he has a black eye.*

Zac was hiding out across the street at *Cole's* house? And he'd parked his car down the street so she wouldn't see.

Her jaw ticked. Before she could think better about what she was doing, she marched out the front door and across the street. She tried to knock gently, but her fist basically pounded the wood.

The door opened, and a very tall and handsome Cole stood on the other side. Her heart thumped but she shook it off. She couldn't focus on how the man belonged on the cover of a magazine right now. She needed to talk to her kid.

"Where is he?"

Cole studied her closely for a moment before stepping back. He nodded toward the stairs. "Up there, first room on the right."

She moved inside, careful not to touch him because that would just be too much of a distraction. The second she was up the stairs, she pushed through the door without knocking.

Both Zac and Anthony looked up at her from where they lay on their stomachs on the bed, game controllers in hand.

Aria gasped at the black eye. "Zac! What the hell?"

She probably could have lightened her words or spoken with a bit more tact, but her head was filled with rage and worry.

He sat up, game controller dropping from his hands. "How did you know I was here?"

Anthony dropped his controller too, but at least he had the good sense to look guilty.

She ignored his question. "Why did I just get a call from Principal Haywood telling me you started a fight with that Benny kid at school today?"

"Because I did."

There was no remorse. Not a single, itsy-bitsy scrap of it. *All right, Aria. Calm down. You can't kill the kid in front of witnesses.*

"We're going home." *That's* where she'd kill him.

He stood. "We need to go to Gianni's house to work on a group assignment that's due on Monday."

She felt Cole's presence behind her as she crossed her arms. "No. Not until you tell me what happened today."

"What happened today is *Benny* was showing everyone the video of him touching your ass, and he was doing it to piss me off. So I hit him. And I let him know that if I saw that video circulating again, I'd break his bones."

Her lips parted on another gasp. Cole spoke before she could. "The recording wasn't deleted?"

Zac's hands fisted. "No. They added cheesy background music, and he was spreading vile shit about her."

*Oh, Jesus.* Her voice gentled. "Why didn't you tell a teacher or the principal?"

He laughed but there was no humor behind it. "Like that would have done anything. Look, we need to go to Gianni's house—"

"Zac—"

"I'm sorry the principal called you, but I'm not sorry about what I did. I'd do it again." His voice softened and he stepped closer. "Please, Mom? I'll be fine and back home tomorrow morning. We're just working on school stuff."

She dragged in a breath. It was Friday, so they had the entire weekend for a school project. She could push this. She could fight Zac some more. But boy, she was tired of fighting with her son. She stepped closer and touched his cheek. "Just...be careful. Please."

"Of course."

Anthony rose from the bed and grabbed his bag. Zac kissed her cheek as he moved past her, while Anthony dipped his head.

"See you later, Ms. Callas. Cole."

She stayed exactly where she was as the boys moved down the stairs. There was the thud of the front door opening and closing, then silence.

When she finally turned, she saw Cole standing there watching her. She didn't know what she expected to see on his face. Sympathy? A bit of pity maybe? But nope. His face was annoyingly clear.

He nodded his head toward the stairs. "Come on. You need a shot of whiskey."

"Just a shot?"

# CHAPTER 7

*T*he whiskey burned Aria's throat and caused her eyes to water. Her glass had barely hit the table when Cole poured her another.

She lifted the shot and swirled it around, watching as the liquid spiraled. "Teenagers are hard."

Cole sat beside her, almost close enough for their shoulders to touch. He had a small bar in the corner of his living room with tall chairs. Maybe she needed a setup like this in her living room.

Ha. With all the shots she'd need to take, she'd turn into an alcoholic.

Cole downed his own whiskey, but if the stuff burned his throat, he didn't show it. "He seems angry about something."

"You noticed?" She was aiming for humor, but the words came out with more twisted sarcasm. "We move a lot. He hates it."

"Why do you move a lot?"

Oh, the stories she could tell this man. For a moment, she *wanted* to tell him. Share her deranged ex stories with him and let another person get a glimpse into the world that was her life. But she gave herself a mental shake. It was too heavy for someone she barely knew.

"It's just a rhythm we've gotten into." Not a complete lie. But not the complete truth. She turned and studied his intense brown eyes. "I heard you were in the military."

She watched the way he cradled the empty shot glass. He even had sexy hands. Thick knuckles, visible veins. Powerful. Just like the rest of him.

"Who told you that?" he asked.

"Lenny."

A small smile stretched his lips. What she wouldn't give for a full, uninhibited grin. Did he have dimples? Did he have laugh lines?

"I was special forces. Loved it. Until I didn't."

She tilted her head. "What made you stop loving it?"

"On our last mission, our location was compromised. We were attacked. I was pushed out of a second-floor window during a hand-to-hand fight and broke my back. Declan was shot. We almost didn't make it back to the US military base. It's the closest any of us have come to death."

God, that sounded awful. "How's your back now?"

"It's good, but it took a year of rehab for me to get here." His gaze moved between hers. "I'm used to being active, so it was a big adjustment. Then when I could be active again, it took me a while to work my fitness back up. But I'm finally there."

She lowered her gaze to his thick biceps. Yes, he was.

"I'd be the same," she said. "Exercise is a huge part of my life. It's my endorphin kick and what I look forward to. I can't imagine a year of barely being able to walk."

Fat raindrops hitting the roof gave their conversation a feeling of insulation.

"Let's hope you never have to."

She tilted her head to the side. "How did you come to care for Anthony?"

"That's a long story. The short version is his mom left him, his sister died, and his grandmother didn't want him. He sort of fell into our laps after that." He lifted a shoulder. "He's an easy kid, though."

So this beautiful man was into saving teenagers who needed a home. Great. Another check next to his name. "You're a good man to take care of him."

He lifted a shoulder like it was nothing.

They spent the next hour talking about nothing and everything. It was nice to connect to Cole, who was usually so closed off. He told her old military stories. Some funny. Some downright scary. And she told him about her fitness business and stories of her and Zac's life.

She'd just downed her third shot when she licked the remnants from her lips. His gaze dropped to her mouth. Her pulse jumped. The rain had grown heavier outside, pounding on the roof, but when this man looked at her, she could almost convince herself the rest of the world didn't exist.

With a quick swallow, she pushed the shot glass away. "I should get going before the storm gets worse."

His nod was slow. They both stood at the same time, and when she wobbled, her hand went to his chest. His very hard, muscular chest.

He held her arms, his heat penetrating the material of her sweatshirt.

For a moment, she didn't move. She should step back. She knew she should. But instead, she stayed exactly where she was, caught up in the intoxicating mix of whiskey heating her blood and this man heating her skin. She swept her hand up his chest to his shoulder, before settling back down on his thick arm.

When her gaze rose, his eyes had darkened.

Suddenly, his hands shifted to grip her hips. She thought he was going to push her away. Put some much-needed distance between them. Instead, his fingers tightened. "Aria..."

She breathed in his masculine, woodsy scent. Her belly flopped.

Her other hand rose, slipping behind his neck and sweeping through his surprisingly soft hair. Then she tugged his head down, slowly.

His eyes flared. Her lips parted. But just before their mouths touched, he turned his head away.

"We shouldn't," he said softly.

She sucked in a puff of air, embarrassment swiftly replacing every other emotion. She took a step back. Then another.

"Aria."

He stepped toward her, but she turned toward the door. "Sorry, I…" *Read it wrong? Had too many shots and thought you felt the same burning need to kiss me as I felt for you? Oh God.* "You're right. I should go."

She'd just wrenched open the door when strong fingers latched onto her arm with surprising gentleness. "Aria, I'm so—"

"It's fine," she interrupted. She looked over her shoulder and forced a smile. "My mistake. I'll see you later."

She tugged on her arm, and when he let her go, she hurried across the road through the rain.

Time to dig herself a hole and hide inside it.

COLE HIT THE BAG HARD. His blood was pumping fast through his veins, and he had music pounding through the room.

*Right cross, right cross, jab.*

He wanted to exhaust his body. To be so damn tired that he forgot. Forgot the hurt in Aria's eyes after he'd turned his head. The embarrassment that had reddened her cheeks.

He hit the bag harder.

He'd wanted to kiss her. Fuck, he'd wanted to sweep the woman into his arms and take her. The need had been a roar inside him. But then what? What came after the kiss? She wasn't a one-time kind of girl. He didn't need to know her well to know that much.

And even if she was, if he tasted her, there was every chance he'd get addicted. Hell, just seeing her across the road every day was wreaking havoc on his system.

Nope. He couldn't do that.

*Hook, hook, right cross.*

Feelings were dangerous. If his father's love for his mother had taught him anything, it taught him *that*. His sister's love for her late husband had further cemented it in his mind. Love could destroy you. It could turn you into a shadow of the person you once were.

He'd promised himself a long fucking time ago he wouldn't allow himself to fall victim like his father had.

*Jab, jab, side kick.*

He shouldn't have offered the whiskey, but when her son walked away, and she'd stood there looking at nothing, like a part of her had just left with Zac, every inch of him had wanted to dull her pain. Fix it.

What the hell was it about her that had him so intrigued? He'd been with gorgeous women before. What made her so different?

*Right cross, jab.*

Everything. Everything felt different.

Thunder rumbled outside the house. When a large figure loomed in the doorway, he finally paused. Air moved in and out of his chest in quick succession. But he wasn't too tired to remember. And dammit, he hated that.

"Everything okay?" Ryker leaned his shoulder against the doorframe.

"Everything's fine." If you called losing your damn mind over a woman you barely knew *fine*.

"Saw some shot glasses on the bar."

"Aren't you observant."

His friend raised a brow.

"Zac was here." Cole swallowed. "He'd had a rough day. Aria came by to take him home."

"And did she?"

"Nope. Zac and Anthony left to study at a friend's place."

"So, the whiskey was a way to make her feel better."

"Yep." He pulled the gloves from his hands and grabbed a towel. He hadn't made her feel better though, had he?

"What happened?"

He left the room and Ryker followed. "She tried to kiss me."

"She *tried* to kiss you…but didn't."

"You're good at this."

His friend didn't even crack a smile. "You didn't want to kiss her?"

In the kitchen, he grabbed a bottle of water from the fridge, and of course his damn gaze caught on the house across the street. God, he couldn't stop.

"Why?" Ryker asked.

Another question he didn't want to answer. He drained half the bottle.

When Cole looked at his friend, he almost groaned. Ryker was looking at him like he saw exactly what was going on in his head.

"Ah," he finally said.

*Fuck.*

"You didn't kiss her because you like her."

Bingo.

Ryker's brows tugged together. "You can actually imagine yourself in a relationship with her, can't you?"

He needed out of this conversation. "I'm taking a shower."

He started to walk out of the room, but Ryker snagged his arm. His friend's voice softened. "Hey. I know that what happened to your dad affected you. But his story isn't yours."

"I know. Because I won't allow it to be."

He pulled his arm from his friend's hold and took the stairs two at a time. He didn't pause at the distinctive sigh from the kitchen.

The second he hit the bathroom, he stripped off and stepped into the shower. More thunder boomed outside. Damn, they'd be lucky if they kept power for the night.

He closed his eyes and let the water hit his head and wash over his face. He needed to call his sister and check in. He hadn't called Naomi in over a week. And his mother... He gritted his teeth. The woman called him often, but he answered as little as possible. Most of the time, he just couldn't bring himself to.

When he stepped out of the shower, he caught a flash of lightning from the window. He dried off, threw on some clothes, then grabbed his phone. Before he could stop himself, he shot off a text to Aria.

*You okay over there?*

The woman was by herself in a storm, and the chance of everyone's power going out in the neighborhood was high. It didn't make him feel good.

He shot a look out the window again. Maybe he should go check on her.

His stomach clenched at the thought. The way she'd looked at him when she'd walked out of here...like she'd stood on a ledge for him and he'd just pushed her off.

*Goddammit.*

He moved down the stairs and into the kitchen. He needed to eat. Maybe that would take his mind off everything.

He heated up a meal from Michele's shop, his gaze skirting over to Aria's house again and again. He couldn't stop himself. When he wasn't looking out the window, he was watching his phone for a response.

He cursed under his breath as he lifted his phone and shot off another text.

*Aria, just tell me you're okay.*

A few minutes later, as he waited for a response, the lights flickered. They came back, but only for a second. Then everything switched off again. Power was gone.

His gaze returned to the window and the house across the road, only to see Aria's place pitch black too.

Fuck it. Cole rose from the chair, shoved his phone into his pocket and headed to the front door.

# CHAPTER 8

*A*ria closed her eyes as she leaned back in the tub. She'd been hoping the bath would relax her. But nope. Her mind was moving a million miles a minute, and there was no amount of Epsom salts that could clear it from the embarrassing almost-kiss. Could she even call it an almost-kiss if the guy hadn't also tried to kiss her?

*No, Aria. No, you can't.*

Argh. It would forever be her very embarrassing moment with her neighbor. A moment that would never, under any circumstances, take place again, no matter how much her hormones were in overdrive.

She sank lower in the tub as thunder growled outside. It was official. She had to move, and for once it had nothing to do with Zac's father. She had to move so that she never had to step foot outside her house again and die of embarrassment when she saw Cole.

She was just blowing out a long breath when the lights in the room flickered. If reports were correct, this storm was a big one. Great, it would match her mood.

Another round of thunder erupted. Her insides rebelled

against the noise. She hated storms. When she was little, she used to hide under her blankets with a flashlight and her dog, Teddie.

She didn't have Teddie anymore, but hiding under her sheets with a flashlight didn't sound terrible. That was still acceptable, right?

Okay. This bath was not distracting her. But then, she was sure nothing in the history of mankind would.

She grabbed her phone from beside the tub and saw the message from Cole.

*You okay over there?*

Was he asking her that because of the storm, or the kiss fiasco?

The man was probably messaging because she'd embarrassed herself in front of him. He likely pitied the ever-loving hell out of her. Yet, even after his rejection, his touch on her arm when he'd grabbed her by the door had still made a little sizzle rush through her veins.

Pathetic. She was pathetic.

*Well, Mr. I'm-not-into-you, you don't need to worry about me. I'm fine.* And maybe if she told herself that enough, she would be.

She was just about to lower the phone again when it rang. She frowned. The call was coming from the police station.

"Hello?"

"Hi, Ms. Callas. It's Officer Hanon."

She straightened. "You can call me Aria. It's a bit late for a phone call, isn't it?"

The officer sighed heavily. "You're not wrong. I'm only just leaving the office. There's too much shit going on. A new drug on the market and some escalating juvenile behavior..." Another sigh. "Anyway, I'm just calling with an update on that kid from the bar."

"There's an update?" Nerves tingled her spine. *Please tell me the asshole's been caught and put behind bars.*

"There is."

The hope turned to dread. By the officer's tone, it wasn't going to be the news she was hoping for. "Tell me."

"We discovered the guy's identity because a missing person's report was filed," Hanon said gravely.

"He's missing?"

"He is. His name's Rufus Maddon. He's a twenty-one-year-old and lives in Yakima with his two parents and younger brother. Kid's had a few brushes with police, but nothing serious. Parents are pretty worried about him."

The kid had probably figured out he was screwed and skipped town. "Okay. So you guys are looking for him?" It probably went without saying, but still, she felt the need to ask.

"Yes. And I'll keep you posted if we learn anything else."

"Thank you."

She hung up and sank deeper into the water. The storm raging in her chest rivaled the one outside. This week had been a lot. Her arguments with Zac, his father's calls, and now Cole...

She and Zac would have to leave soon, before her ex suddenly showed up. She'd spent a chunk of the morning researching where they might go. She couldn't just move anywhere. She needed to consider safety and schools. Choosing without thought or planning meant they could end up in a high crime area or in a dangerous school district. No. She needed safety above all else.

Carmel, Indiana. That was where she'd decided on next. It was safe. Had a great school district. It was also far away from Lindeman...something she made sure of. She'd already emailed a few real estate agents. Now she just needed to wait and see if they had any rentals available.

Zac immediately flickered through her mind. He'd hate moving. He'd been dragged around the country like a rag doll his entire life. He deserved to settle somewhere. Finish his education with at least a couple of good friends.

Mom guilt was a bitch.

And then there was Cole. Why did the thought of leaving him make her chest ache?

She was just closing her eyes again when the lights switched off.

Great. No power. Just what she needed.

With a deep sigh, she climbed out of the tub and turned on the flashlight function on her phone. Then she grabbed a towel and wrapped it around herself before taking the phone to the bedroom.

This was exactly why she had candles. She wasn't a big light-a-candle-to-alleviate-stress kind of person. She was a keep-a-candle-in-case-there-was-a-storm kind of person. So practical. She was a practical woman.

Once several candles were lit, the small flames cast a mellow light throughout the room. It was almost romantic. Huh. Shame she had as much romance in her life as those oldies in the retirement homes.

She was just reaching for the knot in her towel when she noticed the message on her phone. Another one from Cole. She almost didn't open it. But at the last second, she clicked on the screen.

*Aria, just tell me you're okay.*

She frowned. Was he really that worried about her? It was just a storm. She'd experienced worse in her thirty-two years of life. *A lot* worse.

She was about to respond when something at the window caught her attention. A small flicker of light. She squinted at it, but it disappeared.

Her heart gave a little thud. It had almost looked like...a phone light?

No. Absolutely not. That couldn't be right.

With slow steps, she walked toward the window. The curtains were closed, but there was a sliver of a gap in the center. That's where the light had come from. She never worried about gaps much, not with her room being at the back of the house.

Slowly, she pressed her face between the curtains. The yard was dark, and that, along with the rain, made it impossible to see anything.

It must have been a flash of lightning.

Almost on cue, another bolt flashed in the distance, and a second later came the roar of thunder.

It was already going to be a long night. She didn't need to trick herself into thinking someone with a phone was peering into her bedroom window. God.

With one hard tug, she closed the gap in the curtains. There. No more imaginary intruders.

When a shudder coursed down her spine, she wasn't sure if it was because of what she'd just thought she'd seen or the cold. Either way, she needed hot cocoa to calm her nerves. Thank God for gas stoves. She'd set the milk to heat, then get dressed.

She crossed the room and had just stepped into the hallway when she collided with something tall, hard and wet.

Not something. *Someone.*

A scream ripped from her throat. She was a second away from thrusting her knee into the man's balls when he spoke.

"Aria. It's me!"

She went still. Then a huge puff of air blew from her chest, and she pressed a hand over her heart. It actually hurt. That's how hard it had crashed inside her chest just now.

"Holy Mother of Christ. What the hell are you doing inside my house, Cole?"

When she looked up, his face was shadowed, but she didn't miss the crease between his brows. "I knocked half a dozen times, but you never answered, and you didn't respond to my texts."

"I was in the tub. And of *course* I didn't hear. In case you didn't notice, there's a very loud storm outside. Doesn't mean you can just waltz on in. How'd you even open the door?"

He held up a key. "You shouldn't leave a spare under a potted plant."

Her jaw dropped. "There are half a dozen potted plants out there. Did you look underneath each one?"

"It was the second one I checked."

She snatched it from his fingers. "What are you doing here?" Other than scaring her to death. *Again.*

"I was worried about you."

She stared at him, then snapped her mouth shut. Whatever she'd been about to say died on her lips. She quickly shook off the shock. Nope. No, no, no. She was not going to be swept up by his kind words. And she certainly wasn't going to be pulled in by his sexy muscles or his woodsy smell and deep voice. She was immune.

Her gaze caught on the wet T-shirt sticking to his hard chest. His hard, *ripped* chest.

*Dammit. Immune, Aria!*

She swallowed. "I'm okay. It's just a storm." Thank the Lord above she didn't sound like a lovesick puppy. Before he could respond, she frowned. "Wait...was that you outside my window just now?"

His eyes narrowed, his gaze flicking over her head inside her bedroom. "Someone was at your window?"

"I saw a light. I thought..." She shook her head. "I don't know what I thought."

"Stay here."

Her head flew up. "What are you—"

He was out the door before she could stop him.

*Christ.* She hadn't meant for him to go check. He was going to get even more soaked. Why hadn't she just responded to his damn message?

She waited in the dark hallway, fiddling with her phone. After what felt like forever, he finally returned. "I couldn't see anyone." He closed the door, and it thudded behind him.

Holding up her phone, she gaped as the light shone on his soaked shirt and hair and arms. "You must be freezing."

When he didn't respond, her gaze finally lifted. She swallowed. He was looking at her like... God, it was the same way he'd looked at her in his house, right before she'd gone in for the kiss. And just like then, every part of her thought he wanted her. Every part of her shouted, screamed at her, to try the kiss again.

Her skin tingled, a dull ache throbbing in her lower abdomen.

"You should put some clothes on," he said quietly.

His words were like a bucket of ice water on her head. Her gaze shot down. She'd forgotten she was only wearing a towel. And by the tone of his voice, he didn't care for the sight of her in it one bit.

Before he could see the humiliation on her face, she turned. "You can go."

She'd just made it to her bedroom when, yet again, the man's long fingers wrapped around her arm.

"Aria—"

She spun around. "Please. Just go. I think I've embarrassed myself in front of you enough for one day."

His jaw clenched. "You haven't embarrassed yourself at all."

Was he serious? "I tried to kiss you when you're clearly not attracted to me. Now I'm standing in front of you in a frickin' towel. I think that's the very definition of embarrassment."

There was a beat of quiet before he spoke. "You think I'm not attracted to you?"

"Yes." Wasn't that what a man turning away when you tried to kiss him usually meant?

He took a small step forward. Then, slowly, he ran his fingers down her bare arm. The fine hairs on her arms stood on end. "I'm so goddamn attracted to you, all I can think about right now is tearing that towel off your body and pinning you to the wall. Not doing *exactly that* is killing me."

This time, her breath actually stopped in her chest. He took another step closer, crowding her.

*Breathe, Aria. You need to breathe.*

"Problem is, I don't do relationships. And you seem like a relationship kind of girl."

It took her a moment to get the air moving in her lungs again, and then another for his words to infiltrate her foggy, confused mind.

"I haven't had a relationship in a very long time," she said. "So I don't think you could call me a relationship girl." Her words were so quiet, she wondered if he heard them over the storm outside.

She pressed her hands flat against his chest. And there it was. The lava that pooled in her belly every time he was near. The desire that warmed her blood. This man did that with a single touch.

A quiet growl rippled from his chest. "Aria..."

She looked up to see indecision in his eyes. Her gaze dropped to his mouth. To his full lips, which looked all too kissable. The lips she wanted to kiss with everything she was and had.

She'd only dropped her gaze for a heartbeat when another growl exploded from his chest. In the next second, his mouth dropped, crashing onto hers.

# CHAPTER 9

*F* or the first time in his life, Cole ignored the whispered warning in his head. He ignored the fear and the trauma of his past, and he let this woman's kiss consume him. He kissed her like she was the medicine he needed to survive. As if in this moment, what they did to each other was all that mattered.

Aria hummed, and the sound made blood roar between his ears. She grabbed his shirt and clenched the material, leaning into him. He wanted more. He spun them, pushing her against the bedroom wall.

Her hands went to the base of his wet shirt and tugged it up. Their lips only separated for a second, and once the material was gone, he was back with her, only this time he plunged his tongue inside her mouth, gliding it against hers. Damn, she tasted good. He could drown in a river of this woman's sweetness.

When her towel fell away, he wasn't sure if she'd opened it or if it dropped on its own, but she didn't pause to cover herself again. Instead, her hands skirted up his shoulders and around his neck.

Hands under her thighs, he lifted her before pressing himself into the soft curves of her body.

She was everywhere, and she fit so perfectly. Like they were puzzle pieces that had finally found each other.

He grazed his hand up her thigh and side before settling on her breast. When he cradled it, she groaned against his mouth. He found her pebbled nipple and thumbed it. Her mouth ripped away from his, and her head swung to the side on a gasp.

He took advantage of her exposed neck, kissing down her skin toward her chest. He wanted to kiss every inch of this woman, yet he knew that still wouldn't be enough.

When he reached her breast, he cupped the soft mound, latched on and sucked the hard peak.

Her next cry was loud and rippled through the room, deafening the thunder. She ground her hips against him, and he growled low in his throat.

His. This woman was *his* tonight. And that thought made something deep inside him roar to life. He rolled her stiff nipple with his tongue. More sweet moans. "Fuck, those noises destroy me."

*She* destroyed him. She made the banked embers inside him turn into explosions of need.

He released her nipple and lifted his head, once again taking her lips. His tongue dove straight in and dueled with hers. The hand on her breast dropped to her apex.

Her breath stuttered, her fingers digging into his shoulders. He swiped her wet slit, and she jolted, then moaned. So damn responsive. He swiped again, running his thumb around her clit. More moans sounded from her throat, but she never stopped tasting him. Her hips were now grinding against his hand like she needed more. He knew exactly what she needed.

He touched a finger to her entrance.

"Yes," she whispered.

He pushed inside her. The sound that emerged from her chest

was primal and raw and made him ache with the need to take her. But first, he wanted to feel her come apart. He needed to watch her beautiful face as she broke in his arms.

He slid out before thrusting his finger back inside, his thumb circling her clit.

Her moans grew louder, her fingers digging so deep into his shoulders they almost broke skin, holding him tightly as if afraid he'd let go.

Not a fucking chance. He couldn't even if he wanted to. The woman did something to him that was impossible to walk away from.

Another thrust of his finger. When her lips tore from his and her head flew back once again, he pushed a second finger inside her. Her eyes scrunched tight, her lips parted, and she broke.

Fucking perfect.

～

ARIA'S BODY throbbed from what Cole had done to her. She felt heavy, like she couldn't lift a single limb on her own.

Lips pressed to her cheek, then her neck. Air moved around her. Then she was on her back on the bed.

A weight pressed on top of her. More kisses. Warm hands skimmed her body.

*Oh God.* It was starting again. The deep need. The desire that spiraled from her limbs down into her core.

How that was possible so fast, she had no idea, but when fingers once again started thrumming her nipple, she arched her back.

Her eyes fluttered open to see the man hovering over her, caging her to the bed and kissing her neck. She reached for him, threaded her fingers in his hair and pulled him back to her lips. When she felt his hardness press against her core, her lower body clenched. Somehow, even though they'd only known each other a short period of time, he felt so familiar.

Her hands went to his buckle and zipper, and when his jeans were open, she didn't hesitate. She reached inside and grabbed him. He went still above her, a deep moan vibrating from his chest.

She stroked him, feeling him grow thicker in her hold. At the same time, she trailed a line of kisses across his cheek, then nipped his ear. A growl this time. God, she loved that sound.

Suddenly, he pulled her hand away and leaned to the side. When she lost the heat and weight of his body, she wanted to whimper. She watched him remove the last of his clothes.

When he was naked, her insides turned molten. He was so big. All of him. The man radiated strength and power.

She rose to her knees, pulling him to the bed. When he lay down, she climbed on top. She set a knee on either side of his waist and kissed him. Unlike the others, this was a slow, exploratory kiss. She wanted to take her time with him.

She ground herself against his length and, man, it felt so good.

"Aria..." He bit out her name. "What do you do to me?"

If it was anything similar to what he did to her, then she had no idea. All she knew was she wanted him more than she wanted anything else in this moment.

"I don't know," she breathed between increasingly desperate kisses.

His hand returned to her breast, flicking her nipple back and forth. She cried out, and on the next rock of her hips, he was at her entrance.

The hand on her hip tightened. "I'm not wearing anything."

Dammit. She hadn't been thinking. She reached across to her nightstand and rummaged around before pulling out a foil square. Without losing his gaze, she ripped it open with her teeth. Cole's eyes darkened. Then, slowly, she slid it over him, making sure to graze every inch of his length as she went. The feel of him in her hands made heat dance in her belly.

Then, she positioned him at her entrance and slowly lowered her body.

Sweet baby Jesus. He stretched her in the most delicious way. Why did it feel like this man was made for her?

His fingers dug into her hips. And when he was completely seated inside, she paused. Their gazes met, and something deep and intense passed between them.

She wriggled her hips. The man sucked in a sharp breath. A smile curved her lips. She liked that too. Carefully, she leaned over him and cupped his cheek as she kissed him. Then she rocked against him.

Desire rippled through her core. She rocked again, lifting her hips and driving them back down. Cole's tongue plunged into her mouth. Her breasts brushed against his hard pecs, and the friction set her chest on fire.

She increased the speed of her thrusts, but it wasn't enough for him. He rolled them and began to drive into her. *Yes.* She tossed her head to the side and cried out. "Cole..."

His thrusts made every inch of her body tingle. Every time he pushed forward, he brought them back together with a power she'd never felt before.

He nipped her lip, then his hand moved between them, and he caressed her clit. She jolted and cried out.

Christ, she was close. She felt like she was on the edge of a cliff, moments from tumbling off.

But she had no fear. She wanted to fall. She wanted to crash to the bottom with this man and see what happened next.

His thumb moved faster, his thrusts relentless. On one final swipe, her back arched, her nails dug into his shoulders, and she shattered into so many shards, she wasn't sure she'd ever be whole again.

He continued to power into her, and her orgasm continued to pulse.

Cole groaned, his muscles rippling as he tensed and shuddered, buried deep inside her. Then he rocked slowly, sinking into her three more times before finally going still.

The storm continued to rage outside, but it was nothing compared to the storm inside her.

The second they were still, uncertainty began to weave its web inside her chest. She'd just had sex with her neighbor. Hell, sex didn't even feel like the right word. What they'd done felt like so much more.

But he was a neighbor who had very explicitly told her he wasn't interested in a relationship. And she'd basically told him that was fine.

Would he leave now? Just get up and walk out? Jesus, why was she even thinking about it while he was still inside her?

Gently, he pulled out of her and dropped to her side.

Maybe she should get up first.

The thought had no sooner entered her mind when his arm wrapped around her, and he tugged her against his side.

The fear and uncertainty in her chest eased as she leaned into him. His arms felt like a warm sanctuary. In the middle of a storm with no power, no heat, and no light other than the dim flicker from the candles, she knew he was all she needed.

# CHAPTER 10

$\mathcal{T}$he first thing to pierce his sleep was the smell of lilacs. It was a sweet fragrance that hit him right in the chest. The next was the feel of a small hand pressed to one side of his chest, and a soft cheek on the other.

His eyes shot open. Shit. He'd fallen asleep. He never fell asleep. He was known for his self-control and fierce discipline… but last night, with her, all of that disintegrated.

His gut knotted as he lowered his gaze to the top of her head. She was sprawled across his chest, her cheek on his heart, and it just felt…right. His hand twitched to graze her cheek, move the blonde lock of hair from her face.

His heart hammered loudly in his chest.

No. He couldn't do that. Any of it. He couldn't fall for the woman. He couldn't fall for *anyone.*

Carefully, he slid out from under her. The soft hum from her chest was almost his undoing. The way she snuggled into the blankets and her hair fanned around her head like a halo. All of it made him want to return to her. Press her to the mattress. Bury himself deep inside her once again and *claim* her. She was like a damn forbidden fruit he wasn't supposed to touch.

He traced the outline of her delicate jaw with his eyes, his gaze catching on the small scar on her chin. Even that was beautiful.

Fuck. He needed to get out. *Now.*

With tense muscles, he tugged on his still-damp clothes and moved to the door. Before stepping out, he threw one final look her way. His heart slowed as he watched the gentle rise and fall of her chest. The air around him thickened, and he actually took a step back toward the bed. Then he came to his senses.

Clenching his jaw, he snatched his phone from where he'd left it on the dresser and moved. Every step away from her felt heavy and so much harder than it should have been.

He glanced at the time on his phone. Five a.m. Thank God he'd woken up before her. He knew the woman was an early riser from her morning runs. He wouldn't be surprised if she was up within the next few minutes.

Quietly, he opened the front door before clicking the lock and pulling it closed behind him.

He needed a cold shower and a good hour in the ring. Hell, even an hour wouldn't do it.

The sky was still dark, and rain pattered around him as he crossed the road. The second he was inside his house, he flicked a light switch, pleased to find the power restored. He continued up the stairs. His shower was quick, and once he was dressed, he went back down, all the while trying to get Aria out of his head. It was impossible.

As he reversed out of his driveway, he couldn't stop his gaze from flicking across the street. No lights on. Was she still asleep? What would she think when she woke alone?

He shook his head. He'd never worried about that before—he shouldn't be worrying about it now. He'd told her he didn't do relationships. She knew where he stood.

As he parked in the Mercy Ring parking lot, his phone rang. He ground his jaw when he saw who it was. His mother.

God, this morning was kicking his ass.

He almost didn't answer. But if he didn't, she'd just call again. He'd already missed her last three calls in as many days.

He yanked the phone to his ear. "Hi, Mom."

"Darling, hi. Sorry to call so early."

His mother lived in Wisconsin, the state where he'd grown up. She was also an early riser because of her yoga classes and had probably just gotten home from her class.

"I'm up, Mom. What's going on?"

"I have wonderful news. Gerard and I are engaged."

He scrubbed a hand over his face. What was this? Engagement number six? And if they did make it down the aisle, husband four? "Gerard?"

"Oh, you'll love him. He's a mechanic. He has three kids of his own. All grown up. And he's just a sweetie."

"That's great." It wasn't. Not in his mind. But he hadn't told the woman how he really felt about her relationships since he was a teenager. What was the point?

"Cole, I want you to come home and meet him."

His jaw clenched. "Things are pretty busy at work at the moment, with setting up the new business and everything." The guys could easily cope without him. But he'd already spent a year in his hometown with his mother. It wouldn't be terrible if he didn't return for a good long while.

She hadn't been dating Gerard then, so this was a quick engagement. But then, most were.

"Well, how about we come to you?"

He blew out a long breath. "Now's not a great time."

"Darling—"

"I have to go, Mom. Congratulations though. I'll chat later."

The second he hung up, he climbed out of his truck and slammed his door harder than necessary. When he stepped into the gym, he stopped at the sight of Ryker already inside, hitting a bag. Cole had just assumed he was home, still in bed. Had Ryker's car been parked in the lot and he'd missed it? Probably. His mind was too busy with other stuff.

He dropped his bag near the desk. "What are you doing here so early?"

Ryker paused, turning his head and looking at Cole. "Couldn't sleep. Didn't want to work out at home and wake Anthony."

"Everything okay?"

Something flashed in his friend's eyes. That was all the answer he needed.

Everything *wasn't* okay. Demons had been hounding Ryker since their final mission. The second they'd returned home, Ryker had received a call informing him that innocent families had been murdered. One of which, Ryker had grown close to.

"Nope." That was all he said before yanking off his gloves, grabbing two focus mitts, and stepping into the ring. The man clearly didn't want to talk about it, so Cole didn't push. He grabbed some gauze, wrapped his hands and stepped into the ring. Then he started hitting.

"Where were you last night?" Ryker asked between hits.

Cole threw two jabs and a cross punch. "Aria's power went off, so I went to check on her."

"And you stayed the night."

It wasn't a question.

"It was a mistake." The words tasted like acid in his mouth. Sounded wrong in his ears. But how could they be right? How could *she* be right, when he'd convinced himself long ago that no one ever would be?

"Why was it a mistake?"

He hit the mitts with enough force to push Ryker's hands back. "Because she's not like the other women I've been with." Not to him, at least.

For a moment, Ryker was silent. The only noises in the room were the repetitive sounds of his fists hitting the mitts. He got about five more hits in before Ryker spoke again.

"You know, it's okay to change your mind."

Cole paused, his breathing heavy. "About what?" He knew *what*, dammit, but he didn't want to talk about it.

"About relationships not being for you. About not wanting to explore a commitment with someone."

He let the words sink in. They felt heavy in his head. He raised his fists again, and Ryker lifted the mitts.

"Mom called."

*Cross punch, hook.*

"What did she say?"

"That she's engaged again. That she wants me to meet him." Nothing changed with her. Nothing ever would.

"Will you?" Ryker asked. He swiped at his head with the mitt and Cole ducked.

"I'll put it off for as long as I can." Two more jabs. "The call was like the universe reminding me exactly why last night was a mistake."

The universe reminding him of his past. That love was powerful. That love could annihilate the strongest man.

HE WAS GONE. Aria didn't need to open her eyes to know that. The sheets were cold beside her and there was silence. Not another breath in the room.

Slowly, she opened her eyes, and yep, the other side of the bed was empty.

She shouldn't care. The man pretty much insinuated what would happen, and she'd gone ahead and let last night take place anyway. With a long sigh, she climbed out of bed. The dull ache in her core was an unwelcome reminder of what they'd done.

Unwelcome? Ha. Memories of last night would be with her for a very long time, and certainly not for bad reasons. She could almost still feel Cole's hands on her. His mouth on her skin.

Her body was warm as she pulled on running shorts, a sports bra and some shoes. She shot a look to her side tables, then her dresser. No note. When she made her way into the living room, she noticed there was no note there either. And no text message on her phone.

Okay, her heart definitely dropped a little at that.

When she got outside, the sun had already risen. It was later than usual, but that didn't bother her. She had no client appointments today and no workouts to film or coordinate. She'd been planning on catching up on some admin work.

Was Cole already at work?

*Stop, Aria. Stop thinking about him.*

She pumped her arms, turned up the music and ran. She ran twice as fast as usual and got home in half the time. Her breaths soared in and out of her chest. She was just about to go inside when she stopped at the sight of the security camera above her door.

Broken. She frowned. Had the storm done that? The entire lens was smashed. Maybe a rock had been tossed up by the high winds? She'd have to order another.

Then something else suddenly hit her—a memory from the previous night of the light by her window. She'd told herself it was nothing, and Cole hadn't found anything when he'd checked. Still...no harm in checking in the daylight. Right?

With quick steps, she jogged back down the porch and moved around the house. She studied the path as she went. No footprints, but then, there'd been so much rain she wasn't surprised. When she reached her bedroom window, she studied the ground beneath it. Nothing.

God. She was being silly.

She was about to walk back inside when something caught her eye. Frowning, she crouched beneath the window.

A button. A small brown button. Not one of hers that she knew of. Was it Zac's?

When she straightened, she scanned the area.

Quickly, she whipped out her phone and accessed the video storage from the house surveillance. She hadn't checked last night because it was powered by Wi-Fi, so the second the power went off, the camera would have too. But maybe it had caught something before that?

She clicked into the footage, finding the section from about an hour before the power outage. The camera's view extended all the way to the road. It was a safety precaution she never went without. Not with Zac's father out there somewhere, always showing up out of the blue, wherever they went.

She sped up the footage, looking for anything that might stick out. A couple of cars drove past, but other than that, nothing. She was about to click out of the video when yet another car drove past. She paused the footage.

Not another car. The same car that had driven past minutes before.

The footage was blurry through the rain, but it didn't stop her from noticing that it was the same red sedan.

Swallowing hard, she jogged back around the house and went inside. When she reached the kitchen, she tossed the button in a drawer. She made a mental note to mention both the car and the footage to Hanon. It could be nothing. But at the same time, she wanted the officer to know, just in case.

After a quick shower, she made a smoothie and sat down in the spare room. The space was both her office and her home gym.

She started with her emails, and ten minutes in, all she'd done was read and reread the same email three times. She hated admin. Exactly why she left it until dead last on her work list.

When the front door opened, she swiveled around on her chair. Footsteps sounded down the hall, then Zac stepped into the doorway, backpack on his shoulder.

She gave him a small smile. "Hey."

"Hey, Mom."

"How was your night of studying?"

He lifted a shoulder. "It was fine."

Fine. That was all. She was too tired to push for more today. "That's great."

She turned back to her laptop and started reading the same email for a fourth freaking time when Zac spoke again.

"Mom." His voice had softened.

She turned. "Yeah, hon?"

"I'm sorry."

She frowned. "Sorry for what?"

His gaze lowered to the floor, and he seemed to take a moment to consider his words. "I've been...angry lately. And I've been taking it out on you."

"What's made you angry?"

"I don't know. Everything. I think of Dad a lot and what he's done to us..."

His words made her heart hurt. She hated that she couldn't fully protect her son from his father.

Zac shook his head. "And I just...I feel so pissed at him. That he couldn't be the father and family man he should have been. That he hurt you. That he's forced us to leave every home we make because he can't stay out of trouble."

"Zac..." She stood. She hated that he shouldered this. All she wanted—all she'd ever wanted—was for him to be safe and happy. "I'm sorry."

"And *that*. I hate that he makes you feel like you're somehow responsible when it's all on him." He shook his head again. "What I want to say is, I'm sorry, and I'm going to try to do better. You *deserve* better, Mom."

Her heart gave a giant thump. God, she loved this kid. "Thank you, Zac. But I want you to talk to me. Whenever you feel *anything*. Guilt. Sadness. Anger. I want you to tell me, and we can work through it together."

Her son's chest rose and fell, then he nodded. When her phone buzzed from the table, her gaze shot down. Zac's father. Again. Quickly, she canceled the call.

"Who was that?"

She swallowed, but before she could answer, he got that knowing look on his face.

"It was him."

She nodded gravely. "It was."

His throat bobbed, and she could tell he was struggling to hold onto his anger. "I'm going to take a shower and change."

"Okay. I love you."

"Love you too."

Yep, another kick of her heart. She'd never tire of hearing him say those words.

"And Zac..."

He paused and turned.

"It'll be okay." She'd make sure of it.

He gave her a small smile before walking away.

For the next ten minutes, she tried and failed to concentrate on the admin work in front of her, until she finally gave up. Screw admin. She'd research rentals instead. Maybe Indiana wasn't far enough. Maybe it was time to move far, far away. The North Pole didn't sound so terrible.

# CHAPTER 11

*M*eals Made Easy caught Aria's eye. It was lunchtime and she'd driven into town to go for a walk. The little shop in the center of Lindeman sold precooked meals. She hadn't tried the place before, and she had no idea why not. She wasn't a good cook. Never had been, probably never would be. In fact, unless tuna salad or a club sandwich was on the menu, she pretty much sucked.

Luckily, Zac never complained about her pathetic attempts at whipping up a Bolognese for dinner.

She could see two women talking inside the shop. They were hunched over, looking at something on the counter.

She pushed the handle to open the door, but unlike every other shop in Lindeman, it was locked. Strange. Was the place closed? It was Saturday. Not much was closed in town on a Saturday.

She spotted the little button on the side wall. A buzzer. Interesting. Seemed like a big safety precaution for a small town. She hit the buzzer and a second later, the women turned and the door clicked.

"Good morning," a brunette with blue eyes, brown hair and

freckles across her nose greeted from behind the counter. She offered a friendly smile. "I'm Michele, owner of Meals Made Easy."

"Morning." Aria closed the door behind her.

The other woman was a bit taller and had the blackest eyes and hair Aria had ever seen. Both women were beautiful.

"Hi, I'm River, the best friend. Definitely not the cook. That would be devastating for business."

Aria stepped up to the counter and was hit with a pang of familiarity. Where had she seen these women before?

Michele tilted her head. "You live across from Cole, Ryker and Anthony, don't you?"

Ah, that was it. "Yes. That would be me. You're friends with the guys?"

"I'm dating Jackson," River said. "The tall, dark and handsome one."

"Aren't they all?" Aria asked wryly.

Michele chuckled. "Yes, they are. She's also Ryker's sister. I'm with Declan. He lived there until a week ago, and I stayed with them for a little while, but we're now living with River for a little bit."

River leaned in conspiratorially. "Less testosterone."

Aria chuckled. "Well, I just live with my son, Zac."

Michele's lips parted. "Zac, as in *Anthony's* friend Zac? He's your son?"

She was used to the reaction. Especially after moving as often as she had and experiencing surprise from so many. "He is. I was sixteen when I had him." She usually added that part in automatically, because if she didn't, she was hit with the "but he looks so old, and you look so young," and she was left to answer the question anyway.

"Zac actually came in the other day and interviewed for a position here," Michele said.

Now it was Aria's turn to be surprised. "He did?"

"Yeah. Anthony recommended him to do some after-school shifts." She paused. "Is that okay?"

She forced a smile to her lips. "Of course."

She'd applied for a couple of rentals today, so there was a chance he wouldn't be here for long. Is that why he hadn't told her? Because he knew what she'd say?

"I bet having a teenager is amazing." River sighed. "I can't wait to have babies, then have those babies turn into big people who can dress themselves and are forced to be my best friends."

Michele laughed. "I'm not sure that's how it works, River."

"Oh, it's definitely not how it works," Aria said quickly. "Some days our home's a battlefield, but it's all worth it for what the kid gives me." Especially mornings like today, when she got the big "I love you." Those were the best.

Michele's smile softened. "That's awesome. Now, what can I get you today?"

Her gaze skittered to the fridge behind the woman. "I'm guessing people order meals from you in advance? I haven't made an order, sorry."

She waved a hand. "I get walk-ins all the time and always have meals in the freezer for that reason."

"Oh, great. Have you got anything teenage-boy friendly?"

"You mean carbs?" She grinned. "I sure do. I have pasta, including lasagna, lots of meat-based dishes. They all have Anthony's seal of approval, so I'm sure Zac will love them."

"Wonderful. Could I grab maybe five different meals? I'm happy for you to surprise me."

"You got it." She turned to the huge fridge.

River lifted a large camera bag from the counter. "I should get to my shoot."

"You're a photographer?" Aria asked.

"Yup! I do a lot of food and beverage photography for cafés and bars, but I've also started doing some of my own landscape stuff."

"That sounds awesome." A thought hit her. "Actually, I've been wanting to update some of the shots on my website. I run an online fitness business. Any chance I could hire you for a day? I'd love to get some shots of me working out in nature."

"Absolutely." She whipped out a card from a pocket in the bag. "Text or call whenever you'd like. I know some great places around here that would be amazing for that."

"Great. Thank you." She slid the card into her pocket as Michele put the meals into a bag and slid them across the counter. "And thank you for the meals, Michele. Zac's going to kiss my feet when he realizes he doesn't have to force down another half-cooked tuna bake."

"Not a problem. Come back anytime."

She'd just paid when Michele glanced at something over Aria's shoulder and smiled. A big, something-just-melted-my-heart kind of smile. She hit the buzzer, and when Aria turned, her own heart stopped.

Cole. And behind him, four other guys.

Two of them went straight around the counter, one wrapping an arm around Michele, the other pressing a kiss to River's lips.

Aria took a large step away from the counter, glancing up at the three remaining men. "Hey."

She wanted to focus on Cole but worked hard to shift her gaze between them.

One of the guys dipped his head. "Hey, I'm Ryker."

Ah, River's brother.

The other nodded. "Erik."

All she got from Cole was a tight smile. A tight. Freaking. Smile. No "hi." No "how are you today?" Not only that, his hands were in his pockets and he barely met her gaze.

Her stomach tumbled. Really? After sleeping with her, he left without a word, and now he could barely look her in the eye?

She knew he didn't do relationships, but this was ridiculous. She kind of wanted to scream at him. Either that or grab his shirt and demand to know what the hell was wrong with him. But no way was she going to sacrifice her dignity like that.

Instead, she straightened her spine and turned back to the women.

River smiled. "This is Jackson, and that's Declan."

She remembered them from Mercy Ring. Both men gave her warm grins. She could barely lift the corners of her lips. But she did. Kind of.

"Hi." She looked at Michele, then River. "Thank you again for the meals, and for agreeing to do the photos. I'll call you."

She turned and left the store without another glance at Cole.

*Asshole.* He was a huge asshole. And the fact she'd ever thought he was anything else just made her feel stupid. And *he* was a stupid mistake that would never be repeated. It couldn't be. Because, yes, he may not be a relationship guy, but hell, she deserved a freaking *hi* when he runs into her after a night together...at the bare minimum.

She neared the curb, preparing to cross the street, when tight fingers wrapped around her arm and stopped her. That was becoming a habit. She turned her head to see a very tall, very stony-faced Cole looking down at her.

"What do you want?" Her words were short and clipped. She was all out of polite today.

"I'm sorry."

"Sorry for what? Sneaking out of bed without leaving a note, or pretending like I didn't exist back there?" She'd thought guys stopped doing that when they left high school. Apparently not.

She took a step onto the road, but he tugged her back. His jaw clenched. "Both."

When she remained silent, his gaze rose above her head. Was he searching for answers on the street behind her? "I'm sorry I can't give you what you want."

Her stomach did another of those rolls. "I don't want *anything* from you." Lie. Big. Fat. Lie. "I need to go." She spun away from him.

"Aria..." He didn't grab her this time.

She was halfway across the road when she heard the roar of an engine. She looked up—

And saw a car speeding toward her.

A hard body collided with hers, and for a second, she was flying through the air. She expected to hit the unforgiving concrete, but at the last moment, Cole twisted, angling his body to take the brunt of the impact with the road. Aria landed on top of him.

He quickly rolled them closer to the curb and studied her face. There was anger mixed with worry in his eyes. "Are you okay?"

She gave a quick nod, swallowing a few times. "I felt... I felt the air from the car on us." That's how close she'd come to being roadkill. His head shot up and his gaze narrowed. The car turned a corner and disappeared.

He carefully tugged her to her feet, pulled out his phone and began typing something.

"Did you get the plate numbers?" she asked.

"Yeah. I'm going to text them to Officer Hanon."

She gave a quick nod, but it felt stilted. In fact, her entire body felt shaky.

As he typed, she grabbed the fallen food containers, which had scattered across the pavement. Nothing seemed to be damaged, but if it had been, that would have been the last of her worries.

She was just reaching for the last container when Cole grabbed it first and handed it to her. Then he cupped her face. "You sure you're okay?"

No. She really wasn't. But instead of leaning into him like she wanted, she stepped back. "I'm fine. I need to get back to work."

"Aria—"

"Thank you, Cole." Another step back. When he made to move forward, she held out a hand. Damn, she hated that it was shaking. "Don't follow me. I'm fine. Thank you for saving me yet again."

His jaw clenched. "I'd like to walk you to your car, at least."

"No. I'm parked just down the street, so you don't need to. I'll call Officer Hanon about that car later. I'll see you around." She turned and quickly walked away. God, today was a mess.

She'd almost reached her car when something in the distance caught her eye. She stopped in her tracks. Was that...someone's *phone* poking around the corner of a building at the end of the block? She squinted.

The phone disappeared.

# CHAPTER 12

*C*ole's feet pounded against the pavement. He'd received another call from his mother last night. A call he hadn't answered, which was quickly followed by a text from his sister. They both wanted him to visit.

No. That wasn't something he was interested in doing. Especially not now, while his head was a damn mess with all this Aria stuff. He was an ass to her yesterday at Michele's shop because the second he'd stepped inside and seen her, all he'd wanted to do was touch her. Talk to her. Tug her body close and show the world she was his.

He pumped his legs faster.

That had never happened to him before. Separation was always easy. With Aria, it was anything but. And that scared the shit out of him. So, he'd looked away. He'd shut his mouth and not said anything because he'd had no idea *what* to say.

Mistake. Big fucking mistake. He'd seen the hurt and anger cross her face before she'd stormed out of the shop.

He sped up again, ignoring the tightness in his chest and the ache of his muscles. Wind whipped across his face.

His friends had given him hell when he returned to the shop, just like he'd known they would. They'd witnessed him running after a woman, something none of them thought he'd *ever* do. The pressure from his friends to just give in to how he felt...it was intense. They knew why he was fighting this so hard. They knew all about his fucked-up family history and why he stayed away from relationships.

When he turned the next corner, his chest expanded on a gasp. Because there, up ahead, was Aria.

It was barely six a.m., so he shouldn't be surprised she was out running. But he was surprised to see her *here*. He'd thought she ran west from her house...exactly why he'd run east.

His gaze caught on the tight shorts hugging her ass. They were so short, he could see every inch of her long, creamy legs. And that sports bra showed almost her entire back. Jesus, even her bare back was sexy.

Unless he turned around, he was going to catch up to her.

As he grew closer, he slowed his legs. She jumped when he reached her side, her gaze shooting up. She hadn't heard him coming because she was still wearing those damn earbuds. At least it wasn't dark.

Without stopping or slowing, she tugged them out of her ears. "Hey."

"Hey. Glad to see you're not running in the dark anymore."

"You were right—it wasn't safe." She kept her gaze forward and lifted a shoulder. "I can't give up my music, though."

She moved gracefully when she ran. Her arms remained close to her body while her strides were powerful, yet her footwork light. It almost looked like she was gliding.

Effortless. She made running look effortless.

"I thought you ran west." He regretted his words instantly.

One side of her mouth lifted. "Is that why you're running east? Trying to avoid me?"

*Yes.*

"Sorry, Cole. I don't always stick to the same route." She smiled. "Guess I'm not as predictable as you think."

His cock twitched at that smile. Damn, this woman was dangerous. "I have a sister. I know better than to think any woman's predictable." Hell, women were among the most impulsive creatures on the planet. Men, he understood. And not just because he *was* one, but because he'd spent sixteen years serving with guys almost exclusively.

He felt her eyes on him briefly. "You have a sister?"

"I do. She's a couple years younger than me. She lives in Wisconsin."

There was a beat of silence. "Do you visit often?"

"I lived there for a year while my back was healing, but I didn't go home often before that, and I haven't been back since." Because that town suffocated him, and so did his mother. If he never returned, he probably wouldn't care.

"What's she like?"

"Naomi? She's great. A good mom to her son, Chris, and strong." She was doing a lot better than she had been.

"She's a mom? That's awesome. So you're an uncle. Is she married?"

His stomach coiled. "She was. He died."

There was a small gasp, and her feet slowed. "How?"

"He was a tow truck driver. He was crushed between the fixed headboard and toolbox behind the cab of a tilt-tray tow truck. My sister got a payout for his death, but..."

"Money doesn't bring him back," she finished for him.

"It doesn't. And it took her a long time to be okay again." But God, he was glad she'd gotten there. He'd been worried for a while.

When he felt Aria's eyes on him again, he sped up. She matched his pace. "You got any siblings?" he asked, wanting to change the subject.

She looked forward, and finally he could breathe again. "No. I always wanted a brother or sister. My childhood was...lonely."

His brows tugged together. "I'm sorry."

"It was mostly because my parents were so absent. Plenty of kids without siblings have great childhoods."

"You still keep in contact with them?"

She laughed, but there was no humor in it. "No. Getting pregnant so young pretty much got me disowned."

"You were a kid who needed help, and they *disowned* you?"

"Yep."

Shit. What kind of life had this woman led? How had she raised a kid when she'd been just a child herself?

"The father help you out?"

The muscles in her body visibly tensed. Did she not get along with the man? Or maybe she just didn't want to talk about him?

"I moved in with him and his family until we saved enough to get a place of our own."

When she didn't say more, he frowned. He wanted to ask questions. Who was he? Was he still in her life? Had he been a kid too? But everything about her body language and voice told him she wasn't open to the conversation.

"How's Zac doing?"

Finally, a slight lift of her lips. "Good." She looked over at him. "He's a good kid."

"Never said he wasn't."

"He's just had to deal with a lot in his life."

"Like what?"

"Like a mother who was so young she had no idea what she was doing. A lack of family. Instability."

When her breathing got louder and faster, he bit back a curse. He was running too fast, and she was trying to match him. He slowed gradually to a walk.

Frowning, she slowed with him. "What's wrong?"

"Nothing. Just want to walk for a bit." They were on their street anyway. "You're doing a great job."

"At running? Thanks, but fitness is my job, so I'd hope so."

He shook his head. "At raising and looking after Zac."

They'd just reached the front of her house when she stopped, and he stopped with her. There was a beat of silence before she spoke. "All you've seen is the two of us arguing."

He met her gaze. "Not true. I've seen that you work hard to put a roof over his head. I've seen that you make his well-being a priority." He took a small step forward because he couldn't stop himself. "I've seen in the way you look at him that you love him, and he's your first priority."

"Most days, he's my only priority," she said quietly.

Because he was weak, he swiped a finger up her arm and felt the tremble beneath his touch. "It makes me wonder...who's been taking care of *you* all these years?"

His finger trailed back down, then moved to her waist. Her bare waist. He shouldn't be touching her, but he literally couldn't stop. Everything he learned about this woman made him want her more.

"I have."

Her throat bobbed, and his gaze shot down. Suddenly, all he could think about was how that throat had tasted when he was sucking on it that night. How her back had arched and her eyes shuttered when his mouth ran across her soft skin.

His fingers tightened on her waist.

"Cole...what are you doing?"

He had no fucking clue. When it came to this woman, he had zero control. "I'm talking to you."

She pressed her hands to his chest, and the heat from her palms penetrated his skin. "You're doing more than that."

"I shouldn't touch you," he said, speaking his thoughts out loud. Yet even as he said them, his other hand went to her neck.

She leaned in. "Then why does it feel so right?"

"Good damn question," he whispered.

She wet her lips.

Fuck it.

His lips slammed onto hers. And there it was again. The roar inside him. The need to tug her closer. Claim every part of her.

She moaned and her fingers bit into his shoulders. When he slipped his tongue inside her mouth, he growled. She tasted so fucking sweet. It was a taste he could get addicted to. Hell, he already was.

He tugged her hips snug against him. His fingers slid behind her head. He wanted to stay right here. To block out the world and just get lost with this woman—

"*Mom?*"

Her muscles tightened in his hold. Then she gave his chest a push. It took everything in him to let her go. To step back and put space between them.

He turned in time to see Zac standing in the open doorway of their house. He was dressed in track pants and a shirt. His hair was a mess, like he'd just woken up...and he was scowling at Cole.

"Crap," Aria whispered under her breath. She looked up at him. "I'll see you later, Cole."

She moved across the yard and onto the porch, where there were quiet words spoken as Zac's gaze kept flicking over her head toward him. Then she hustled him inside, firmly closing the door.

And it took everything Cole had to not go after her and promise things he had no business promising.

# CHAPTER 13

"*O*h, man. You're not even breathing heavily, while I'm over here huffing like a steamboat and moving like a giant sloth."

Aria chuckled at River. The other woman definitely was not doing either of those things. "Have you seen a giant sloth move? I guarantee you, you're moving faster."

"Oh, I've seen many sloths move. I make a habit of watching sloth videos, then forcing Jackson to watch them with me."

Aria laughed again. This woman was hilarious. "Doesn't sound like the worst use of time. And in case I haven't said it yet, thank you for bringing me out here for this shoot."

"No problem. I love hiking out here, even if I do sweat my face off."

River had suggested the Atlas Woods right here in Lindeman. There was a well-used trail, but River was leading them off the beaten path to a particular clearing she liked. They'd already taken a few photos of Aria hiking on the way up, and a couple of her stretching. When River pulled her camera out, she was intensely focused.

"So, this is a secret location that only locals know about?" Aria asked.

"Ha, locals *wish* they knew about it. I mean, some probably do, but not many. I just love nature and found it one afternoon when I was exploring new areas."

Aria sidestepped a large bush. "Exploring new areas sounds fun."

"Yeah, I don't do it as often as I used to, though. Jackson's big and beautiful, but he's also my fun police. He doesn't like me being out here in the middle of nowhere on my own. Hell, it was an effort to get him to agree to us coming here today without him. I mean, I know I was shot, but I still need to live."

Aria tripped over her own feet. "You were *shot?*"

River swung her head around. "Yeah, some rookie cop missed the bad guy and got me instead. But I'm fine now."

Aria was sure her eyes were almost bugging out of her head. "When was this?"

"Hm, maybe two months ago? I've lost count of the days."

And the woman was already hiking? "Maybe we should stop here?"

"No, no. I'm fine. Trust me, Jackson made sure I rested plenty after the whole getting-shot-and-kidnapping ordeal."

Okay, this time she actually *felt* her eyes bug out of her head. "You were kidnapped too?"

"Kidnapped might not be the right word. Can you call it kidnapping when you voluntarily hide in the bad guys' truck, and they drive away with you still inside?"

The woman was messing with her, right?

River shot her another look, and her lips twitched. "We live exciting lives here in Lindeman."

Aria opened her mouth to ask one of the million and one questions racing through her head, but River spoke first.

"We're here."

She followed through a break in the trees, and her eyes

widened. "River, this is beautiful." And such a great spot for some photos. It was a large, open clearing of grass nestled between thick trees. Amazing.

River's eyes softened. "I know. I love it here. You can almost forget the outside world exists. These pictures will be perfect."

The woman seemed to have a real passion for nature photography. She'd told Aria a bit about it on the way up here, how she'd only recently started selling her nature shots, and before that, her entire income had come from food and beverage photography.

River dropped her gear, keeping her camera in hand. "All right. You do your thing, and I'll snap away."

Aria took off her jacket. Luckily, after the walk, she wasn't cold at all. She started with some lower body resistance exercises, then got into some upper body stuff. Every so often, River would ask her to stop and hold a pose, but other than that, every photo was authentically her working out, exactly the way she liked to run her business.

When she started her cool down, she smiled. The stretching at the end was her favorite part. The slowness after a huge hit of endorphins… Yeah, it was awesome.

River bent down and snapped a photo as Aria stretched her quads. "We have some amazing shots here."

"I can't wait to see them. I've been wanting to get some nature shots done for a while."

River changed angles. "You're a machine. You just did a full workout after a huge hike and didn't even break a sweat."

"The cold helped keep my temperature down."

River scoffed. "I could be in a blizzard, and I'd still be a pool of sweat if I did that workout. Bet you already did some mammoth run this morning too."

She *had* done her run. Her very eventful run, which had ended with her being lip-locked with Cole before Zac found them.

She nodded. "I *did* run this morning."

River lowered the camera. "Everything okay?"

Did she not look okay? "Of course." If you call having a thing for your commitment-phobic neighbor—and a teenage son being not so happy about it—okay.

She switched to stretching her hamstrings.

"Because if it isn't, I'm a great listener," River said. "I know we don't know each other that well, but people have said I give out some pretty awesome advice."

Aria chuckled.

"Okay, less people and more Michele. But the woman knows what she's talking about."

Well…it would be nice to talk to someone. As infrequently as she dated, she made even fewer friends.

"Cole and I had sex," she blurted.

River's brows rose. "Wow. That's huge. When?" There was no judgment in her voice, just surprise.

"The night of the storm. Then he ignored me in Michele's shop yesterday—"

"He *did*! That asshat."

"Then this morning, he caught up to me on my run and kissed me."

River's brows rose higher. "If that doesn't give you whiplash, nothing will."

"I know! I don't know what's going on or what to do. I mean, the sex was great." Not just great. Out-of-this-world amazing. "But literally just before that, he told me he wasn't a relationship person. Whereas I…"

"You are."

Was she? "Well, I don't really engage in casual sex"—until now, it seemed—"so I guess I am. My relationships have always been a mess, though. I tend to choose the assholes, for some reason. Every relationship since I was a teenager has been short-lived and kind of a disaster." Not kind of. Egg-in-the-face, should-have-never-tried-it disaster. "The last guy I dated cheated on me."

River scowled. "He *was* an asshole."

"Zac got home while he and I were in the middle of a huge fight over it. He'd grabbed my arm, and Zac went nuts."

God, she hated even thinking about that day. She'd had to hold Zac off the guy while he fled.

"Then this morning," she continued, "Zac saw me kissing Cole. He held himself together pretty well, but he wasn't happy."

"Because he loves you and wants you to be safe, but he doesn't know Cole well enough to trust him with you," River said gently.

"Exactly." She grabbed her water bottle and took a sip. "If I was smart, I'd stay away from him." But any time Cole was near, she didn't want to be smart. She didn't want to use her brain at all.

There was a beat of silence before River spoke again. "Maybe." She lowered the bottle. "You don't agree?"

"Depends on how much you like him. You *could* stay away, or..." She lifted a shoulder. "You could peel back his layers. Find out why he doesn't date. I mean, he obviously likes you. I haven't heard of him sleeping with someone, then going back and kissing them. Like...*ever*."

Her skin heated at River's words. She liked Cole. It was actually crazy how much, considering how little they knew each other. The kiss this morning had been unexpected. But it had also been explosive and raw and hot.

She moved over to a large tree and lifted her leg, pressing her toes against the wood to stretch her calf. "You are very wise."

River's smile grew. "Told you."

Aria switched feet. Her shoe brushed against something hard when she put her first leg down. Frowning, she glanced at the ground, brushing away some of the dead leaves with her foot. She paused.

Wait. Was that—

"Is that a *shoe*?" River asked, moving behind Aria.

Carefully, Aria brushed more leaves away—and her heart stopped.

The shoe was connected to a leg. It was a person.

"Oh my God!" River gasped.

With shaking limbs, Aria crouched and carefully brushed piles of dead leaves away from the body. When she reached a face, she screeched and scrambled back. A man, his eyes open and lifeless. But it wasn't just any man.

It was the kid who'd slipped Klonopin into her drink in the bar. Rufus Maddon.

~

"So...you kissed her."

Cole scrubbed a hand over his face as he and Jackson walked to the coffee shop. He hadn't even told his friend anything yet, but he somehow knew. "Who told you?"

"Ryker. He saw you from the window."

*Asshole.* "Yeah, I kissed her."

Best damn kiss of his life, and he hadn't stopped thinking about it since. The only reason he'd let her go was because of Zac. "I don't know what's going on with me."

"I do. You're falling for her."

The panic was instant, and it spidered through his limbs, making him twitchy.

Jackson clasped his shoulder. "Hey. Take it from me, a guy who fought his feelings for River for *years*. Once you stop fighting it, life gets easier."

"It's different. You've known River since you were teenagers." And Cole wasn't falling for anyone.

Jackson laughed. "Time isn't a factor. I've loved River since the day I met her. I just fought it for too damn long."

They stepped inside the café, which was the closest coffee

shop to Mercy Ring. When Cole spotted Officer Hanon sitting at a table with a mug of coffee, he moved straight over to him.

"Hanon."

The officer looked up. "Turner. How are you doing today?" The guy looked tired. He had dark circles under his eyes.

"I'll be better if you tell me you've caught Maddon."

The guy grimaced and shook his head. "Not yet. He's still on everyone's radar, though, so it won't be long."

Cole had his doubts. "What about the car that almost hit Aria?"

"Stolen. It was dumped on the outskirts of town, and there were no prints."

Shit. Cole scrubbed a hand over his face.

"The car had a strong stench of alcohol," Hanon continued. "Whatever happened, I don't think it was malicious. It was likely some drunk scumbag who wasn't in control of what he was doing."

A waitress stopped in front of them just as Hanon answered a call.

"What can I get you?" she asked Cole.

"Black coffee to go."

"Latte for me," Jackson said. "And two cappuccinos."

Cole raised a brow at his friend. "Latte?"

"Fuck off. River got me onto them."

He chuckled. "I got nothing against you ordering a latte. It's just not your usual black. What's River doing today, anyway?"

Jackson's lips twitched. "She's doing some work for Aria, actually."

That had him pausing. "She's taking photos for her?"

"Yep. In the Atlas Woods."

Cole frowned. "Where's that?" He'd only been living in Lindeman for a few months, so he wasn't as familiar with the area as Jackson, who'd grown up here.

"Not too far east. A bit remote," Jackson offered.

He frowned. "Is it safe for them to be hiking out there on their own?"

The hesitation from Jackson was enough to have Cole tensing.

"It's not *unsafe*. Just isolated. I don't love River going out there when she's alone, but the women should be fine together. River knows the woods well and it's daylight."

"This goddamn Black Dust is causing me to lose too much sleep. We need to find the damn dealer, and we need to find them *now*."

Cole frowned at Hanon's last words into the phone before he hung up. "Black Dust?"

Hanon scowled. "The street name of a new synthetic psychoactive drug. Very powerful. Very expensive. A lot of kids who've managed to get their hands on it are already dead."

"And someone's dealing it in *our* town?" Cole asked.

"Yes."

Shit. He didn't want that stuff anywhere near Anthony. "We'll keep an eye out."

Hanon was just nodding when his phone rang again. He looked at the screen before sighing and answering. "Hanon speaking."

The man immediately swore under his breath and shot to his feet. When his gaze flew to him and Jackson, Cole's muscles tensed yet again.

"Leaving now." He hung up.

"What is it?" Jackson asked before he could.

"Aria Callas and River Harp just found the body of Rufus Maddon in the Atlas Woods."

Cole's stomach dropped. Jackson cursed and whipped his phone from his pocket.

# CHAPTER 14

The sight of Aria made Cole's gut clench. She sat under a tree beside River, arms wrapped around her waist, her face white. They were in the parking area for the trails. Police cars were scattered everywhere, but Aria almost looked like she was in a world of her own.

He parked his vehicle, and the second River glanced their way, she stood and ran to Jackson as he exited the truck. Aria didn't look up at all.

When Cole reached her, he crouched in front of her. Still, she didn't lift her head. Carefully, he moved some hair off her face and tucked it behind her ear.

"Hey."

Finally, she focused on him. A frown marred her brow. "What are you doing here?"

"Jackson and I were in the coffee shop with Hanon when he got the call."

She nibbled her bottom lip and nodded. "It was the guy from the bar."

"I know."

"He's dead."

"I'm so sorry you had to see that." Finding a dead body in the woods would give most people nightmares.

She swallowed and looked away, toward the trees. "He had dried blood on his head. I think someone hit him."

He cradled her cheek, and she looked back at him. "Let's get you home."

Her eyes skirted between his for a moment. Then, without a word, she nodded.

He helped her up, then slid an arm around her waist. She didn't bat an eye at his touch. He hated how pale she was.

He looked around and found River already in the passenger seat of her car. Aria's Beetle wasn't here, so River must have driven them. Jackson gave him a nod before sliding into the driver's side.

He helped Aria into his truck before lightly caressing her cheek once again. It seemed that every time he did, some of the color returned to her face. "I'll be back in a sec."

She swallowed and gave another nod.

He closed the door and moved over to Hanon, who was talking to the officers who'd reached the area before them.

"Guy's been dead for a while," one of the officers said. "Maybe a week."

"A week?" Cole frowned. "That would put his time of death very near the night he slipped the Klonopin into Aria's drink."

Hanon blew out a breath, scrubbing a hand over his jaw before giving Cole a look. "Turner, don't go getting any ideas. As far as we're aware at the moment, these are isolated incidents."

"When will the coroner know the exact time of death?" he asked, ignoring Hanon's warning.

"Within twenty-four hours," the young police officer said.

Nodding, he turned back to Hanon. "I want to know what they say, and any other information you can give me."

He frowned. "Turner—"

"She's part of this," he interrupted, his voice low. "It's too much of a coincidence. And I have to know she's safe. *She* deserves to know she's safe."

A beat passed before the guy answered. "Fine. I'll let you know."

"Good." He'd been prepared to stand there and argue for as long as he had to. The officer had saved him time, which he appreciated, because he wanted to get Aria home as soon as possible.

He turned away and moved back to his truck. Aria was looking out the windshield without really focusing on anything. He hated seeing her like that.

He waited until they were driving to try and talk to her. "The hike up there go okay?"

Her brows lifted. She hadn't been expecting that question, but hell, he wanted to get her mind off the dead body. He wanted to see some color back in her cheeks and have her look at him like she was actually *seeing* him.

"It was good," Aria finally said. "River made me laugh a lot. She was joking that she's not fit, but she is."

He smiled. "She's got a great sense of humor. The other day, she told me I was about as deep as a puddle. But not the kind left from a storm, the kind of puddle you get after a small sprinkle of rain."

Aria chuckled. The sound had his own lips tugging up.

"She felt the need to be that specific?" Aria asked.

"Oh yeah. I don't even remember what I said to warrant such an insult."

Another chuckle. For the rest of the drive, Cole worked hard to keep her mind off Maddon's dead body. And, for the most part, it worked. By the time he pulled into his drive, there was more color to her cheeks.

He was about to reach for his door when she stopped him with a touch on his arm. "Thank you. For driving me home and taking my mind off things."

He covered her hand. "I don't like seeing you upset." For some reason, it made him want to go to battle for her and fight every enemy she had, real or in her head.

They climbed out and he crossed over to her side of the car. When he pressed a hand to her back and started heading across the street, she frowned. "You don't have to come with me."

"I am." Every part of him knew this woman shouldn't be alone right now.

"I'm okay," she said softly.

"That's good. But I'd still prefer to stay with you for a while."

She opened her mouth, and for a moment, he thought she was going to fight him on it. Until she simply said, "Thank you."

THE SECOND ARIA stepped out of the shower, she smelled Mexican spices.

She frowned. Was someone cooking? She didn't have ingredients to make Mexican food. And as far as she was aware, the closest Mexican restaurant was a good hour's drive away. Which was strange for the west coast.

She dried off quickly before wrapping herself in a big pink towel and sneaking to her bedroom. The shock of finding Maddon had finally worn off. Mostly.

She'd seen a dead guy. Not just any dead guy. The one who'd drugged her and tried to whisk her off to God knew where. She'd probably never get his vacant eyes out of her head. They'd be permanently ingrained in her memory forever. But at least she didn't feel like she was going to be horribly sick at any second.

She quickly checked her phone, noticing a message from River.

*Are you doing okay?*

River had saved her today. Where Aria had wanted to fall

apart at the scene, River had taken charge, leading her back to the car, where they had cell reception, and calling the police.

She quickly responded to River's message.

*I'm okay. Thanks for checking in. You?*

*Yeah, Jackson's hovering like a crazy person. I keep telling him I'm fine, but he doesn't believe me. Hope Cole's taking good care of you. Let me know if you want me or Chele to pop over.*

God, the woman was sweet.

*Thank you, River. I'll let you know.*

She'd also gotten a text from Michele earlier, just before she jumped into the shower. Apparently, news traveled fast around here. She had no idea how the woman had gotten her number, but it was nice to have people checking in on her.

She walked into the hall and stopped in her living room when she saw Cole standing by the stove, stirring something with his back to her. Her gaze flicked to the island, where there was diced tomato, lettuce and onion, a jar of salsa, some soft tortillas and a bowl of guacamole.

"When you insisted on staying, I thought you'd wait on the couch, make sure I didn't pass out in the shower, and then leave."

She certainly hadn't expected this. Maybe she *had* passed out somewhere between the dead body and here, and now she was dreaming about this gladiator of a man cooking for her.

He looked at her over his shoulder. He was still stirring whatever he had cooking on the stove, and the muscles in his arm flexed. Man, why did a domestic Cole have to be even sexier than a moody, brooding Cole?

"I wanted to make sure you ate. Bit risky when I don't know what you like. I'm hoping you're going to tell me you're a fan of Mexican."

She took slow steps forward and gave her thigh a little pinch. *Ouch.* Nope. Not dreaming. "I love Mexican food. Guacamole especially is a favorite of mine. But I didn't have ingredients for this food in my house, and this looks like a feast. And it's only lunchtime."

"Ryker ran everything over from our place for me." One side of his mouth lifted. "And nothing wrong with eating Mexican for lunch."

No, there wasn't. There wasn't anything wrong with any of this. It was just one big fat shock. She'd had a few of them today. "It looks like your culinary skills go beyond breakfast food."

He grabbed a trivet from the drawer. How the man knew where stuff was in her kitchen, she had no idea.

"I have a limited number of recipes in my repertoire." He set the trivet on the island and smiled at her. Good Lord, that smile... "I don't tell many people. It's a bit of a secret."

He was sharing secrets with her now?

She slid onto a stool at the island. He sat beside her and started assembling a taco on his plate.

She didn't understand him. At all. He didn't do relationships, but sex, followed by kisses and cooking her food, was okay?

"How are you doing after this morning?" he finally asked.

She dragged her eyes away from him and scooped a heaping spoon of guacamole onto a tortilla. "I don't feel like I'm about to pass out anymore, so that's good."

"That *is* good," he said softly.

"It wasn't just the shock of seeing the dead body that affected me..." She paused, feeling his eyes on her.

"What else?"

Her throat felt tight, but she forced the words out. "I'm pretty sure he was wearing the same clothes as...as that night."

He clenched his fork so hard his knuckles turned white.

"It was just jeans and a T-shirt," she added quickly. "So, they might not have been. But I couldn't help but wonder what would have happened to *me* if he'd gotten me out of Lenny's Bar."

She finally looked at his face, and it was to see Cole's eyes, hard and steely.

"And if something had happened to me," she continued, "what would have happened to Zac?" He was only sixteen. She had a restraining order against his father, so she didn't think he'd go to him. But...then what? Foster care? The thought made bile rise in her throat.

So much for no longer feeling sick.

Cole touched her shoulder, and that small bit of contact brought her back to him. It made the fear in her chest fade and something else grow. Something warmer.

"I wouldn't have let that guy leave with you."

"You didn't even know me," she said quietly.

"Maybe not, but I saw you push him away. I wouldn't have let you walk out of there with a guy you'd clearly tried to get rid of."

The hand on her arm slid up to her neck. She inhaled a deep breath.

"And I know you a lot better now."

She frowned. "You don't know me *that* well."

"I know you're a good mother who loves her son. I know you're passionate about health and fitness, and a hell of a businesswoman to have supported you both for so long. I know you don't like boxing, or at least seeing *Zac* box makes you nervous, but I don't know why."

Her stomach knotted and she tried hard to keep the emotions off her face.

"A few minutes ago, I learned you love Mexican food. And I know you have this particular spot on your neck...and when I swipe my thumb like this..."

She shuddered when he swiped his thumb gently over her flesh.

"You react to my touch like I've burned you."

"What are you doing?" she whispered.

She wasn't talking about just now. She was talking about the whole day so far. The kiss. Caring for her.

If the question bothered him, he didn't show it. "I'm talking to you. Getting to know you. Making sure you're okay."

"That almost sounds like courting. But you don't date, Cole."

His eyes flashed something dark. It came and went so quickly, she almost didn't catch it. "Since meeting you, I'm not so sure about that decision. I'm starting to think…maybe you're worth the risk."

Her belly did a massive flip. She wasn't sure what the man meant by "risk", but she liked that she might be worth it.

"Cole…"

His name had barely left her lips when he dipped his head and kissed her. It was soft and gentle, like he was exploring her. But it also touched a spot deep inside her that hadn't been touched for a long, long time…possibly ever.

# CHAPTER 15

*M*ercy Ring was busy today. All men, all hitting their own bags, some in pairs, some alone.

Cole crossed his arms over his chest. They hadn't opened their business that long ago, and it felt good to be helping people. There weren't enough boxing gyms in Washington, let alone the nearest towns.

Declan came to stand beside him, a huge smile on his face. "It's busy."

"I was just thinking that." Cole scanned the room. He'd already done a round, talking to new clients, correcting people's forms, and giving tips and pointers.

"I heard a rumor."

Cole's lips twitched at his friend's comment. "A rumor? We in high school or something?"

Declan's smile didn't drop.

"You gonna tell me what this rumor is, or you gonna make me guess?" Cole finally asked. He knew what his friend was going to say. But why make it easy for him?

"I heard you've been spending a lot of time across the street over the last week," he finally said.

"You hear this from Ryker or Anthony?"

"They've both mentioned it. Michele too."

Yeah, Cole knew Aria had been growing close to the women. "It's true. We've been spending a lot of time together."

"Kind of like...dating?"

Cole still got a small flicker of panic at the mention of the word, but it wasn't as consuming as it once was. "We haven't put a label on it. Just enjoying each other's company for now."

He'd even stayed over at the woman's house a couple of times during the last week. It was...nice.

Declan's grin got even wider. "I called it. Jackson owes me fifty."

"You guys bet on us?"

"We made a bet on how long it would take you two to get together. Jackson said a year." He shook his head. "The guy thinks everyone's a slow mover like him."

"Assholes." But even as Cole said it, one side of his mouth lifted.

"How does Zac feel about it?"

"The kid keeps his cards close to his chest, but I hope I'm growing on him. He's been working at Michele's shop with Anthony, so Anthony's probably telling him about all my good traits."

"Good traits?" Declan shoved his shoulder with a laugh. Then his face turned serious. "Hey, they ever find out anything about who killed that kid in the woods?"

The smile left Cole's lips, and a familiar heaviness sat in his gut. "No. Just that he died from a blow to the head."

What really had Cole's muscles twitching was that the autopsy report confirmed his time of death as the night he'd slipped Aria those drugs. It made Cole uncomfortable as hell. He wanted answers into what the fuck had happened, and he wanted them now.

"They found his car parked at the west end of the woods,"

Cole continued, grateful that Hanon had kept his promise to share what he could. "Other than the hit he received, there was no other evidence of foul play."

The police were still looking into it, but so far, they had nothing. Frustrated didn't even begin to explain how he felt.

When the door opened, Cole turned his head to see Aria stepping inside. Desire slammed into his gut at the sight of her in shorts and a workout top. At the gorgeous hair cascading over her shoulders.

He wanted her, plain and simple. More than he'd ever wanted anyone. So he was going with it. He wasn't labeling it. He was moving slow. Exploring whatever this was between them.

She walked toward them, and he immediately slipped an arm around her waist when she was within reach, tugging her close.

"Hey."

A huge smile stretched her lips. God, he loved her smile. "Hey. I just drove in to grab some meals from Michele and a coffee to fuel me. Thought I'd stop in and see if you guys want me to grab you one?"

He lowered his head and kissed her. He wasn't a PDA kind of guy, but he couldn't *not* kiss her. "A coffee would be great."

More because it meant she'd be back in ten minutes.

He kissed her again. Then he heard Declan behind him.

"Shit. What have you done to him, Aria?"

Aria pulled away. He wanted to growl and yank her back.

"What do you mean?" she asked.

"This is not the Cole I know." Declan slapped a hand on his shoulder. "But I like it. Maybe next you can make him laugh. Throw a few smiles our way every so often."

"I'll work on it," she said. "Right now, I'm spending all my time convincing him to cook for me."

"He *cooks?*"

Okay, talking time was done. "Straight black, please."

"You got it." She looked at Declan. "Coffee?"

"Cappuccino, thanks. And if you could bring me a side of whatever superpowers you have, that would be great."

Aria laughed. "A straight black and a cappuccino. Not sure they'll have superpowers, but I'll ask."

The second Aria left the building, Cole shoved his friend. "You need to stop."

"Not a chance, my friend. Not a chance."

Declan walked off toward a group of younger guys while Cole continued to survey the clients. He spent the next ten minutes moving around the room before a text came through on his phone.

He pulled it out, and the warmth that had settled in his gut from Aria's visit turned cold. It was Naomi.

*Hope you're doing okay today. Thinking of you and Dad. X*

His gaze shot to the date. The tenth. It was the anniversary of his father's death.

His heart pounded, and his chest suddenly felt tight.

With everything that had been happening with Aria, he'd just...forgotten.

He *never* forgot. That date was permanently ingrained in his mind. The date he'd found his father's lifeless body. The date his father had given in to the pain caused by his ex-wife and checked out, leaving Cole behind.

He held his phone so tightly he could have crushed it. He was still trying to control the turmoil rushing through his body when the door to Mercy Ring opened.

He shoved his phone into his pocket with a shaking hand and forced the emotion down. Then he walked toward the door to greet their new patron. The guy who stepped inside was big, both in height and breadth. About as big as Cole and his teammates.

"Hey," he said as he approached the guy. "I'm Cole, part owner."

"Hi. Marcus." His gaze scanned the room. "I was wondering if there was a spare bag I could train on this morning?"

"There's one bag left. I just need you to fill out some forms." Cole rounded the desk, his muscles still bunched from Naomi's text, but he did his best to ignore the tension vibrating through him. "You from around here?" Cole was pretty sure he'd never seen the guy before, but at the same time, there was something familiar about him.

Marcus shook his head. "Just here visiting family."

Cole nodded. "You boxed before?"

"I have. Did professional stuff for a while."

Maybe that was why the guy looked familiar. He handed over the forms. "Just fill these out."

He let the guy fill out the paperwork, then got him set up with a temporary pass before taking him over to the last free bag. "You need equipment?"

Marcus dropped his shoulder bag, pulled off his sweatshirt and took out gloves. "Nah. I'm good."

"Gonna be in town for long?"

Marcus frowned, fitting the first glove on his hand. "Not sure. Maybe."

Cole gave a slow nod. There was something about the guy that put him on alert. Something in his eyes and the way he spoke. A dangerous edge. He reminded Cole of some of the assholes he'd taken down while in the military.

Marcus's first punch was hard and precise. Exactly what a professional boxer's hit should be. Cole watched as he threw a few more. They were all the same.

He stepped back but kept his eye on the man, all while thinking about the text from his sister and the reminder of what this day was…and that, for the first time in his life, he'd forgotten about his father.

ARIA RANG the buzzer of Meals Made Easy. She had a huge smile on her face that she just couldn't wipe off. It had been there for days. Cole had been everything she'd needed this last week. Kind. Attentive. Everything about him, and them, felt so right. She knew she shouldn't get ahead of herself. They were new and they hadn't labeled what they were yet...but man, she was happy.

Michele pressed the button, then smiled at her as she walked through. "Hey, hon. You look like you're having a good morning."

"I'm having a great *week*." So great, she'd actually managed to not fret about everything that *wasn't* going right in her life. Like the rental application rejections and finding Maddon's body.

With the rental stuff...maybe she was secretly relieved that, for the moment, she was stuck. Stuck with Cole. But even if she wasn't stuck, she almost wanted to stay and take a risk so that she could explore whatever this was between her and her neighbor, and so Zac could finish high school in one place.

Michele's features softened. "Oh, that's wonderful. I knew if that big grumpy soldier would just let his guard down, he'd find someone amazing." She turned and went to the fridge. "Zac mentioned he's been over at your place a lot," Michele said as she brought a handful of meals to the counter.

"He has. So has Anthony, actually. Although sometimes I think the boys don't want to see us together, so they go across the road." She didn't blame them.

"Teenagers." Michele chuckled. "Hey, we should have a girls' night. Maybe go get a drink. Or have a girls' night in."

Aria paid for the meals. "Oh my gosh, yes."

She'd been in Michele's shop a couple times in the last week, and not just to get meals or to see Zac. Michele and River had also been texting and calling. The women were both quickly becoming good friends. And Aria loved that.

Michele's smile widened. "Great! I'll text River and we can make a date."

"Perfect."

After a quick goodbye, she dropped the meals in her car and walked a couple doors down to the coffee shop. Memories of her week with Cole skittered in her mind as she waited for the drinks. Her only concern about the time they'd spent together was that, even though they'd talked a lot, they hadn't really talked about *important* things. She hadn't told Cole about Zac's father, and he hadn't told her where his aversion to relationships came from. They'd both just spent the time enjoying each other's company. Which was fine for now.

She *wanted* to tell him about Marcus. He was the first person she'd ever wanted to tell, in fact. Usually, she kept any and all information about her ex private. For once, she wanted to let someone else in. Share what she and Zac had been living through. Was it too soon for that burden?

The coffee shop wasn't busy, so the drinks didn't take long. The closer she grew to Mercy Ring, the bigger her smile became. Man, she was screwed. Maybe she liked him *too* much. She knew she was more sure about him than he was about her. There were odd occasions when she saw something that looked a lot like fear flashing through Cole's eyes. Fear of what, exactly, she wasn't sure. But it kind of terrified her in turn. That he'd succumb to it. And that would mean the end of them.

*No. Stop, Aria. Stop thinking about worst-case scenarios. Things are going well.*

She just needed to keep reminding herself of that.

She stepped inside the boxing gym. Stopping at the desk, she set the coffees down and scanned the space. It was packed this morning. Her gaze caught on Cole on the far side of the room. His back was to her, but she would recognize him anywhere.

Her gaze swung to the man beside him...and she frowned. There was something about the way he moved, about the outline of his body that—

He took off his sweatshirt. And Aria's entire body went cold.

Because there, spiraling around his left bicep, was a tattoo. A tattoo of an eastern diamondback rattlesnake.

She took a step back. Rattlesnake. It was what they called him in the ring because he was so deadly. There were more rattlesnake tattoos on his back. She remembered the exact date he'd gotten each one of them. He'd probably added more since.

Fear flooded her body, followed quickly by panic. He'd found them. And he was right here, in the same room, talking to Cole.

Her legs were moving before her brain could catch up.

Out. She had to get out before he saw her.

The second her feet hit the sidewalk, she was running. She slid into her car and pulled out of the parking lot. Her hands trembled with a violence she couldn't control.

Did Marcus already know where she lived? Or just what town she lived in? How had he found her this time? What kind of trouble had he brought with him?

The second she got home, she called Zac. When he didn't answer, she sent him a text.

*Are you at school?*

She couldn't tell him Marcus was here over text. Zac would lose it. Where Aria felt fear whenever Marcus was around—fear for her son, and of the trouble his father brought with him—Zac always felt anger. The kid would probably go search him out.

When her phone beeped, her eyes shot down. But it wasn't a message from Zac—it was Cole.

*Everything okay? I saw the coffees you dropped off but you didn't take yours, and you didn't stop to chat.*

No. Everything *wasn't* okay. But that wasn't something she could explain through text message, either.

God, where would they go? They had nowhere to live yet. They could drive through the night and find a motel somewhere out of town. That would have to do for now. It would have to be cheap, because she didn't know how long she'd need to stay there or at other motels, waiting to hear back on a rental. If it was too long, she'd drain their savings.

But Cole...

Her heart ached. She'd only just met him. It shouldn't be so hard to leave him. Yet it felt impossible.

She sent back a quick text.

*I'm okay. Just had to get home quickly. There's something important I need to talk to you about when you finish work.*

It would be her goodbye. Tears pressed at her eyes, but she blinked them away.

She plugged her phone into the charger in the kitchen and went to the hall closet, where she pulled out her suitcase. It felt heavy in her grasp.

Half an hour later, she'd packed about half her clothes when her phone buzzed from the other room. She ran out to get it— and came to a sudden stop when she saw a man standing in the center of her living room.

The man she'd spent most of her son's life running from. The man who continued to find her, always bringing trouble and danger with him.

# CHAPTER 16

*F*or a moment, she couldn't speak, and it took every scrap of strength she had to remain upright. But she forced the words out. "What are you doing here, Marcus?"

Every part of her twitched to get away from him. To get out.

His hands were in his pockets, and his muscles rippled. So much about his physique was similar to Cole's. But where Cole was a protector, this man was a predator.

"I'm just dropping by, Aria."

Bullshit. He always found them for a reason, and those reasons were always selfish. "The last time you *dropped by* was because you owed money to very dangerous people. I gave you all I had."

Then she'd disappeared, but not before those people had shown up at her house, looking for Marcus and more money. A shudder rocked her spine at the memory. They hadn't hurt her or Zac, but the threat had been there.

"The time before that, you were hiding out from *other* people. Were they gang members or black-market gamblers, Marcus? I can't remember." There'd been so many visits over the years, she'd lost track.

"It's not like that this time."

Did he expect her to just believe him?

His gaze shot to the door, then back to her. "Thanks for leaving the door unlocked for me."

*Shit.* She'd left the door unlocked? God, she'd been such a mess when she got home, but how the hell had she made *that* big of a mistake?

"How'd you find us?" she asked quietly.

The last time he'd found them, they'd been living in Charlotte. She'd intentionally moved to the other side of the country, thinking she'd be safe here.

"Come on, Aria. You could leave tomorrow, take our son to the other side of the world, and I'd know your exact location by the time you got there. I make it a point to have eyes on you. Always."

Was he saying he'd known where she and Zac were this entire time? For almost a year? The thought made a toxic mix of dread and panic pool in her belly.

He took a small step forward, and it took everything in her not to step back. The man liked to incite fear. It was the boxer in him. The predator.

"You're lying."

"I'm not. That restraining order you slapped on me all those years ago never worked. Running never worked. Just accept that I have known, and will always know, exactly where you are. And when I need you, I come to you."

Anger surged in her chest. Yeah, the restraining order hadn't worked because the guy thought he was above the law.

"Of course, if you were trying to hide from me, that TikTok account definitely doesn't help."

She frowned. Her business was on Facebook and Instagram, but not TikTok. And she was always careful to never share her location or post any parts of the town that would expose her. Did Zac have a TikTok account? Had he posted something? God, she didn't even know how TikTok worked. All she knew was that people posted videos.

"What TikTok account?"

He smiled but ignored her question, running his fingers over her couch. "Zac looks happy. He's working in a kitchen now, isn't he? A place called Meals Made Easy."

Nausea coiled in her stomach. "You stay away from him!"

"Come on, Aria. He's my son as much as he's yours."

She wanted to laugh in his face. "You may be his father by blood, but you've *never* been a father to him. You've been too busy chasing money. Getting involved in criminal activities."

The second he'd started to win some boxing matches, she'd seen the changes in him. At first, it was little things. Getting home late. Money disappearing from their account. Soon, she learned about the gambling. The drugs. The cheating.

She could still remember that first time people had come to their home looking for Marcus. Zac had been five, and she'd been so scared for his safety. It was then she'd known she had to get out. She had to protect her baby.

"He's tall, like me. He'd probably make a good boxer."

"He's not going anywhere near the boxing world." Her son wasn't his father. But even so, the idea of him anywhere near that stuff made ice sweep through her veins.

Marcus took another step forward. "He might."

"You need to leave. *Now.*"

"Come on. You can't even stand to be in my presence for five minutes? I was here earlier, actually. Must have just missed you."

"What?" He was lying.

"Climbed in through a back window. Checked out the little home you've built here."

Oh, God. She felt violated.

"When you weren't here, I thought I'd check out the boxing club in town and come back later."

"You're leaving." She moved toward the door, but she only got a couple steps before he snagged her wrist and tugged her against his chest. Her breath caught. He was big, but he was also fast. Deceptively fast. Another reason for his nickname. Because the eastern diamondback rattlesnake wasn't just lethal. It also had the fastest strike speed of any other snake in the US.

"I've traveled a long way to see you."

"Go to hell," she growled.

He touched her cheek, and the bile crawled up her throat. She twitched to kick him in the balls. Hit him. *Something*. But she knew that was exactly what he wanted. He wanted a reaction. And he probably wanted to hit her back.

"Aria—"

"Let. Go."

"There was a time you loved my touch."

"You mean when we were kids, before the world of professional boxing went to your head and you got mixed up in things you should have stayed the hell away from?"

"I was trying to support my family."

"No. You were trying to feed your greed. You made your choice. And that choice wasn't me or Zac. So get the hell off me, and get out!"

The sound of an engine roared from the front yard.

Her stomach dropped. Zac. God, was school finished already?

This time, she *did* try to tug herself out of Marcus's hold, because she knew what seeing it would do to Zac. His hand dropped from her face, but the hand on her arm remained.

The door opened. Zac stopped dead in his tracks, his eyes narrowing. There was a heavy pause. When he spoke, he didn't sound like the baby she'd raised. He sounded like a man ready to go to war with his asshole of a father. "What the hell are you doing here?"

"Hello, Zac. I was just telling your mother how much I missed you both."

Zac's gaze dropped to where Marcus touched her arm. The

veins in his neck stood out as he looked back up. He dropped his bag to the floor and slammed the door shut. "Let her go."

One side of Marcus's mouth lifted. "I'm just talking to her, kid. Actually, I was thinking about staying for dinner."

Zac took a step forward, and Aria's breaths moved faster inside her chest, fear suffocating her.

"Let her go. *Now.*"

Marcus arched a brow. "Or what?"

"Zac," she tried calmly. "Can you give us a moment?"

Zac's gaze never left his father. "No. I'm not leaving you with this monster. Get out, Marcus."

He laughed. "Marcus? I don't even get 'Dad' anymore?"

"I've seen you hit Mom one too many times to ever consider you a father."

Oh God. She needed to end this before Zac did something that made Marcus shift his focus from her to him.

She pressed a hand to his chest. "Leave now, Marcus."

"No."

In the blink of an eye, it happened. Zac ran at his father.

"Zac, no!" She yanked on her arm, and Marcus finally released her. She stepped in front of Zac. "Stop!"

He tried to reach around her. "The asshole needs to pay for what he's put us through!"

She heard Marcus laughing behind her. Her blood boiled, but she ignored him. She touched Zac's cheek and lowered her voice. "Zac, please. Stop."

Finally, he looked at her. And something passed between them. Quiet words that said exchanging fists with this man wouldn't win them the fight, and it certainly wouldn't win any wars.

When she was sure Zac was calm, she finally turned. "You leave now, or I call the police. Your choice."

Marcus still looked amused. And she wanted to kill him for

that. Was this a game to him? Had he shown up just to intimidate them?

Finally, Marcus nodded. "Fine. I'll leave. For now. But I'll be back."

She held Zac's arm tightly as the man walked around them. Her son could easily pull out of her hold, but she was hoping that her touch would keep him calm.

Marcus opened the door, then stopped and turned. "Don't think about leaving, Aria. It wouldn't take me long to get to you again—and you'd regret it."

When the door finally closed, she breathed her first gulp of air in what felt like hours. Then she turned to Zac. "Are you okay?"

He was still watching the door, anger all over his face, as if waiting for the man to return. "I hate him. I fucking *hate* him!"

Oh, she did too. Zac deserved a good father. A man who'd be there for him. Who'd give him the world. He'd gotten the opposite. "I know, baby. I'm sorry."

So sorry, her heart felt broken.

He ran his hands through his hair. "Are you okay?"

"Yes."

She wasn't. But admitting to her son how damn afraid she was of the man wouldn't help anyone.

The thing that terrified Aria the most wasn't him grabbing her. It was his words. Were they true? Had he really always known their location? That meant staying and running were the same. And as long as Marcus was alive, she wasn't safe.

COLE PARKED IN HIS DRIVEWAY. His chest was still painfully tight over the realization that he'd forgotten the anniversary of his father's death, but he tried desperately to push it down as he crossed the road. He needed to check on Aria. Something was wrong. It wasn't just the fact that she'd left three coffees on the counter, including her own, without a word to him. Or her text insisting they needed to "talk." It was a feeling deep inside him that something wasn't right.

A black Audi in front of her house had him pausing. Did she have a visitor?

He was just walking up the driveway when he saw her through the front window. He stopped. She *did* have a visitor. A man, and he was holding her arm. Cole couldn't see her face, but he could see the guy's.

It was the same one who'd been at Mercy Ring that morning. Marcus.

Instantly, he tasted acid in his mouth and his heart began to race. Was Aria the person he was here to see? Were Aria and Zac the *family* he'd mentioned?

Suddenly, it hit him. That's why he looked familiar. He looked like Zac.

Marcus cupped her cheek, and Cole's throat closed. Images flashed in his mind. Of his father, describing how he'd found his mother in bed with another man. Of his mother, admitting she didn't love him anymore. And then the downward spiral and destruction of the strong father he'd always known.

*Push him away, Aria. Show me you're different.*

The words were a shouted plea in his head.

But...she didn't. She stayed exactly where she was, allowing the man to touch her. To stand so close, their bodies were almost fused.

Blood roared between his ears, deafening his world. He took a step back. Then another. When he couldn't watch any longer, he spun around and stormed back to his place.

Cole had promised himself he'd *never* become his father. He'd lived by that promise every damn day of his life since his dad's death. Until he hadn't.

There was the sound of an engine behind him, and he heard Anthony and Zac say goodbye to each other, but he didn't look at them. He was too angry. Not just angry at Aria. At *himself*. For allowing himself to slip. Allowing himself to entertain the idea of having a relationship.

*That* was what she'd had to get home for so quickly? Was this also what Aria wanted to talk to him about? Had she seen Marcus in the gym and…what? Felt guilty that she hadn't told him about him? Did he work out of town, and this was an unexpected visit?

He slammed the door closed behind him and walked straight toward the home gym. Ryker stepped out of the kitchen as he passed. "Everything okay?"

It was far from fucking okay. "No."

In the gym, he grabbed some gloves, shoved them on his hands and started hitting the heavy bag. He didn't think. He just threw punches. He hit the bag until his muscles ached. He didn't know how long he went at it. An hour? Longer?

It wasn't nearly enough.

His phone buzzed from where he'd dropped it on the weight bench. A text from Aria.

*Hey, are you finished at work? Can we chat?*

She wanted to *chat*? About Zac's father being home? About where that left them?

Hell no.

Almost on cue, his phone rang. Not Aria this time, his mother.

*Really?* She was calling on the anniversary of his father's death? It was like the entire universe was laughing at him.

He needed to get out. Out of this house and far away from everything.

# CHAPTER 17

*a* few hours later, Aria stepped out of the station. The report was filed. Marcus had broken his restraining order. Again. Now there was a warrant out for his arrest. That was the best she could do. She had to believe it was enough and that they'd catch him.

Such a large part of her wanted to pick up and leave. To escape this town and hide from Marcus like she always did. But his words...

*Don't think about leaving, Aria. It wouldn't take me long to get to you again—and then you'd regret it.*

She didn't want to believe him, but she did. He always found them.

He hadn't said what he wanted. Why he'd suddenly shown up again. Which made her nervous as hell. Because he always wanted something. Money. A place to hide.

She slid behind the wheel and sent a quick text to Zac. When he confirmed he was still okay and with Anthony, she started driving home.

Zac. Her hands tightened on the wheel. Thank God no one had thrown a punch today. Marcus had hit her before, more than once, but he'd never hit Zac. Pushed him? Yes. That's how he'd gotten the cut on his face, he'd landed on the corner of the coffee table. But never a fist to the face. She'd always dreaded the day Zac was angry enough to swing on his father. She knew it was coming, and the thought made her break out in a cold sweat. Marcus was a demon in the ring. He'd sent guys to the hospital with a single blow.

*Don't think about that, Aria.*

She shot a look at her phone in her middle console. No text from Cole. She'd sent him two since Marcus had left, both asking to talk. She *needed* to talk to him. Tell him what was going on. The idea of pulling him into her mess made her feel sick to her stomach, but at the same time, she suspected he would know how to protect her.

Something inside her calmed at the thought. Something that had been tight and anxious since seeing Marcus in that gym. Hell, she'd been anxious for the last sixteen years.

She turned onto her street but frowned when she didn't see Cole's car in his driveway. Could he have parked in the garage?

She pulled into her drive and got out, once again glancing across the street. When she saw movement in Cole's living room window, she headed to his house. Every step she took made her feel lighter. Made the trickle of hope that everything would be okay get that much bigger.

But as she knocked, something started to nudge at the hope—fear. She was about to tell Cole everything. About her dangerous, abusive ex. About how often she and Zac had run from the man. He already had cold feet. What if this was too much? Too heavy and complicated?

When the door opened, a breath she hadn't realized she'd been holding whooshed from her chest. But it wasn't Cole. It was Ryker.

He frowned. "Hey."

"Hey, Ryker. I was wondering if Cole was around."

Something crossed Ryker's face. It came and went so quickly, she didn't have time to place it, but one thing she *was* sure of…he looked uncomfortable. And that made little flecks of panic flicker in her belly.

"He went out."

Her brows twitched. "Do you know where?"

Maybe he saw the desperation on her face or heard it in her voice, because he tugged his phone from his pocket and typed something. Immediately, it beeped back. He ran a hand through his hair.

"He's at Lenny's Bar," Ryker said quietly.

Aria frowned. Why would he be there?

"He wasn't in the best mood when he got home today," Ryker added.

Oh God. Had Marcus said something to him? About her and Zac? She took a step back. "Thank you."

"Maybe you should give him some—"

"I really need to speak to him now. I'll just go to the bar." Even though Lenny's was the last place she wanted to go after what had happened during her previous visit.

She ran home and changed into jeans and a T-shirt before getting into her car and driving to the bar. The entire way there, her heart raced, because she just knew something wasn't right. This last week, Cole had responded to every single one of her texts within minutes. And now, he hadn't responded to the last two…but he'd responded to Ryker's. And he was at a bar?

She parked in the lot and got out. When she reached the door, she paused, taking a moment to calm her racing heart. After finding Maddon's lifeless body in the woods, she'd had dreams about this place. Bad dreams. About Maddon pulling her out of the bar while she was almost unconscious. Of him taking her to those woods and her ending up dead instead of him.

She took a deep breath. *Don't think about that, Aria. Think about Cole. You need to talk to him.*

With a straight spine, she stepped inside. Lenny's gaze swung over to her from behind the bar. He frowned, looking surprised to see her. She gave him a small, forced smile before scanning the bar.

When she saw Cole, her heart stopped.

He had his back to her, and beside him was a woman. A woman who looked just like the redhead who'd been all over him the last time Aria had been here.

For a moment, she didn't move. Just like she had outside, she took a few seconds to breathe. To get herself under control before walking forward.

When she stopped at the bar table and Cole's gaze hit her, her stomach dropped. He wasn't looking at her like he had that morning. There was no warmth in his eyes. No tenderness.

"Hey," she said, her voice small.

"How'd you find me?"

No *hi*. No, *are you okay*? "Ryker."

He nodded.

The woman beside him leaned over, pressing her chest into his shoulder. And Cole didn't pull away. Not even slightly. She smirked at Aria. "I'm Violet."

She couldn't even muster a fake smile for the woman. She looked back at Cole. "You couldn't answer my texts?"

"You looked a bit busy when I dropped by this afternoon."

She frowned. "You came over?"

"I did. And I saw you and *Marcus* in the window."

She pulled back at the derision in his voice. "You saw me and Marcus together?"

"He had his hand on your cheek. Looked like quite the intimate moment. I didn't want to interrupt."

She tried not to flinch at his mention of Marcus touching her. God, she could still feel the man's hand on her skin. It made her want to scrub her face raw.

"Cole, let me explain—"

"It's fine, Aria. I put the pieces together."

She paused, confusion swirling inside her. "What pieces?"

"You two are together, right? So, when you saw him talking to me in Mercy Ring, and realized he was in town, you got scared."

"No. That's not true," she started. "We're not together."

And the fact he thought she'd date him while she was already dating someone else hurt so badly, she wanted to keel over. She didn't. She forced herself to remain upright.

"Marcus and I haven't been together since Zac was five years old. He's—"

"You don't need to lie to me," Cole interrupted. He didn't sound angry or upset. In fact, there was no emotion in his voice at all. "I've seen this before. My father lived it in front of my fucking eyes. I get it."

His father?

"We were never that serious, and it was never going to work between us anyway," Cole continued. "You can go home to him, and I'll stay here."

She frowned. His words were designed to hurt, and they did their job. They punctured her chest, making it hard for her to draw a breath. She ignored Violet's smile, the way the woman casually stroked Cole's back.

"Really? You're not even going to listen to my side?"

For the first time, he looked her dead in the eye. But his gaze was almost vacant. "Go back to him, Aria."

No. He wasn't going to listen.

She took a step away. Then another. Tears pressed at her eyes, but she blinked rapidly to stop them. She didn't want to cry. Not here. Not in front of him.

Aria turned just as Violet wrapped her arms around him from the side. She needed to get out, before she completely fell apart. Before the events of the day suffocated her.

With quick steps, she weaved around the tables and out of the bar. Lenny called her name, but she didn't stop and turn. He would see the devastation on her face, and she didn't want that. She wanted to be away from everyone. From Cole. Marcus. From the world.

She'd just reached her car when the first tears fell. How had she woken up this morning on top of the world, only to have everything crash down around her now?

Her phone buzzed, and she had to wipe the tears away to see who it was. Zac.

*Hey, Mom. I just got back from Anthony's but you're not here. Everything okay?*

She closed her eyes. Not *everything* was crashing down around her. She still had Zac. He was safe. And that was the most important thing.

*Just coming home now. X*

She wiped another tear from her cheek. God, she had to stop crying. Zac was already angry about his father. He didn't need to see her like this.

With a deep breath, she started the car. She was just pulling out of the lot when she looked into her rearview mirror to see Cole standing outside the bar door, watching her.

# CHAPTER 18

*H*e was an asshole. Every step Aria took away from Cole had him feeling worse. And that look on her face when he'd told her to go...

His stomach clenched.

When he felt Violet's breath in his ear, he pulled away.

"Hey!" she pouted.

He didn't want the woman touching him. Never had. What the hell was wrong with him? "Like I told you the other night, I'm not interested."

"But—"

Before she could finish, he got up and moved out of the bar. He felt Lenny's eyes on him the entire time. The judgment was like a fucking arrow in his back.

*Yeah, I hate myself too, Lenny.*

The second he made it outside, he couldn't stop himself. He searched for her car in the lot. When he spotted the Beetle, his muscles bunched. She was wiping her eyes because he'd made her cry.

*Fuck.* He wanted to kick his own ass. He took a step forward, not entirely sure what he planned to do, but she quickly pulled out of the lot.

With clenched fists, he moved to his own vehicle. The second he was inside, his phone rang. It was his sister, Naomi. God, he didn't feel like talking to anyone right now, but he'd missed her last four calls, and he knew from experience they would just become more frequent.

"What is it, Naomi?"

His sister's soft voice sounded across the line. "Hey, Cole. I just wanted to check that you're doing okay today?"

No. He was far from okay. "I'm fine."

"I don't believe you."

"How are you and Christopher doing?" He didn't want to talk about him and his mess of a day.

She sighed. "We're okay. Good days and bad days, as you know." Cole heard his nephew's little voice in the background before his sister called out to him. "Yes, Chris, you can have some more strawberries."

The first real smile in hours tugged at his lips. He loved his nephew.

Her voice quieted. "He still asks for his dad a lot, but it's becoming less frequent."

The smile fell. He hated that the kid had lost his father so young. He knew that pain, but hell, Cole had been sixteen when he'd lost his own father, and Chris was only four at the time. Ted had died last year, just before Cole left the military.

"What about you?" he asked quietly. "How are you doing?"

There was a short pause. "Still seeing my therapist, which helps. And Mom comes over a bit and helps around the house."

Naomi had never held the same bitterness toward their mother for what had happened to their father. But then, he and Naomi had never really seen the world quite the same way. Cole's view was a lot more black-and-white than his sister's.

"Oops, Chris just spilled his glass of milk. I've got to go. But you're okay?"

"I'm okay. I love you, Nae. Tell Chris I love him too."

"We love you back. And Cole...whether it's Dad that has you down today or something else, I hope it passes soon."

His sister knew he didn't like to talk about his problems. She never pushed, just checked in, and he loved her even more for that. "Thanks."

Cole pulled out of the parking lot. His sister did sound better. She'd been in a bad way after Ted died. A single mom of a four-year-old, heartbroken over losing her husband...it would tear down most people. Another example of love hurting.

He pulled into his drive, but he only had eyes for Aria's house.

He itched to go over there. Talk to her. Was it possible he'd gotten everything wrong?

The image of Marcus's hand on her cheek flashed in his mind. Of his hand on her wrist. Of her not moving out of the man's embrace...

He climbed out of the car and slammed the door closed. When he stepped inside, Anthony's gaze shot up from where he sat at the kitchen table.

"Everything okay?" Anthony asked.

"It's fine." He moved toward the stairs as Anthony spoke again.

"Zac and I just got back from a long drive. He told me his dad's in town."

His fingers clenched into a tight fist. "Right. I saw his dad and Aria together."

"Yeah. He told me the asshole was touching her. Is she okay?"

He paused, his gaze shooting to Anthony. "Why wouldn't she be okay?"

Anthony looked confused. "Because of everything he's done."

He moved into the kitchen, a sick feeling swirling in his gut.

Anthony's brows twitched in surprise. "She didn't tell you?"

"Tell me what?"

"That they've been running from him since Zac was five. He's got problems with gambling and drugs and other stuff. Aria's got a restraining order, but it doesn't help. Zac said the last time he found them, she told him to leave, and the asshole punched her. And it wasn't the first time."

Cole's skin iced. "He *what?*"

"I can't believe she didn't tell you. Aren't you guys dating?"

He hadn't listened to her in the bar. In fact, he'd outright refused to let her speak. Was that what she wanted to talk to him about?

"Apparently, Aria and Zac have lived in more than a dozen towns since they left him over ten years ago. But he always finds them and always brings trouble. Like, really dangerous trouble."

*Fuck.* He'd made a mistake. A *huge* damn mistake.

His gaze shot out the window and across the street. When he saw the car in the driveway, and that man at the front door, a dark fury roared to life inside him.

Before he could move, Aria's door opened, and then Zac was there—throwing a fist.

*Shit.*

BY THE TIME Aria got home, she almost looked normal. Almost. There was a slight reddening of her eyes and cheeks, but that was it. With any luck, Zac wouldn't notice she'd been crying. And if he did, well, he might just assume she was upset over Marcus. Which was true. He just wasn't the driving force of her tears.

With one final glance at her reflection, she climbed out of the car and moved into the house.

Her gaze swung around, taking in the empty living room and kitchen. She stepped into the hall and spotted Zac in his room. He lay on his bed, phone in his hands.

He looked up at her and frowned. "Hey. You okay?"

"No. But I will be. I spoke to Officer Hanon. He wrote a report and said to call if Marcus returns."

"So, we're not leaving?"

She nibbled her bottom lip and glanced out the window. She had no idea what the best option was. "I don't know." Sometimes, having to make all the decisions sucked.

"I'll do whatever we need to do, Mom," he said quietly.

Oh God, this kid…

She crossed the room, sat on his bed and pulled him into her arms. When his arms wrapped around her, she felt the wetness in her eyes again, but this time for completely different reasons.

"I love you, Zac."

"I love you too, Mom."

She pulled away. Thankfully, no tears had fallen.

"What did Cole say when you told him?"

Her stomach rolled. She tried to keep what she felt off her face, but when Zac straightened, she knew she hadn't succeeded.

"What happened?"

She shook her head. "Nothing."

"Don't lie to me, Mom. I can see something's wrong."

Yeah, she definitely hadn't hidden it well. "We broke up." Not that they'd been dating. And the man had kind of stomped on her heart. But her son didn't need to know that last part.

"Why?"

She shook her head. "You don't need to wor—"

"I'm not a kid anymore. You can tell me things."

Her voice softened. "You'll always be my baby, and it will always be my job to protect you."

Some of the softness crept back into his face. She looked down at his phone, which now lay on the bed. Remembering something Marcus said, she frowned. "Do you use TikTok?"

"Nah. A lot of the kids at school are into it, but I'm not. Why?"

She opened her mouth to tell Zac about Marcus's comment when a knock sounded at the door.

The back of her neck prickled. "Are you expecting company?"

He shook his head. "Maybe it's Anthony."

She left Zac's room and moved over to the door before looking out the peephole. Ice trickled into her veins, and she took a quick step back. What the hell was he doing back here?

She turned to see Zac had followed. His gaze shifted from the door to her. Then his expression hardened. "It's him, isn't it?"

It wasn't a question.

"Zac—"

He brushed past her to the door.

"Zac, don't. We'll call Officer Hanon—"

He pulled the door open, and an arrogant-looking Marcus stood in front of them.

Before Aria could comprehend what was happening, Zac swung.

Aria cried out as Marcus easily dodged the hit. He laughed, which seemed to enrage Zac further. He swung again, but this time, instead of just dodging the hit, Marcus grabbed Zac's wrist, swung him around and swept an arm around his neck.

"I was wondering when you'd take your first swing at me."

Aria flew forward. "Let him go!"

He shoved her with one hand, and she fell to the hard concrete of her front porch.

"Let me go, asshole!" Zac growled.

Aria jumped to her feet just as Marcus shoved Zac against the front wall of the house. She grabbed his arm, but Marcus swung his hand back, catching her in the eye. She cried out and stumbled again—but instead of falling to the porch a second time, strong hands caught her.

She looked up to see Cole standing behind her. Even though his hands were gentle, there was a quiet fury on his face.

"Are you okay?" he asked through gritted teeth.

She gave a short nod. He set her away from him, then grabbed Marcus from behind and yanked him off Zac. Aria moved straight over to her son and wrapped her arms around him.

Marcus growled. "What the fuck—"

This time, Cole shoved *him* against the house. At the sound of feet pounding concrete, she looked across the yard to see Anthony running toward them, Ryker right behind him.

Cole got close to Marcus's face. "What the hell are you doing fighting a kid?"

"*My* kid," Marcus growled. "I'll do whatever the hell I want to him!"

Rage pummeled through Aria's limbs. "He's not your kid! He hasn't been yours for years."

Cole's voice lowered to a deadly quiet. "You're going to leave this property. Drive away and never return. If I hear that you bother them ever again, I *will* find you, and you won't like what I do."

Marcus's eyes narrowed, the muscles bunching in his arms like they often did before he threw a punch. Aria's fingers tightened on Zac's arm.

When Ryker stepped up behind Cole, she released a quick breath. One on one, Cole and Marcus would probably be an even match. Yes, Marcus was a former professional boxer, but Cole was former Delta. With Ryker there, she was almost certain Marcus wouldn't try anything.

"What are you to her?" Marcus asked.

"That's none of your business." Cole moved his head closer. "Stay the fuck away." He released him, then positioned himself in front of Aria and Zac.

She watched as Marcus stormed to his car, dropped in and drove away. She still had no idea why he'd come back. But she didn't care. All she wanted was Zac safe. And maybe Cole and Ryker had scared him away for good. God, she could hope.

She turned to Zac. "Are you okay?"

He nodded, but the anger on his face hadn't disappeared. He studied her left eye. "He got you." Zac grazed her cheek, and she tried not to flinch at the sting.

"I'm okay." It wasn't exactly a lie. Physically, she'd had worse. But emotionally? Man, this day was taking it out of her. "Go inside, baby. I'll be there in a sec."

Zac shot a quick look over her head, then gave a nod and moved inside.

When she turned, she saw the chin lift between Ryker and Cole, before Ryker and Anthony moved back across the street. Then Cole stepped toward her.

Before he could get too close, she pressed a hand to his chest.

"Aria—"

"Thank you for helping us." She kept her voice formal, not wanting any emotion to seep in. "I appreciate it."

He lifted his hand to graze her cheek, gaze zeroing in on her injury, but she tilted her head away.

"You should go," she said quietly.

A pained expression crossed his face. When he opened his mouth, she moved toward the door. She couldn't listen to anything he had to say. He'd said enough at Lenny's. And this had already been the longest day of her life.

"Aria. I'm sorry. Can I just talk to you?"

"No." She didn't have the energy for that. "Goodbye, Cole."

# CHAPTER 19

*a*ria's gaze caught the rearview mirror. Cole. He was still behind her. It wasn't a huge surprise. She was almost certain they were both heading to the same place. But the fact he'd walked out of his house at the exact moment she'd walked out of hers made her suspicious. Was it self-indulgent of her to wonder if the man had waited inside his house for her to leave?

If he was heading to the same place as her, that meant they'd both received similar calls from the high school teacher.

She blew out a breath at the memory of that call. It had come from the boys' history teacher. Apparently, there'd been an altercation in class. Again. An altercation between Zac and Anthony, and Ezra and Benny. The teacher wanted all parents to come in to have a *chat.*

Argh. This was not what she needed. Not after yesterday.

She scrubbed a hand over her face. She'd had extra locks put on all the windows today. She'd also put Hanon's cell number on speed dial, with his permission, and ordered a new security camera. Marcus was right. He'd just keep finding her. It was time to stop running. Time to do whatever she could to prove to Marcus that he was *not* welcome in her life.

COLE

And that decision had absolutely nothing to do with not wanting to leave the man in the car behind her.

She pulled into the school parking lot and, of course, Cole parked right beside her. He'd both called and texted her today. She hadn't responded to either. She couldn't. The man had lost faith in her so quickly and so easily. And the things he'd said...

She blew out a breath and climbed out of her car to find Cole waiting for her at the front of his.

"Cole—"

"I just want to walk you in," he said quietly.

The sound of his deep, smooth voice... God, it rolled over her skin. She hesitated for a second, then stepped forward. He didn't touch her as they walked inside, but the heat from his body almost felt like he did. Even after yesterday, there was still such a large part of her that wanted to lean into him. Touch his arm. His hand.

Pathetic. She felt pathetic. She had to be, to still want him after how he'd treated her.

They took the stairs up to the second floor and stopped in front of a classroom. Cole reached the door first, and once he opened it, he pressed a hand to the small of her back to guide her inside. Her skin burned like he'd touched bare skin.

*No, Aria. Don't think about what he does to you.*

She forced her body to calm as she approached the middle-aged man behind the desk.

"Hi, I'm Aria Callas, Zac's mother."

The man stood and shook her hand. "Rod Walker. Nice to meet you."

The hand on her back finally dropped, and she lowered into a spare seat in front of the teacher's desk. A woman was already sitting, but when Aria smiled politely at her, the woman didn't smile back. Was it Benny's or Ezra's mother?

"Cole Turner," Cole said, shaking Walker's hand. "I'm here for Anthony."

143

"Thanks for being here."

Cole sat beside her. Had he dragged the chair closer?

The teacher lowered into his seat. "Dorothy, Cole, Aria, thank you for coming. Unfortunately, neither of Benny's parents could make it, so it's just us. I want to discuss ways we can help the boys get along in class."

There was a beat of silence. The other woman, Dorothy, tapped her foot while her arms remained crossed over her chest.

The teacher cleared his throat. "As I mentioned on the phone, there was another fight. It happened in the middle of my class. I don't know who started it. Both sides said it was the other—"

"It was obviously Zac."

Aria swung her head toward the woman. "Excuse me?"

The woman's eyes were borderline hostile as she looked at Aria. "Ezra's told me all about your kid. How he attacked Benny at Mercy Ring, then again in the schoolyard the other week." She turned back to the teacher. "He's clearly violent. What are you doing to protect my child?"

Okay, this woman was pissing her off now. She opened her mouth to tell her exactly what she thought, but Cole beat her to it.

"I was at Mercy Ring that day. Zac was provoked."

"And that makes it okay?" She leaned forward. "Teenagers are going to provoke each other. If everyone threw punches every time they were *provoked*, we'd live in a pretty messed-up world."

Oh, this woman...

"I'm sure your son hit back today," Aria said.

"To defend himself."

The teacher held up his hands. "Please. I'm not trying to start a debate over who started what. From what I saw, all four of them played their part. I just want us to work together to see how we can help the boys remain amicable while at school. They don't have to like one another. They just need to stop using their fists."

There was a heavy beat of silence throughout the room.

"I'll talk to Anthony," Cole finally said.

Aria took a breath before looking back at the teacher. "I'll talk to Zac too."

It was true. He shouldn't be retaliating with his fists. But, God, he was going through a lot.

When Dorothy remained silent, Aria almost rolled her eyes. Now she knew where the woman's son got his attitude.

The teacher sighed. "Dorothy—"

"No. I guarantee you, whatever happened today was not Ezra's fault. Just like the previous altercations have not been his fault." The woman stood.

The teacher stood with her. "Please—"

"If there's nothing else, I'll be leaving now. I trust you'll make sure my son is not on the receiving end of any more fists, otherwise, I'll be forced to take this further."

Aria shook her head in exasperation. Did the woman honestly think her precious son was the victim in all this?

The teacher blew out a long breath as the door slammed behind the woman. "I'm afraid this meeting hasn't gone quite to plan." He lifted two sheets of paper and handed them across the table. "This is some information on how to help the boys from your end. And as always, we'll do what we can here."

Aria took the paper and folded it. "Thank you, Mr. Walker." She stood and pushed it into the back pocket of her jeans, then shook his hand before leaving the room. Cole didn't touch her on the way down the stairs, and she wasn't sure if she was happy or disappointed by that.

She'd just reached her car when he finally touched her arm. Then the heat of his front pressed into her back.

"Aria."

She stopped. She stopped moving. Breathing. Thinking.

This is why she hadn't answered his calls or texts today. Because she'd known how hard it would be to say no. To walk away. From him and everything he made her feel.

COLE WAITED until she reached her door before touching her. "Aria."

For a moment, she was still. He took a small step closer and gently touched his lips to her neck before whispering, "Forgive me."

He felt the distinct shudder course through her body. At her hesitation, his heart thudded.

*Say yes, Aria. Give me another chance.* He needed her forgiveness. Because he needed *her*, even if he couldn't explain why.

"Cole, I..." She stopped.

*Can't?* Is that what she was trying to say?

He slid a hand up her side, and he was almost certain she leaned into him.

"I hate myself for what I did," he whispered, before pressing another kiss to her neck.

"I need time," she breathed.

Even though she said those words, she didn't pull away when he kissed her again. The next two kisses trailed up her skin, and when he reached her cheek, she turned her head for him.

He didn't hesitate. He kissed her lips.

Her soft groan made lava burn through his veins. It made him want to claim her right here in the parking lot.

Slowly, she turned to face him, and he plunged his tongue into her mouth, tasting her.

God, he needed this. Since yesterday, he'd felt like he was drowning without her. The memory of what he'd done to her was like a physical pain to his chest. But touching her right now, kissing her, it was healing.

He swept his hands under her ass and lifted her up against him. Then he pressed her to the car, leaning into her softness.

Another deep moan sounded from her throat, and it made more desire slam into his gut. For a moment, he forgot where he was, why he was here, and everything else outside of this kiss. She was all that existed.

He'd just cupped her cheek when she pressed her hands against his chest. "Cole. We shouldn't."

Her words were like a bucket of cold water. Shouldn't? Everything in him said this was all they *should* do.

"Aria—"

"Please. Put me down. I need to go."

He held her for another beat. Then, using every scrap of strength inside him, he lowered her to the ground, removed his hands and stepped back.

Her gaze flicked up to his. She opened her mouth like she was going to say something, then closed it again. There was something in her eyes. Regret? Regret at what they'd done? Or that he'd screwed things up and she could no longer be with him?

Before he could figure it out, she slid into the car and drove away. And he was left wondering what the hell he was going to do.

# CHAPTER 20

*a*ria's fingers flew across the keys on her laptop. Man, she was doing an awesome job at distracting herself today. Maybe it was the change of scenery from working in the coffee shop instead of at home. Or maybe it was that she'd turned her phone off and felt somewhat detached from everyone who may try to contact her. Everyone being Cole.

He'd been messaging her a lot over the last few days. Multiple times a day. Checking in. Asking if they could talk. He'd even shown up at her house a couple of times, and she just...hadn't answered. Because what he'd said to her in that bar, and that woman pressed up against him...both were burned into her memory like a physical pain.

She'd been a fool to think she could change him. He'd told her he wasn't a relationship guy. So it shouldn't be a surprise that his faith in her had been rocked so easily. Still, it hurt.

She scrubbed her hand over her face. Yet she'd still kissed him in the school parking lot. And that kiss...God, it had been every-thing. Hot. Intense. A whole-body kind of consuming.

Okay, she wasn't doing such a great job at distracting herself anymore.

But it wasn't just Cole she was trying to distract herself from. There was, of course, Marcus.

He hadn't contacted her again, thank God. A part of her hoped—*prayed*—that Cole had scared him off. But the realist part of her, the part that knew Marcus so well, knew he didn't scare so easily.

Leaning back in her chair, her gaze flew around the busy coffee shop.

"Shit! Have you seen this new video on Tander's TikTok?"

Aria's coffee stilled halfway to her lips at the words from the kid at the table beside hers. She still had no idea what Marcus had been talking about with his TikTok comment. That was something else she needed to figure out.

"What's he done this time?"

She turned to see two kids huddled over the phone, but the screen was facing away from her.

"No fucking way! How does he not get arrested for this stuff?"

Aria lowered the mug to the table. She was just about to ask the kids about the account when the café door opened.

Her pulse jumped. River, Michele, Declan, Jackson, Ryker... and Cole.

Immediately, Cole's gaze zeroed in on her. Apart from the small glimpses through her peephole, it was the first time she'd seen him in days. Certainly, the first time they'd been in a room together. She hadn't gone on her normal morning runs around the neighborhood. She'd gotten creative, driving to different locations or working out in her backyard. Today, she'd parked a few miles from the coffee shop and jogged here, with all her stuff in a backpack.

It was probably time to jog back now.

She closed her laptop as Michele and River approached her table.

"Hey," Michele said, smiling at her.

Aria rose. "Hi. Sorry, I was just leaving."

Lie. And the women probably knew it.

River's gaze softened. "That's okay. We just wanted to check that you're doing okay after that jerk went to your house. No more visits?"

News had traveled fast. A couple of hours after Marcus's little visit, she'd had messages from both of them checking in and asking if she was okay.

"No more visits, thankfully." She shoved her laptop into her bag and swung it onto her back. When she looked back at the women, it took all of her strength not to glance behind them at Cole. Was he looking at her? Probably. She felt hot and tingly… and like she needed to get out of here, now. "I should go."

She went to step around the women, but River touched her arm. "Are you sure you can't stay for a coffee?"

"I'm sorry, I need to jog back to my car and get some more work done before Zac gets home from school."

At least that wasn't a lie. She did need to get some work done. She'd just been planning on getting it done here.

"I'm almost finished editing those photos we took," River said. "I'll give you a call when I'm done."

Her tummy did a little roll. The photos they'd taken in the woods before they'd found Maddon's dead body. She forced the smile to her lips. "That would be wonderful. I'll see you both later."

River gave her arm a little squeeze before Aria weaved her way out of the café. Cole and his friends were now sitting in a booth. She didn't look at him but could feel his eyes on her. When he didn't get up, she wasn't sure if she was relieved or not. She certainly wasn't disappointed when she stepped outside and the door closed behind her, and he didn't follow. Nope. Definitely not. She wanted it this way. It was safer. She couldn't go falling in love with a man who would question his trust in her at every turn.

She tightened the straps on her backpack and started jogging.

She'd only passed a few stores when a figure suddenly appeared beside her. Her body jolted and she almost stumbled over her feet.

Cole.

~

"Go, talk to her."

Cole shook his head at Declan's words. "She wants distance from me." And he didn't blame her. Not after how he'd treated her. But damn, it still hurt like razor blades to his insides.

He watched as she shoved her laptop into her bag. She wasn't looking at him, and her movements were rigid. She was leaving because of him. She couldn't even stand to be in the same room.

Jackson leaned across the table. "You messed up. Go make things right."

"She's been ignoring my calls and texts. She won't answer her door. She hasn't even been going on her morning runs."

Maybe that was because of that asshole ex of hers, but he was almost certain it was at least partly because of him.

He'd been keeping a close eye on the house because of Marcus. He'd even asked Zac when he was over, hanging with Anthony, to call him if Marcus ever showed his face again. He'd expected the kid to say no, but Zac had agreed, thank God.

When she walked through the maze of tables toward the door, Ryker nudged his shoulder. "Go."

She stepped outside. And dammit, he couldn't sit there any longer. He rose from the booth and raced out of the store. She started jogging, and he was damn glad they'd all just been at Mercy Ring and he was already in workout clothes.

He ran forward, catching up with her easily. The little jolt from her had his insides coiling. That's what he did to her now.

She didn't stop. In fact, she sped up. "I need to get home, Cole."

He kept pace with her easily. "You haven't responded to any of my calls or texts. Can you at least tell me Marcus hasn't contacted you?"

Her voice softened. "He hasn't."

"Good." He waited a beat before saying the words he'd said before. "I'm sorry."

"You've said that already."

"I'll say it as often as you need to hear it."

"I can't…" She stopped mid-sentence.

He frowned, watching her more than the path ahead of them. "You can't what, honey?"

Her brows twitched. Then she stopped. He stopped with her.

"I can't afford to tangle my heart up with someone who's scared to love. It's a risk for me. And as you've clearly seen, I can't afford any more risks in my life right now."

He swallowed. "I'm not scared to—"

"You *are*. I've gone over this in my head a million times. You told me yourself you've never dated anyone. That you *don't* date. You won't tell me why, but I've seen your fear. You mentioned your father in the bar, but other than that, nothing."

He tasted acid in his mouth at the mention of his dad.

Sympathy shone in her eyes. "I'm not saying you don't have good reasons. You probably do. But your fear of falling for someone means that you and me are never going to work. Because I *want* to fall in love. I want—no, I *need*—to be with someone who sees the world the way I do. Who's been burned but still hasn't given up."

Another thud of his damn heart.

"And more than that, I need someone who trusts me. You believed a perfect stranger over me, then you didn't even give me a chance to explain. How can I trust someone who's so eager to believe the worst in me?"

She looked like she wanted him to disagree with her. To say it wasn't true, but dammit, it was. He was fucking terrified to have his heart chained to anyone, only to have that person tear it from his chest and leave him hollow inside. He'd seen it. Hell, he'd found his father's dead fucking body in their home. Because *he'd* trusted someone with his heart.

Aria offered a sad smile. "You and I—we just weren't meant to be, Cole."

Then she jogged away. And watching her leave him… Fuck, it hurt. But he couldn't stop her. He couldn't tell the woman the way she'd described him was a lie when it wasn't.

Instead of jogging, he walked back to the coffee shop, all the while wondering what the hell he was going to do. He couldn't get her out of his head. And he was damn worried about her—worried about her ex getting to her, and worried about her leaving town without telling him.

His skin chilled at the idea of never seeing her again.

He pulled his phone from his pocket. He needed to sort out his damn head, and there was only one person who could help him do that.

# CHAPTER 21

"*H*ey, stranger. It's nice to receive a call from you for a change."

Instead of walking back to the coffee shop, he headed to his car. He'd driven Ryker but his friend could get a ride home with their friends. "Hey, Nae. Just checking in."

Wind blew in the background. "Really? Well, I'm just at Chris's Little League game. You should see them in their over-sized jerseys. They're adorable."

"I'm sure he's killing it."

"Oh, he is. And last night, we had dinner at Mom's with her and Gerard. That was nice too."

"Sounds great." It didn't. Not for him. But he was glad they'd had a good time. He unlocked his car and slid behind the wheel.

"Chris drew you a picture at school this week. It's of the two of you and kind of looks like two stick figures, but the taller stick figure has cantaloupes on his arms."

Cole chuckled again. The kid had drawn him many pictures when he'd lived in Wisconsin for a year. They looked like Naomi described. And he'd loved every one of them.

"How am I doing?" she asked. "Have I filled enough space yet for you to tell me why you called? If not, I have more. I have some wicked stories about my new favorite hobby."

"Do I want to know?"

"Pole dancing."

"You're joking?"

"Nope. Every Thursday night. It's so much fun."

God, he didn't need a visual of his little sister dancing on a pole while probably wearing very little clothing.

Naomi's voice softened. "What's going on, Cole?"

He watched two women walk past the car without really seeing them. "There's a woman..."

"About damn time." He could almost hear the smile in his sister's voice. She was just like the guys. She'd always sworn he'd break his no-dating rule when he met the right person. "What's her name?"

"Aria. She lives across the street. We were kind of seeing each other, but then I screwed up and she doesn't want anything to do with me anymore."

And her distance felt so damn heavy in his chest. He'd never felt like this before. The need to be with someone. The ache over a distance every part of him instinctually knew shouldn't be there.

"What did you do?"

He hesitated. That's how bad it was. He didn't even want to say it out loud. "I saw her with another guy and assumed she was cheating. I let her find me at a bar with a girl crawling all over me. Said shit I didn't mean."

"Oh, Cole."

Yeah. He blew out a long breath. "I just...I need to know how you did it, Nae? How did you see what happened to Dad and still remain open to love?"

His sister had lost her husband, and here she was, still capable of smiling and joking.

He shook his head. "I saw Dad become a shadow of the man

he used to be. Love did that."

"Cole, not a day passes where I don't think about Dad. And I am so sorry that you were the one who found him that day. I can't even imagine what that must have been like." She paused, and he could hear the tears in her voice. "Mom cheating on Dad, Mom not loving Dad...it killed something inside him. We both know it. You lived with him and watched it firsthand. It was a tragedy. I wish he could have pulled himself out of the darkness he'd found himself in."

Cole had wished that same thing every fucking day since.

"But that was *his* life," she continued. "Not yours, and not mine. We are allowed to love. We are allowed to feel all the beautiful things that come with giving ourselves to another person. Because it *is* beautiful. Love is the most beautiful emotion in the world. And I may have lost Ted, but even if I knew how my story with him was going to end, I would do it again."

He clenched the wheel so hard that his pulse thrummed in his fingers.

"I would do it a hundred times over. Ted gave me everything. He gave me love and memories that I hold close to me on my worst days. And he gave me Chris. If I had let what happened to Dad stop me from experiencing all of that..." She took a breath. "*That* would have been the tragedy."

He closed his eyes and rested his head back. These were the words he needed to hear. This is why he'd called his sister. "You're so damn strong," he said quietly.

He'd seen her pain and devastation after losing Ted. And the fact that she was doing so well now, that she was living her life and being such a wonderful mother...the woman was amazing.

"I'm strong because I have to be," she said firmly. "Please don't let what happened to Dad stop you from living your life."

Her words were somewhere between a plea and a challenge. To be his own person. To get over his fucking fears. And damn, he wanted to. "I need her to forgive me first."

Naomi scoffed. "With your big brown eyes and sexy soldier muscles, how could she not?"

He smiled.

Her voice softened. "And try not to be so hard on Mom."

"Nae—"

"I know you blame her for what happened to Dad. And no, she shouldn't have cheated. But Mom has her own issues. We both know she struggles to find happiness with *anyone*. She's on her sixth fiancé, and her fourth marriage. Her issues go beyond cheating and Dad. And there's nothing either of us can do about it." Another pause. "And I know that she holds a lot of guilt over what happened to Dad."

He swallowed. She was right. He knew she was. "I'll try."

"Good. Now, go get your woman."

Aria reached her car, breathing through the pain rippling through her body. Once inside, she started the engine and pulled onto the road.

She'd wanted him to tell her it wasn't true. That they *were* meant to be together. God, her heart had begged for the man to admit that. But he hadn't. He'd remained painfully quiet. And the expression on his face—an expression that had told her he knew everything she said was true. That they wouldn't work. They couldn't. Not with his current mindset.

The problem was, as much as she didn't want to admit it to herself, she was falling in love with him.

It was official, she was a magnet for heartbreakers.

Not that Marcus had ever broken her heart. They'd both just been young and naive. Falling pregnant too young. Playing house for a few years until her fear of him had forced her to run.

She rounded a corner. Marcus's silence made her nervous. Usually, once he'd found them, he wasn't quiet. In fact, he would endlessly harass them. Draw them into his problems until Aria and Zac fled, or Marcus got what he wanted.

Blowing out a long breath, she lifted her phone. No message from Cole. But of course, there wouldn't be. She'd left him less than half an hour ago. Was it sad that she still wished for different circumstances? That she knew who he was, yet she still hoped and prayed for him to want her? Want *them*?

Argh. She was just being pathetic now.

For the rest of the short drive home, she pushed him from her mind. The second she pulled into her driveway, she whispered the words in her head she'd been telling herself for days. *Do not look at his house.* She'd surreptitiously looked out the window so many times over the last few days, she was practically a stalker. It had to stop.

She walked to the door and slotted her key in the lock. She'd just opened it and taken two steps inside when she stopped. The breath stalled in her throat.

Oh God...the place was *trashed*.

The coffee table was turned upside down, the cupboards in the kitchen open and contents spilled everywhere. The couch pillows were scattered around the living room, slashes through them. Even the attic hatch door in the ceiling, leading to the attic, was open.

She took slow steps toward her kitchen. Every freaking drawer was pulled out and empty.

Her gaze shot to Zac's bedroom, just visible from where she was standing. Same thing. It was a mess.

With trembling fingers, she pulled out her phone and used Officer Hanon's direct number for the first time. Calling someone she knew instead of dispatch felt safer and faster.

"Officer Hanon speaking."

"It's Aria Callas. Someone broke into my house. The place is trashed."

He cursed. "They're gone now?"

Gone? Aria hadn't even considered the possibility of someone still being in the house! Quickly, she moved back out the front door. "I think so. I couldn't hear anyone." Her chest rose and fell in quick succession. God, she could barely breathe.

"Stay outside. I'm coming now."

Aria hung up—and the second she did, she wished she hadn't. She wished she'd kept him on the line, because a chill suddenly swept over her skin. What if someone *was* still in the house?

She moved all the way to the curb, then perched on the edge, crossed her arms over her chest and waited. She'd only been alone five minutes, tops, when a car pulled into the house across the street. Cole's car.

He got out, his eyes shifting to her house, then to her. He immediately moved toward her, and damn her treacherous heart for wanting him close.

"Aria?"

When she didn't answer, he lowered to the curb beside her. All she wanted to do was lean into him.

"What's going on?" he asked, his tone one of concern. "Why are you sitting here…and why the hell are you so pale?"

She wasn't surprised she was pale. She'd felt the blood drain from her face the second she walked into the house.

"Wait—is that asshole Marcus here?" Anger edged his voice.

He started to stand, but she touched his arm. "No. Someone broke into my house and wrecked the place."

Man, she wished her security camera had survived the storm. The one she'd ordered wasn't due to arrive for a couple more days.

The muscles in his arms visibly tightened. "Did you call the police?"

She nodded. "I did. But I didn't feel safe waiting inside in case…"

Cole's eyes turned steely. "Wait here."

"No!" Her fingers tightened. "Hanon's coming. We should wait for him."

He touched her cheek, and his eyes softened. "I'll be okay."

That small touch... It went a long way toward soothing the storm of fear and panic inside her. She swallowed, and after a moment, she nodded and released him.

He rose and disappeared into the house. She had to force herself to remain calm. She sat her chin on her knees, trying not to dig her fingers into her skin.

Finally, Cole returned, sitting beside her once again. "The house is empty."

She gave a small nod, and Cole tugged her against his side. She should pull away, she knew she should. But in that moment, when all she craved was warmth and safety, pulling away from Cole's heat and strength felt impossible. So she sank into his side and closed her eyes, letting the feel of him anchor her.

# CHAPTER 22

$\mathcal{C}$ ole remained close to Aria as Hanon, his partner, Jenkins, and three other officers moved through her house. All he wanted to do was wrap her in his arms and comfort her, but he needed to move slow.

He *hated* this. If this was the work of her ex, what had he been looking for? Or was this just to scare her?

"You really don't need to wait with me," Aria said quietly, breaking the silence.

"I'm waiting." No way was he leaving her by herself.

She watched him for another moment, and when she looked away, he exhaled a long breath. She was accepting his company, just like she'd accepted his comfort when he'd arrived. When she'd leaned into his side, something had kicked in his chest that was as unfamiliar to him as everything else she made him feel.

His conversation with his sister played over in his mind. Naomi was right about everything. The second he'd met Aria, he'd known she was his. But he'd fought it. How it had taken him so long to realize what an idiot he was, he had no idea.

He didn't try to talk to her as they waited. Something told him she needed the silence right now. To process. To accept that her home, her safe place, had been violated.

When Hanon stepped out, he moved over to them with a grim expression. "The guy entered through the back. He broke a window and crawled inside."

Yeah. Cole had seen that. "I've already called someone to fix it. He should be here within the hour."

Aria's gaze swung to him. He'd called while Aria had been talking to Hanon earlier. She had enough to deal with, and if he could lighten her load, at least a bit, he would.

"We've taken some prints, and we'll run them through the system. You don't have a home camera?"

She looked at her front porch. "I did, but it broke in the storm. I've ordered a new one, but it hasn't arrived yet."

At her desolate tone, Cole gave in to the urge and slid an arm around her waist, tugging her into his side. She didn't pull away.

Hanon nodded. "We'll get these prints to the station. You'll need to check your belongings, see if anything's been stolen. If it has, put in an insurance claim and call us." Hanon took a step away but stopped when Aria spoke.

"This was probably Marcus. You haven't found him, have you?"

Something crossed Hanon's face, and Cole frowned. *Had* they located him? Why hadn't Hanon told her already?

"We actually found the hotel he was staying at," Hanon began.

Aria straightened beside him. "So, you have him?"

"No. We received a call from the hotel that there were some... unfriendly visitors, and there was an altercation in one of the rooms. By the time we got there, both parties had left. We watched hotel surveillance, which is how we know it was him staying there, even though he gave a different name. He hasn't returned as of yet."

Aria laughed, but there was no humor in it. "Sounds like Marcus."

"We've still got an APB out on him for breaking his restraining order. If he comes back here again, we'll arrest him."

In the meantime, Cole would be with her. He just had to convince her to let him stick around.

When the officer left, Cole walked beside Aria to the door, but before they could move inside, she stopped and turned. "Thank you for this afternoon, Cole, but you don't need to stay with me."

"I know I don't need to, but I *want* to." He didn't want to leave her for a second. Not when her ex had possibly trashed her home.

Her gaze jumped between his eyes, but she remained silent.

"Let me stay and help you clean up," he said quietly, shifting closer. "At least for now."

She nibbled her bottom lip, and he cupped her cheek. When she leaned into his touch, his gut gave a protective kick.

She opened her mouth, but before she could say anything, a car pulled into her drive. He turned his head to see Zac climbing out of the driver's side, and Anthony the passenger.

Aria pulled away from him.

Zac's gaze shifted between them, then to the house. "What's wrong?"

"Someone broke in while I was out," Aria said quietly when the boys were in front of them. "The house is a mess."

Zac's eyes darkened. "Marcus."

"We don't know." She touched his arm. "But we're both safe, and that's what counts."

A storm brewed on his features, but he nodded.

"We need to clean up and let Hanon know if anything's missing. Cole's offered to help."

The pit in his stomach disappeared. She was letting him stay...for now.

"I'll help too," Anthony offered.

Aria smiled as she reached out and squeezed his arm. "Thank you."

Then she looked up at him, and God, that look—it destroyed him.

"Both of you," she whispered.

~

THEY SPENT hours cleaning the place and putting it back together. In that time, the window was replaced and daylight turned into evening. Aria was exhausted, but it was more emotional exhaustion than physical. The only good thing to come out of the cleaning was that neither she nor Zac had found anything stolen. But that begged the question—why had someone broken in at all?

Aria glanced at Cole from below her lashes as he set the table for dinner. The boys had left to pick up food, so it was just the two of them at the moment.

"You really don't need to stay." She felt like a broken record, she'd said it so many times.

His gaze rose, and for what had to be the tenth time that day, she felt that *thing*. It was hard to describe exactly what it was, but it felt hot and intense, and made her want to run away and toward him simultaneously.

"I want to stay," he said, straightening. He started walking toward her. Slow, measured steps. "I want to be close to you, and not just so I can make sure you're safe."

She swallowed. "We've had this conversation already, Cole." And the man hadn't disagreed with her. He hadn't told her she was wrong or that he'd fight for them. His silence had been deafening.

He stopped in front of her. When his hands went to her hips, awareness was like lightning down her spine. The kitchen island pressed to her back. She knew she should pull away, but right now, she just couldn't. He made her feel safe like no one else could, and she desperately needed that feeling.

"I heard what you said today." The way he held her gaze as he spoke demanded all of her attention. "And this is what I should have said in response. I care about you, Aria. And yeah. It goes against everything I've ever sworn I wanted or would allow myself to have. But that's only because I hadn't counted on *you*."

Hope bloomed in her chest, but she pressed it down. She had to hear all of his words before she let herself believe they might work.

"My father loved my mother," he continued quietly. "He loved her so much, it became almost his entire identity."

Her brows twitched, dread pooling in her belly at what she felt was coming.

"When I was fifteen, my father got home early from work and found my mother in bed with another man." There was no pain in Cole's words, just a dark acceptance. "That was the day my mother admitted she didn't love him anymore. That she'd stopped loving him a long time ago and wanted a divorce."

God. Her heart ached for the man she'd never met.

Cole's hand skirted beneath the material of her shirt, holding her bare waist. "He moved out, and I went with him. He was my best friend, and I didn't want him to be alone. My sister stayed with Mom. But Dad wasn't the same. Even though he tried to be okay for me, he just wasn't. He started drinking. He stopped smiling. And about a year later, I found his body on his bedroom floor. He was dead."

She sucked in a sharp gasp of air. "Oh, Cole."

"They said it was due to a combination of painkillers, anti-anxiety drugs and sleeping pills, which shouldn't be taken together. And alcohol, of course. He'd gotten to a point where he was drinking almost nonstop."

"I'm so sorry." She touched his chest.

"I don't know if it was an accident."

"Cole…"

He shook his head. "I was so angry. And I've *been* angry ever since. I blamed my mom for breaking him. For years, I've held the belief that love makes us weak. That it makes us vulnerable and puts us at the mercy of another person. Then a little over a year ago, my sister Naomi's husband died, and my sister was a mess, and that just confirmed it for me."

"Of course it did," she whispered.

"I promised myself I would never fall into a situation like that." The hand on her waist smoothed around to her back, inching up. "But it took *you* coming into my life to make me realize...we don't get a choice. And I can't let fear rule my entire existence."

Tears pressed at her eyes, but she blinked them back.

"I told you I wanted you, and then I hurt you. When I saw you with Marcus..." He blew out a heavy sigh. "That day was the anniversary of my father's death. When that asshole touched you, all I could think about was my mom cheating on my dad. And I'm *so damn sorry* for that. But I won't make that mistake ever again."

Everything about his expression and his voice made her believe what he said was true. She understood now why he'd jumped to what he assumed was the obvious conclusion. And she *wanted* to believe he wouldn't do it again. With everything she was, she wanted to believe him.

As if he heard her thoughts, he lowered his head so his temple touched hers. One of his hands went to the back of her neck. "Please." His breath brushed her skin. "Give me another chance."

Her heart beat faster, and her blood soared in her veins. She took a couple of seconds to let his words filter inside her. To touch a spot no one had touched before.

In that time, his hands slid down to her ass, and he lifted her onto the island. Then he stepped between her thighs. His lips lowered to her cheek, and she wanted to sigh at the kiss he pressed there. God, his kisses made her world brighten.

She closed her eyes and allowed herself to feel it all.

"You're right," she finally breathed. "We don't get to choose."

His head rose, his fingers threading through her hair. "Does that mean you'll give me another chance?"

She flicked her gaze between his eyes before whispering, "Yes."

His mouth crashed onto hers, and he kissed her. He kissed her like it was their first and last kiss. Like she was the beginning and end for him. His tongue slid inside her mouth and tangled with hers.

This time, she didn't hold back. She clutched his shoulders and felt the strength and power beneath her touch. This man... He was the only person to ever make her feel like *this* was it. This was what all the struggle in her life had been leading up to.

Meeting Cole. And falling for him.

# CHAPTER 23

*A*t the sound of movement in the house, Cole's eyes shot open. Aria remained asleep beside him, her chest moving up and down slowly with her deep breaths. Not only did he sleep better knowing she was by his side, but damn, it felt good to hold her while she slept.

He focused on whatever had woken him outside the room. When quiet footsteps led into the kitchen, he slowly slid out of bed, careful not to wake Aria. She didn't stir, but there was a small moan from her lips. His dick twitched but he shut it down, moving out of the bedroom. He was silent the entire way to the kitchen. That's where he found Zac at the kitchen counter, setting down a box of leftover pizza.

The kid's eyes widened when he saw Cole, but he recovered quickly. "Sorry, did I wake you?"

"I'm a light sleeper. It's a military thing." Not only that, but he could go from dead sleep to wide awake within seconds. It could be both a blessing and a curse.

Zac gave a nod, then he turned to grab a glass from the cupboard. "Want some water?"

"Sure."

He watched as the kid filled two glasses before handing one over. Cole didn't miss how closely Zac studied him. He had questions.

"It's real," Cole said quietly, taking a sip of water. "This thing between your mom and me. That's what you're wondering, isn't it?"

"You hurt her. Whatever you said or did after Marcus was here, it upset her."

Those words were like a knife to his flesh. "I did. And I will spend a long time making it up to her. It won't happen again."

Zac's gaze never left his. "She's been hurt a lot over the years."

Another fucking stab. "That ends now."

"You're gonna treat her well? Protect her?"

"Yes." No hesitation. He'd been slow getting to this point, but he was here now. She was his, and he was hers, and he wasn't going anywhere.

Another beat of silence from Zac, then he finally nodded. "Good."

"Anthony said Marcus has hit her." The words tasted like acid in his mouth.

Zac scowled. "He almost broke her fucking nose...more than once. The man's a scumbag who only cares about himself. Every time he comes into our lives, it's for selfish reasons. Money. Somewhere to hide out. Mom's been trying to keep us away from him and his problems since I was a kid. It's drained her, financially and emotionally. But I'm done with running. I want him to know he can't mess with us anymore."

Cole watched Zac closely. The kid almost spoke like he wanted to challenge the asshole himself. "I want to kill him too. Believe me. But you have to be smart. If your father ever comes near you, you call for me. You don't engage him in a fight."

Zac's jaw clenched, but he nodded. He wasn't dumb. Just an emotionally driven teenager. He picked an olive off a slice of pizza but didn't eat it. "I'm not always the best son, but I'm trying to do better."

Cole stepped forward and squeezed his shoulder. "You love her. That's exactly what she needs."

There was the rustle of sheets, then the padding of footsteps. But it wasn't Aria. Anthony had stayed the night too. The boys had stayed up late playing video games. He'd been able to tell from Aria's face throughout the evening that she appreciated their friendship. She liked that Zac had a good friend. That he was doing normal kid stuff.

Anthony stepped into the living room, running a hand through his sleep-mussed hair. "Hey. You guys eating all the left-over pizza without me?"

Zac lifted a slice. "Yep. And it tastes *good*." The kid took a big bite. Jesus, he ate half the slice in one go.

Anthony stopped at the kitchen island and grabbed a slice of his own.

Cole frowned at the teenagers. "You guys are still hungry?"

"Always," Anthony said around a mouthful of food.

Cole shook his head in bemusement just as he heard something from Aria's bedroom. A soft whimper. His insides iced even as Zac spoke.

"It's a nightmare," he said quietly, all humor gone from his voice. "She gets them every time Marcus comes back into our lives."

"A nightmare about what?" He was pretty sure he knew, but...

Zac stopped chewing, and the angry expression on his face made him look far from the sixteen-year-old kid he was. "It changes. But they always involve Marcus. I usually wake her up, but she can rarely get back to sleep. You should go to her."

SHE HAD TO GET OUT. *Not just out of this house. Out of Chicago. Away from Marcus and his damn problems. He'd found them. She'd known he would. Known it was only a matter of time. And whatever he'd gotten himself mixed up in, it wasn't good. All she'd needed to do was take one look at him to know that. There'd been a darkness about him. One that only came when he was desperate. Maybe he'd lost money he didn't have. Maybe he'd pissed off dangerous people. Whatever it was, she didn't want any part in it.*

*Her gaze cut to Zac as she moved about the room. He was sleeping in her bed because she needed him close. She needed him within reaching distance. He was only nine years old, dammit! He didn't deserve any of this. He deserved safety and love and security.*

*They'd left Marcus four years ago, right after the first hit. He'd started drinking and gambling away all the money he earned from his fights. He'd also become angry and just plain scary. The police had barely done anything. She'd learned very quickly that nothing would help her but disappearing. He was becoming too popular in the boxing world, and he made people too much money.*

*She'd thought they might finally be safe here. A year had passed since his last visit. She'd been so hopeful.*

*God, she was stupid.*

*She closed her eyes at the memory of him at her front door when she'd gotten home from picking Zac up from school. She'd smelled the alcohol on his breath. Seen the bloodshot eyes. That familiar dread had flooded her. Her ex was always angry, but when he drank...it was so much worse.*

*She swallowed. Thank God for Ned, her kind neighbor, who heard the commotion and came out with a gun.*

*But now it was just her again. Her gaze caught on Zac's little chest as it moved up and down. Hopelessness and fear tried to drown her. She was responsible for him. Only her. She had no one to help. No family to turn to. No friends. And she felt the heavy weight of that responsibility, a burden she would happily bear.*

She choked down a sob. She loved him so much. He was her entire world. She had to keep him safe.

She shoved aside the desolation and straightened her spine. She would get them out, and she would protect him at all costs. There was no other option. She'd already packed her car. She was throwing together the last bag, which she'd run out to the car, then it was Zac's turn. They'd drive through the night.

Each move to a new town took its toll on them, both financially and emotionally. She'd have to drain their savings once again. But she'd build it back up. Her online fitness business was gaining traction. It was all worth it. For Zac's safety, she'd do anything.

She'd just shoved the last of her clothes into the bag when she heard it. A thud from somewhere in the house.

Her heart leaped into her throat. Every window was locked, but just like the rest of the house, the locks were old.

With trembling fingers, she lifted her phone and made the call she'd been dreading.

"Nine-one-one, what's your emergency?"

"My ex is breaking his restraining order. He's in my house. I need immediate assistance." She kept her voice as quiet as possible, but she couldn't stop the tremble. Before the operator could say anything else, she rattled off her address and hung up.

They wouldn't make it in time. They never did. It was on her to protect herself and her son until they got here.

She grabbed the knife from beside the bag, the one she'd kept with her all afternoon. Then, with slow steps, she moved out of the bedroom and into the hall. There was silence, but she knew the man could be quiet when he wanted.

Two more steps, then she heard the creak of a floorboard.

A second later, Marcus stepped out of Zac's bedroom.

He stopped at the sight of her. A slow smile spread across his lips. It made her stomach crawl. Sixteen-year-old her had found sixteen-year-old Marcus cute. Charming even. Neither of them were the same person now.

*His brow lifted when he spotted the knife in her hand. "You going to stab me, Aria?"*

*She'd do whatever she needed to do to keep her son safe. "Get out of my house, Marcus."*

*The smile slipped from his lips. "I told you. I just need somewhere to hide out for a few days and a little money."*

*So he could put them both at risk from whoever he'd pissed off? No. "You can't stay here." She didn't need to give the asshole a reason. "And I don't have any money."*

*Not entirely true. She worked hard and she squirreled money away whenever she could. But she needed every cent to relocate. To feed her son.*

*He laughed, but there was no humor behind it. "Come on. Let's be honest here. I've seen your online business. I know you're doing well enough, and you've always been a good saver."*

*"What's the money for, Marcus?"*

*He inched forward a step. "I lost some bets. I owe Denny some cash."*

*Gambling. Of course. "I can't help you. I've already called the police. You should go before they get here and arrest you."*

*His eyes narrowed. "Now, Aria, I haven't even brought up the little issue of Zac. You took my kid away from me. And if you don't help me, I might just be inclined to take him back."*

*A wild panic surged through her veins, but she was careful to keep it off her face. Marcus loved to make people fear him. It was just one of the reasons he was such a good boxer. "Get. Out."*

*There was a moment of pause. Her heart thumped. Then, before she could anticipate his move, he lunged forward and grabbed the hand with the knife. He spun them around and shoved her against the wall. Her teeth clattered when her head struck the surface.*

*He clenched her wrists so hard that she cried out and released the knife. Then his hold on her eased.*

*He pressed his face into her hair. "Mm. I've missed you, babe."*

*Her skin crawled at his touch. "I'm sure you've had plenty of women to keep you company," she growled through gritted teeth. "Get off me!"*

"No. I think I'm gonna spend the night with my family." He lifted his head, and his eyes were pure evil. "Now, I want you to call the police and cancel that callout."

Like hell she would. When his hand grazed up her side, she swung her knee and got him right between the legs, hard.

He growled, and she quickly followed it up with a head butt right into his nose. This time he howled as blood ran down his face.

She pulled out of his hold and ran toward the bedroom. She only got three steps when he grabbed the back of her shirt and threw her into the hall table. It tipped, and a large plant in a thick ceramic pot hit the floor beside her with a loud thud.

She barely had time to process what was happening before Marcus was on top of her, turning her over. His fist swung so fast, she didn't see it coming, and he caught her right in the jaw.

Pain exploded through her face. Her head spun and her vision darkened.

"You made me fucking bleed, bitch!" She barely heard him through the buzzing between her ears. "You don't tell me when to leave. I make that choice. Now I'm going to take my son. Maybe I'll return him if you call off the police."

His weight lifted from her. Through her haze, she saw him grab the knife as he stood.

No! She couldn't let him take Zac!

Gathering the little strength she still had, she pushed up and grabbed the potted plant. With shaking arms, she lifted it above her head and ran forward. Marcus turned just as she brought it down onto his skull.

The pot smashed, and he dropped to the floor.

She leaped over him and rushed into the bedroom. She reached for Zac in bed just as a hand grabbed her shoulder. She screamed—

Her eyes flashed open at the hand on her shoulder, and for a moment, all she saw was a dark figure looming over her. She shoved at his chest and opened her mouth to scream again. Then he spoke.

"Aria, it's me! Cole."

Cole. Not Marcus. The scream released as a long, desperate exhale. God, the dream… It felt so real.

Without thinking about what she was doing, she sat up and crawled into Cole's lap. He didn't hesitate. He wrapped his arms tightly around her.

"Thank you," she whispered. The thank-you was for waking her. For letting her seek comfort in his arms. For all of it.

"Will you tell me about him?"

She closed her eyes at his soft words. She didn't want to talk about Marcus. She wanted to forget about his very existence. But Cole needed to know, not only so he could protect them—and himself—but because tonight she'd told him she was in this. That they were in this together.

"Marcus and I were in the same grade at school," she said, swiping a tear from her eye. "He was taller than most of the other boys. Popular and good-looking. We started dating, and as you already know, I got pregnant at sixteen."

She blew out a long breath. Cole started a slow stroke down her back, and it made warmth trickle back into her cold body.

"I told you that my parents didn't want anything to do with me after that, so I moved in with Marcus's parents, and when he finished high school, we found a place and moved out. He'd always been into boxing. At first he was just doing some amateur stuff, but when he turned eighteen, he started working harder and got really good, really quickly." Her next breath was more of a shudder. "Then…it was little changes. He'd stay out longer at night. Come home smelling of alcohol. When we started struggling with money, I began asking questions. He was earning a lot from his wins, and I was doing a bit of personal training on the side, so we shouldn't have been having money problems."

A tremble coursed down her spine at the memory of their first big fight. She felt Cole's lips in her hair, and she closed her eyes.

"We argued…and he did this thing he'd never done before,

where he towered over me like I was his opponent in the ring or something. He didn't hurt me, but I felt the threat of violence. It was the first time I ever feared him."

Cole remained silent, but there was a slight tightening of his fingers.

"Our fights became more frequent. He started drinking more. Taking drugs. We had a few visitors in our house that I just didn't feel comfortable being around Zac. I knew they were into drugs and gambling, and I just wanted them out."

She nestled deeper into his chest, trying to capture as much of his warmth as she could.

"One night, his *friend* came over unannounced. Just walked in when I opened the door. Started talking about some cash Marcus owed him. He didn't say it directly, but he hinted at the trouble Zac and I would find ourselves in if he didn't get his money."

Just the memory, over a decade old now, still turned her skin to ice. "I was stupid. I should have left then. Instead, I waited for Marcus to get home. He was so angry when I brought it up. That was the first time he hit me."

Cole cursed under his breath.

"I left the next day. Took Zac and just disappeared to Texas. It took almost a year for him to find us. Six months the time after that. Thirteen months the third time… I got good at moving in a hurry. Until now." The last words came out quieter.

Cole touched her cheek, and she looked up. "You don't need to run anymore. You have me. I'll protect you."

Her gaze skittered between his eyes. "I don't want to pull you into whatever mess he brings my way. He's dangerous, Cole."

"Let him bring the mess. And let him feel what happens when he does."

There was so much conviction in his voice. For the first time in her life, she felt like she truly had someone on her side. Someone to help protect Zac. Someone to protect *her*.

She laid her head on his chest once more. "Thank you."

# CHAPTER 24

ole kept his elbows tucked and his knees loose. His front leg pointed toward his opponent, a man who could, and had, taken down hundreds of dangerous men in his life.

But he'd taken down just as many. And this morning, he had anger on his side. It coursed through his veins. It turned the world around him from vibrant shades to a dark gray.

He knew anger. He'd tasted it many times. But this was different. Because Aria was different. She'd dropped into his world from seemingly nowhere and changed everything. She'd changed the very trajectory of his life. And the things she'd told him a few nights ago...

His opponent finally swung. A right cross.

Cole dodged it easily. He remained light on his toes.

The man's eyes flashed in challenge. He swung again, this time following it up with a jab. Cole dodged both.

He hadn't swung yet. Not a single hit.

Another right cross flew toward his head. Cole dodged and finally swung back. The punch got his opponent in the side of the head. Not hard. But not soft.

The guy barely seemed to register the impact. But Cole had known he wouldn't. He'd taken harder hits.

An image flashed in his head of Marcus hitting Aria. Cole swung again, this time harder. He just missed his opponent.

The next flash in his mind was of another story she'd told him. Of people showing up at her door. Bad people, demanding money she didn't have, while she tried to protect her son when she was barely an adult herself.

He jabbed at his opponent twice, then threw a cross hit.

And she'd been running ever since. She'd never been able to stay anywhere for too long. Sometimes as little as six months. She couldn't make friends. She couldn't build a long-term home for her or her son.

A fist flew at his head. He wasn't fast enough to dodge and it landed. Pain radiated through his skull. But instead of shying away from the feeling, he absorbed it and threw a jab followed by a hook.

The hook caught Ryker so hard, his friend keeled over.

Shit.

Erik straightened from outside the ring. He'd already done a round this morning with Ryker.

Cole dropped his fists. "You okay?"

Ryker took a moment to catch his breath before straightening. "Yeah. That was a good hit. What's going on with you?"

"Something has to be going on with me to get in a hit on you?" He knew that wasn't what his friend was saying, but he didn't know if he wanted to talk about the shit running through his head or not.

"It's the look in your eyes," Erik said before Ryker could.

"Yeah. You're in your head," Ryker added.

He was.

"You and Aria still okay?" Ryker asked.

"Aria seems to have forgiven my dumb ass." Thank God.

"What is it, then?"

"She keeps having these nightmares about her ex. And every time I learn more about him, about the things he's done to her and the trouble he's brought into her life, I want to kill him more."

Both Ryker and Erik's eyes narrowed. It was Erik who answered.

"Do we want to know?"

"He's been trailing her since she left him when Zac was five." That was eleven damn years. "Every time he finds her, he brings trouble. He always drags her into his messes. Takes her money. And he isn't afraid to use his fists on her."

Wild rage crossed Erik's face. "The guy was a professional boxer for years and he *hits* her?" Erik was once a professional boxer. He knew that world. Knew the man could probably kill a person with a single blow, yet he'd dared hit Aria.

Cole would tear him to fucking shreds if their paths crossed again. "Yes. And I just keep thinking about that day he came in here. If I'd known then what I know now…"

"But you didn't," Ryker said quickly. "And you can't beat yourself up over something you didn't know."

The logical side of him understood that.

"Police still looking for him?" Erik asked.

"For what that's worth. They haven't been able to locate him since he checked out of that hotel."

Ryker shook his head. "Where is she today?"

"Working at Michele's shop."

The place was quiet and had good security. No one got in without Michele buzzing them inside.

The door to Mercy Ring opened, and Cole looked up to see Anthony's classmates entering. This was the third session for the kids. And at each session, the same teens pissed him off.

Cole hadn't wanted Benny to return. In fact, he'd wanted to inform the teacher that he was to leave the kid at school from now on, ever since he'd grabbed Aria's ass. But Aria had asked him not to just in case the kid retaliated by fucking with Zac.

Erik dipped his head. "I'll see you guys later." He nudged Anthony on his way out.

Anthony smiled cheekily at Cole and Ryker as he walked past. Cole grinned back and shoved his shoulder. He was spending a lot of time with Zac, and by getting closer to Zac, Cole was also spending more time than usual with Anthony. The kid's leg was a lot better.

Zac dropped into a seat beside Anthony. As usual, Benny and Ezra snickered as they sat at the opposite end of the row.

When the last kids sat, Ryker stepped forward. "Good morning, everyone. Hope you were all okay after our last session."

Benny snickered again and said something to Ezra that Cole couldn't catch.

"You got something to say, Benny?" he asked.

The look he got was belligerent at best. "Nope."

Cole kept his eyes on the kid until he squirmed in his seat, then finally looked away. "We're working on combination hits today."

He got the session started by demonstrating various combination hits with Ryker, building on the foundation the boys had already learned, then the kids partnered off. Anthony and Zac partnered together, as they usually did, but he didn't miss that Benny and Ezra stationed themselves nearby. The little shits liked to annoy both boys. Particularly Zac.

As Cole walked around the room, he noticed most of the kids were doing well. When he walked to the wall to grab some more gloves, he overheard a conversation from inside the nearby bathroom.

"He did not."

"He *did*. Told me today."

"He said he could get you Black Dust?"

Black Dust...that was the new drug on the market. The one Officer Hanon said was lethal if taken in excess.

"Yep. For the right price."

"He's lying. No one can get that stuff here."

He was about to walk into the bathroom when shouting from behind him snagged his attention. He turned just in time to see Zac shove Benny in the chest. Both boys had removed their gloves, and Zac was getting in the kid's face.

Cole ran across the room, but Ryker got there first, moving between them. The teacher was also there, a hand on Benny's shoulder.

Benny laughed. "What's your problem, Callas?"

Zac lunged forward, but Ryker kept him where he was with a hand on his chest. "Let me go!"

Cole touched Zac's shoulder. "Calm down."

"Aw, that's sweet," Benny cooed. "Your new daddy here to make everything better?"

"Benny!" the teacher growled.

Cole's attention whipped to the kid. "What was that?"

"He's been shit-talking Mom like he always does," Zac said.

Benny laughed. "Only because it makes you cry like a little bitch."

"Hey." Cole moved closer to Benny, his voice lowering. "Stop. *Now*."

Something flashed in the kid's eyes. But it wasn't Benny who answered, it was his friend, Ezra.

"Why? Just because you're fucking her, we can't talk about her anymore?"

Audible gasps sounded throughout the room, and the teacher switched his attention. "Ezra!"

Cole kept very still, but his eyes never left Ezra's. "You don't talk about her again. Got it?"

"Or what?" Ezra sneered.

Cole's eye narrowed. He stepped closer.

The teacher's nervous cough was loud in the otherwise silent room, and he pressed a hand to Cole's arm. "Mr. Turner."

All of Cole's attention remained on Ezra—that's when he noticed the kid's eyes. "You on something?"

All the bravado left the kid instantly. "What?"

"Your pupils are huge. What have you taken?"

"Nothing."

*Bullshit.*

Cole turned to the teacher, who looked nervous and flustered. "He's on drugs. We don't allow people into Mercy Ring who are high. You take those two out of here—now." He turned his attention to Benny. "And I don't want either of these boys in here again."

Benny's brow furrowed, then he scoffed. "Whatever."

Cole ignored the kid. He was trying to get a rise out of him and Zac. Cole wouldn't be giving him that satisfaction. Not today.

ARIA TAPPED AWAY at her laptop while Michele cooked. She was so grateful to the other woman for letting her work here today. It was actually really peaceful. Michele seemed to like the quiet, which worked well for Aria.

She was just sending out a new workout routine to a couple of clients when her phone dinged from beside her laptop. She smiled when she saw who it was. Cole.

*Morning, honey. You doing okay?*

She nibbled her bottom lip. She loved it when he called her that, and it had become really frequent these last few days. He'd also been attentive and kind and basically everything a woman could ask for in a partner.

She quickly typed in a response.

*Other than being tortured by the delicious scents of Michele's butter chicken, I'm doing great.*

And she actually was. It was strange that she could be so happy and content when her home had been broken into and Marcus had shown up in her life again. Cole's presence offered a sense of protection. Even when he wasn't around, like now, she still felt safe knowing he was hers.

Her phone vibrated with another message from Cole.

*That woman's cooking could torture the most hardened soldier.*

She smiled, responding.

*I might be able to weasel some from her for dinner.*

She chuckled at Cole's response.

*So my night would consist of butter chicken and you? Fuck, I'm a lucky man.*

She felt Michele's gaze rise to her before her friend spoke. "Let me guess, Cole's put that smile on your face?"

Aria grinned at her friend. "Yeah. He's been making me smile a lot these last few days."

Michele wiped her hands on her apron. "You must have a special touch, because no way could anyone else have pulled this side out of him."

*Thank God for that.*

"Either that, or he just met his perfect woman," Michele added with a smile.

Aria's smile softened. "Well, he's definitely my perfect man." She pointedly glanced at the cooktop. "Actually, we were talking about your butter chicken."

Michele's brows rose. "Really? You want some?"

"I mean, if you've got a little extra?"

"God, yes, take some. I've made so much. I'm making rogan josh next. I'll give you some of that too, and you can have a little curry feast for dinner."

"Oh gosh, you're making me hungry now."

Michele's smile widened. "Guess we better take a lunch break, then."

Man, she loved this woman. She was still smiling when her phone buzzed, but this time with a call.

The smile dropped from her face. Marcus.

Aria was still looking at her phone when Michele set two bowls onto the table and lowered to the seat beside her. Suddenly she wasn't so hungry anymore. Quickly, she canceled the call.

"Everything okay?"

Her gaze flew up to the other woman. "Of course. This looks wonderful."

She pushed her laptop aside, turned her phone over, and pulled the bowl in front of her, all the while trying to ignore the pit in her stomach that was caused by Marcus.

# CHAPTER 25

*A*ria smiled as Cole's arms slid around her waist from behind.

"That smells incredible." His smooth, deep voice brushed over her skin

She stirred the butter chicken with a wooden spoon. "Yeah, Michele's a great cook."

"I'm not talking about the food."

When the man nibbled on her neck and a hand slid up her ribs, she playfully elbowed him in the gut. "Cole, Zac's home!"

He turned her. When he stroked some hair away from her face, his fingers grazed her skin. She wanted to lean into his touch.

His eyes shifted between hers. "You're so beautiful, Aria."

Oh Lord, could this man get any more perfect?

He kissed her, and yep, he could. This time, she didn't try to stop herself. She leaned into him. When his tongue slipped between her lips, she hummed.

He always did this. Made her go from zero to a hundred with the slightest touch. Maybe that had something to do with the whole falling-in-love thing. Something she felt wholeheartedly but wasn't quite ready to share yet.

She'd just slid her fingers into his hair when a choking sound came from across the room.

*Crap.*

She tore her mouth away and pushed at his chest. He stepped back, but when she tried to step away, his hand slid around her waist and tugged her back to him, his hold on her like iron.

"Zac, I didn't see you there." Embarrassment heated her cheeks as she smiled at her son.

"Yeah, I think you were a bit busy." He scrubbed a hand through his hair and there was a hint of a smile on his face. "That's okay."

She smiled with him. She hadn't dated much over the years, but when she had, Zac never liked the guy. Cole was the first person he actually seemed okay with. A part of her wondered if it was because he could see how happy Cole made her. Or maybe he just saw that Cole was a good guy. Probably didn't hurt that he liked Anthony, and Anthony liked Cole.

Zac set his phone on the island and walked over to the fridge. She frowned at the cell, a thought coming to her. "I know you said you don't have a TikTok account, but does Anthony?" Maybe he'd accidentally posted something with her or Zac, and her location had been exposed.

Beside her, Cole tensed at the mention of TikTok. She'd told him about Marcus's reference to the video site.

Zac poured some milk into a cup. "Nah, he doesn't."

"I wonder…if you created an account, and I'm in a clip somewhere, would you be able to find it?"

Zac considered the question for a moment. "I can find out which accounts kids at school are following. If you were filmed here in Lindeman, then someone local must be responsible." He took another sip before lowering his glass. "I've heard TikTok pushes videos made by people in the same area, which might help."

That sounded promising. "If you have time, that would be great. I just want to know what Marcus was talking about."

Zac scowled. "He's an asshole. I wouldn't listen to a word he said." He rounded the counter and drank the rest of his milk before putting the glass into the sink. "I'm going across the street to hang out with Anthony. Cole, feel free to continue feeling up my mother while I'm gone and get it out of your system."

Cole nodded. "Thanks."

She shook her head and lightly elbowed Cole in the gut before turning back to Zac. "Tell Anthony he's welcome to come over for dinner. Ryker, too, if he's there."

Zac snapped his phone up and nodded as he left. The boys had been eating dinner with her and Cole for the last week. It all felt very domestic. She liked it.

The second the door closed, Cole pulled her close again. She pushed at his chest. "No, Cole, I need to make papadums."

She stepped out of his embrace, but immediately he tugged her back and sat her on the island. She kind of, sort of, pushed him away, but she really didn't. Her attempt was weak at best.

The man kissed her until she was panting. It was only the buzz of her phone behind her that finally had her tearing away from him.

"Ignore it," he said, kissing down her neck.

"It could be Zac."

She reached across the island, giggling as Cole continued his onslaught. Then she frowned. "It's a notification from the school."

That was odd. It was evening. She clicked into it.

The gasp that slipped from her lips had Cole tensing immediately.

"What?"

Her eyes scanned over the letter from the principal.

*Dear parents and caregivers,*

*It is with deep regret that we inform you about a recent loss to our school community. Early this morning, Ezra Kahl lost his life...*

There were more words. Words encouraging parents to talk to their kids about his death. To keep them home if they needed time. But the shock kept her from taking in much else.

Cole lifted her off the island and read the email from over her shoulder. He cursed under his breath.

"Ezra..." Her stomach clenched. Zac hadn't liked him, but this would still be a shock.

He took the phone from her fingers. "It doesn't say how he died."

"Those poor parents," she said quietly. Her heart ached for his family. She may not have liked the mother, but losing her son? God, she didn't know how the woman would survive it.

His gaze shot to the front window and his house. "I might go bring the boys over here. We can see if they know yet, and how they're doing with the news."

She gave a small nod. "Yes, go get them, please. If they don't know, we can tell them together."

He pressed one last kiss to her lips before moving out of the house.

Aria nibbled her bottom lip and went back to the curries on the stove. She'd just turned down the heat when the door opened again.

"That was qui—" The words froze on her lips when she saw who it was. She took a quick step back. "Get out."

Marcus held his hands up. He had a black eye, and he looked like he was limping as he walked toward her. "I'm not here to hurt you, Aria. I've been waiting patiently for soldier boy to leave. Once I have what I need, I'll go."

She frowned, her fingers twitching to reach for one of the knives in the block beside her. "What do you want?"

One side of his mouth lifted. "The first time I broke in, when you weren't home, I left something for safekeeping."

"You *what?*"

"I just needed to leave it somewhere no one would look. It's why I've stayed away for a while. So no one would follow me. But now I need it back."

*Oh, Jesus.* "What is it?"

He smiled, but there was no humor behind it. Instead of moving forward, he grabbed a dining table chair and carried it to the hall before positioning it below the attic hatch door in the ceiling.

As he stuck his head into the cavity, she swiped her phone from the middle console and quickly called Cole. She also inched back so that the knife block was within reaching distance. Before Cole could answer, Marcus growled and dropped to the floor. She quickly turned the volume off on her cell and pulled her arm behind her back.

"Where's the backpack?" he growled.

"Backpack?"

"The backpack, Aria! I hid it in the attic. Where is it?"

Her heart pounded in her chest. She'd only seen that look on his face a couple times in her life, and it never ended well for her. Her gaze shot out the window and across the street. The door was closed. Dammit. Had he answered her call yet? Could he hear Marcus?

She forced her gaze back to him. "The house was broken into three days ago. Everything was raided. The attic hatch door was open when I got home."

He was across the room so fast, she didn't have time to grab a knife. He gripped her shoulders, and his fingers bit into her skin. "You're lying!"

She tried to yank herself out of his hold, but his grip was too tight. "I'm not," she said, voice firm.

Suddenly, she was flying across the room. The back of her

head hit the edge of the dining table and she fell to the floor, hard.

"There was a small fortune in drugs in that bag!"

"Drugs?" she said weakly, clutching her head. When she lowered her hand, she grimaced at the sight of blood.

Marcus dropped in front of her and yanked her up by her hair. She cried out as pain blasted her skull.

"Black Dust, Aria! It's fuckin' expensive."

She grabbed at his wrist. "It was probably someone who followed *you* here! They broke in and stole it," she growled. Not that pleading her innocence had ever saved her before.

She tried to pull his hand away, but he was too strong.

"I stored it here so I could line up my fucking buyers without anyone stealing the shit, like they tried to do at the hotel. If I don't find it"—he leaned closer—"I swear to God, Aria, I'll kill you *and* Zac!"

"I just can't believe it," Zac said quietly. "He was there being an asshole at school all week."

Cole nodded soberly. Someone from school had posted the news on social media just before he'd stepped into the house.

"I wonder if any of the guys know what happened," Anthony said, typing something into his phone.

Cole was just leaving Anthony's bedroom, beckoning the boys to follow, when a call from Aria came through on his phone. He frowned as he answered. "Aria?"

"Where's the backpack?"

Cole's blood ran cold at the sound of Marcus's voice. *Fuck.* He was there. With Aria.

"Stay here," he growled to the boys. He didn't wait to see if they listened. He flew down the stairs and ran out of the house. Fear and panic spiraled through his limbs, but he shoved it down.

The second he stepped inside the home, he saw Marcus looming over a bleeding Aria, her hair fisted in his hand.

"I swear to God, Aria, I'll kill you *and* Zac!"

Cole saw red. He lunged, pulling the asshole off her before throwing him into the living room coffee table. It broke under his weight, and Marcus hit the floor. He was only down for a second.

Zac and Anthony ran inside. They only stopped for a second to take in the scene before running to Aria. Cole's full attention remained on Marcus. He positioned his body to block the others.

"You touched her," he said with deadly quiet.

The guy's chest heaved as he panted. His expression was all rage. "That bitch just lost me a lot of fucking money! I'll do whatever the hell I want with her!"

Cole fought for calm. Instead of hitting first, like he knew the guy wanted, he stepped forward and kept his voice low.

"*Wrong.* Because she's mine now. She and Zac are under my protection. But you know that already, don't you? And you know I could kill you without breaking a sweat. It's why you waited for me to leave. Because you're a fucking coward who only hits people you think are weaker than you."

The hit came hard and fast. Cole dodged—and that enraged the asshole further. Marcus lunged and swung again. Cole darted, but this time followed with a punch of his own, catching the guy in the jaw. Marcus's head snapped back.

A growl roared through the room, and Marcus ran at him. Cole dropped and rammed his shoulder into the guy's gut before taking him down and landing on top of him. He swung again. There was a crunch. The asshole's nose broke.

Marcus howled in pain and rolled them. This time, the punch grazed the side of Cole's head. He barely felt it.

Marcus lifted his fist again, but before he could swing, there was the distinct sound of a pistol slide being racked.

"Get off him!" Zac yelled.

"Zac!" Aria gasped.

Slowly, Marcus rose, his focus switching from Cole to Zac. "You wouldn't shoot me, kid."

Cole pushed off the floor to see Zac standing in the kitchen, a gun in his hand.

"I would. I'd shoot you right between the eyes so you'd never breathe another fucking breath around my mother again!"

Marcus took a step toward him.

Zac fired.

Aria screamed.

But the bullet hit the floor by Marcus's feet. Close. A warning shot.

Cole lunged forward and easily disarmed Zac, but by the time he turned, weapon up, Marcus was gone. Cole took off after him. He'd just hit the street as Marcus slid into a Beamer halfway down the block and sped away.

He stormed back into the house.

"What the hell were you thinking?" he shouted at Zac.

Zac didn't respond. He just stood there, looking angrier than Cole had ever seen him, breathing heavily.

Cole was on the verge of chewing him out when he heard Aria moving behind him. He turned and went to her. Anthony was at her side, carefully helping her stand.

Blood roared between his ears at the sight of the open wound on her head.

"I'm okay," she said quietly.

"I'm taking you to the hospital. You might need stitches."

He lifted her into his arms, and when he turned to look at the boys, his eyes narrowed on Zac. "You're both coming."

## CHAPTER 26

$\mathcal{A}$ ria stared at the moon as it cast dim light over the trees through the car window. They'd spent hours at the hospital. While she'd received four stitches, Ryker had picked up the boys. They were all staying at Cole and Ryker's house tonight, but the boys would probably be asleep by the time she got there.

Four stitches. She knew she'd gotten off lightly. That look in Marcus's eyes... God, he'd been ready to kill.

A shudder coursed down her spine. She wasn't sure if Cole felt it, but his hand tightened on her thigh. He'd been quiet all evening. At the hospital. While she'd spoken to Officer Hanon.

She placed a hand over his.

Seeing him go up against Marcus had filled her with pure terror. Cole had been just as fierce, and she'd known he would be, but that knowledge hadn't helped the fear. Then Zac, holding her gun...the one she kept hidden in the empty flour container in the pantry but didn't think he knew about...

Her breath caught.

"Don't think about it, Aria."

She swallowed, looking over to him. "I should have hidden the gun from Zac better. If that bullet had landed..."

Her heart banged against her ribs. He'd told her he'd only been trying to scare Marcus by pulling the trigger, but there was so much anger in her son.

Another squeeze of her thigh. "It didn't."

*But it could have.*

She swallowed, turning back to the window. Hanon had sent officers to search the streets. He'd been particularly interested in the information about the Black Dust.

Christ, she couldn't believe the guy had stashed *drugs* in her home and she hadn't even known. That had to be why her house was broken into. She had no enemies besides Marcus. And how else would someone have known to look in the attic storage space?

"I'm sorry I left you."

Aria frowned at Cole's words. Wait, he didn't think...

"This *isn't* your fault," she said firmly.

The muscles in his arms visibly tensed as they pulled into his driveway. "I shouldn't have gone across the street and left you unprotected. I knew he was out there somewhere."

"Cole, I was the one who didn't lock my door when you left."

His jaw clicked. He didn't look at her. "Come on, you need to get some rest."

She wanted to grab his arm and tug him back, finish this conversation, but he was already out of the car.

With a deep exhale, she opened her door to find him already there. Gently, he took her arm and helped her out. Zac had packed her a bag with a few things, so Cole escorted her straight into his house, keeping his arm around her waist as they entered and moved up the stairs. She hated how silent he was. And she hated his pained expression even more.

She remained silent until they stepped into his bedroom and closed the door behind them. "Cole. Tell me you know this isn't your fault."

He shook his head. "I hate that he got to you today. And I hate that when I first met him, I welcomed him into my fucking business."

"Cole..."

He blew out a long breath. Tortured. The man was tortured. Was he thinking about his father? About loving and then potentially losing her?

When he took a step away from her, she wrapped her arms around his middle and lay her cheek against his back. He went completely still.

"I'm okay," she whispered.

There was a beat of silence in the room, so heavy and so full of unspoken turmoil that the air felt thick. Slowly, he turned. He studied her face, and she covered his cheek with her hand.

"I'm okay," she repeated. "Thanks to you."

His gaze pulled back to hers. It wasn't just guilt she saw in his eyes now. There was something else. Something worse.

Fear.

Was she right? Was he afraid of losing her?

Before she could analyze it further, he tugged her body into his and kissed her. The kiss was raw and demanding. It was everything they both needed.

His tongue swept inside her mouth, sliding against hers, causing her sex to flare to life. She could almost taste his hunger, tinged with desperation. Like he was frantic to hang on to her. Reassure himself that she was okay.

She slid her fingers around his neck, and he lifted her up against his body. She moaned loudly. His kisses were like little shots of electricity that darted straight down to her core.

Air whipped around her, then she was sitting on his sleek dresser. It put their heads almost at the same height. He stepped between her thighs, his lips never leaving hers. The hard evidence of his arousal pressed into her.

She trailed her fingers down his chest. Everything about him was hard and heated and hers. This man was *hers*. And God, that felt good.

He gripped the hem of her shirt and tugged it over her head. Then he removed his own before trailing kisses down her jaw and neck.

Her breaths came in short gasps. *Yes.* She wanted to feel him everywhere. Skin against skin. She wanted him to surround her. Consume her.

His fingers shifted from her ribs to her back, then her bra fell. She cried out when his mouth dove down to her breast.

*Fuck.* This man's lips on her... They made her feel everything.

She lifted her hands to his neck and weaved her fingers into his hair. She needed to anchor herself. His tongue flicked over her nipple, then he sucked.

She was on fire. Flames spread from her breast to her lower abdomen. He flicked to the other breast, and it was the same thing. The same burning. The same all-consuming need.

After his mouth trailed back up her neck, it settled beside her ear, and his breath brushed over her, causing her skin to tingle.

"Lift for me, honey."

She lifted her body up, and he tugged off her jeans and panties. Then she was pulled to the edge of the drawers, his mouth on hers again. When his finger ran over her clit, her entire body jolted.

He ran his finger over her again. She moaned and ground against him. He continued the onslaught, and she continued to squirm until a finger touched her entrance. Her breath stopped. Slowly, he pushed inside her. Her world tilted and threatened to disintegrate.

Then his finger moved in an almost rhythmic way. That, in combination with his tongue and his taste, drove her right to the edge.

His thumb went to her clit, and he ran it over her as he continued to thrust with his finger.

"Cole..." His name had barely left her lips when her body convulsed and spasmed around him. She opened her mouth, but he swallowed her cry with his lips. The orgasm hit her so hard, her entire body trembled with a violence she'd never felt before.

When his mouth lifted, she slowly opened her eyes and looked at him. The way he touched her, the way he kissed and looked at her, it felt different tonight. *He* felt different.

As if he heard her thoughts, he said quietly, "Everything you are, I want."

Her breath stuttered from her chest. "You have me. I'm giving myself to you."

~

FUCK, Cole wanted to drown in those words. His heart crashed so hard inside his chest, he could swear something cracked. That was what this woman did to him.

He stepped out of his jeans and briefs, and just when he was searching for a condom from his wallet, she grabbed his arm and pulled him between her thighs.

"I'm on the pill," she whispered. "I want to feel you tonight."

He closed his eyes. It took a moment to just control the storm of his emotions.

When she reached down and touched him, his eyes opened, and blood pumped fast inside his veins. She ran her fingers over him, touching everything, from base to tip. When he couldn't take it anymore, he grabbed her hand. Then he plunged his tongue into her mouth as he eased his length inside her body.

He swallowed another of her cries.

Being inside her was like nothing else. It was like his heart and soul and every other fucking fragment of his being was in tune with hers. Like she aligned everything for him, for the first time in his life.

He pulled back before rocking forward. Her groan was a rumble against his lips.

As he continued to thrust, he held her close. His fear had shifted tonight. He wasn't scared of loving her anymore. He was scared of *losing* her. Of not holding her close enough. Of not building a life with this woman.

Of her being taken away from him.

He thrust again. She threw back her head and groaned. She looked wild and unrestrained.

He felt something else in his chest. Something tight and painful and rapturous.

Love. It was love. For her. For all that she was and the man she turned him into.

He increased his speed, kissing her exposed neck. Her pulse raced beneath his lips. He reached for her breast and rolled her nipple between his thumb and finger. Her breaths became shallow, and when her head lifted, he caught her mouth again.

His hand left her breast and traveled down her body. One thrum of her clit and she broke. Her walls clenched him tightly, and she whimpered his name.

His blood roared at the sound. At the unbelievable feel of her around him.

Two more thrusts, then he shattered along with her. Every muscle in his body tensed and vibrated. He continued to thrust until he had nothing left. Until she owned all of him.

Their breaths were loud in the quiet room. And when the world finally slowed and he came back to her, he looked down to see her watching him.

She'd given all of herself to him, just as he'd given himself to her.

Without a word, he lifted her. He didn't slide out of her body until he laid her in the bed. Then he held her close, not wanting a single sliver of space between them.

# CHAPTER 27

*A*ria's eyes flew open, and she jackknifed into a seated position in bed. Her heart beat fast in her chest, and a band of sweat broke across her forehead.

When Cole stepped into the room in only a towel, the air whooshed from her chest.

A nightmare. It was only a nightmare. Not real.

Worry washed over Cole's face. He was across the room in a second before lowering to the side of the mattress. "Hey. You okay?"

When he cupped her cheek, she leaned into him. "I'm okay. Just a bad dream."

This one had been worse than usual, ignited by everything that had happened yesterday.

Cole's gaze softened. "Tell me about it."

Her brows twitched. "Are you sure?"

It would only make him angry, and she knew the man was already right on the edge. Every nightmare was a memory.

He nodded.

"Okay... Zac was twelve. We were living in Charleston. When I got home from dropping Zac at school, Marcus was in our

199

house. At first he was being oddly nice. I told him to leave, and he begged me for a place to stay. Said he'd be on the street otherwise. That they'd kill him. But he didn't tell me who 'they' were. He said if I let him stay, he'd leave in the morning and wouldn't be back again."

Cole remained silent as she spoke.

"I refused. Said I'd call the police. He was so angry. Broke a whole lot of stuff, then left." She swallowed nervously. "It was a couple hours later when I heard them. They came in while I was loading the car. Forced me inside. Held a gun to my head and demanded I tell them where Marcus was. They were drug dealers."

Anger rolled off Cole like a heat wave.

"I told them he wasn't there, and they trashed the house looking for him. Then they gave me a number and said to call them if Marcus showed up again. That if I didn't, they'd kill both me and Zac."

The fear had been unlike anything else. She'd gotten herself and Zac the hell out of there and left most of their things behind. She'd been scared for months, always expecting them to show up again.

His hand trailed down her arm and squeezed. "I'm sorry."

"In the dream, instead of leaving, they took Zac." Panic swelled inside her, but then Cole tugged her against his chest. And that was all it took to calm her. To bring her back to safety.

"Hanon's going to find him soon. Until he does, we're going to make sure you remain safe. You're not running anymore. This is your home, and he can't chase you away."

The idea of staying in one place...God, it flooded her with both terror and hope. She wanted to stay with Cole, and Zac deserved a home and roots. To finish school with friends. But it was so terrifying. Because it was a life she'd never lived. Not in her adult years. Anytime she tried, she'd regretted it.

She looked up at him. "Thank you."

He pressed a kiss to her head, just as his phone rang from the side table.

When he lifted it, she saw "Mom" on the screen. She tried to climb out of bed to give them some space, but his arm tightened around her waist and held her in place as he answered, putting the phone on speaker.

"Hi, Mom."

"Hi, darling. How are you?"

Again, she pushed at his arm and tried to worm away. He was talking to his mother, for Christ's sake. It was a private conversation. The last thing she wanted to do was eavesdrop, especially when she knew how complicated their relationship was.

Instead of releasing her, Cole slipped his hand beneath the shirt she'd slept in, *his* shirt, and his fingers splayed on her belly.

"I'm okay," Cole said. "You?"

"Great. I'm good too. Now, I know you're very busy, and you can't make it up here before the wedding, but I was thinking—"

"Actually, I can."

Aria's gaze shot up. There was a beat of silence from his mother.

"You can come?" she eventually asked.

"Yeah. Not for a few weeks. We have some stuff to take care of here first, but soon. And I'll have a plus-one."

A plus-one? Her? He was taking *her* to meet his mom?

"And possibly a couple of teenagers."

Okay, Aria was still asleep, right? There was no way Cole had just told his mother he was bringing Aria and possibly Zac and Anthony to meet his family.

"Oh...well... I mean, I would love that!" His mother sounded as shocked as she felt.

"Great. I have to go now, but I'll call soon to organize details."

"Okay, yes. That would be great!"

When Cole hung up, Aria couldn't stop staring at him. She

probably looked like a deer caught in headlights, she was so shocked.

Cole rose from the bed and pulled on some clothes before finally glancing her way. "What?"

"I'm just...surprised." Surprised being a gigantic understatement. She was going to meet his mother. Zac too. That was huge.

He bent and hovered his mouth over hers. "Surprised in a good way?"

"The best way," she said quietly.

He kissed her. "Good." He straightened. "Anthony's making everyone breakfast this morning, so I'm going to check how he's doing."

"That kid's amazing."

Another kiss, then he was gone.

Aria smiled throughout her entire shower and as she dressed in her jeans and knit sweater. She was going to meet his family. His mother and sister. See the town where he grew up. And he *wanted* her to see that. All of it. And not just her. He wanted Zac to be part of it.

It almost felt too good to be true.

She'd just stepped out of the bedroom when she ran smack bang into Zac.

"Oh, sorry, honey."

He frowned down at her, then before she knew what he was doing, he tugged her close and hugged her. She didn't question it. Just leaned into her son.

An entire minute passed before he finally pulled back and studied her face. "Are you okay? How are the stitches?"

Oh, he looked so worried. She cupped his cheek. "I'm okay."

"I don't think I said this yesterday because I was too angry, but I'm sorry about the gun."

"Thank you. But don't do it again. We've got to trust Cole to protect us in a situation like that. He has combat training."

"I know. I just... I'm so damn furious around him."

He wasn't the only one. "I know. He'll pay for what he's done. I promise you." Even if the actual crime he paid for was just the drugs.

Zac nodded. Then he pulled her back into his arms. Her eyes misted. He'd been so angry for so long. But this Zac... This was her baby.

When he stepped back, she started to precede him down the hall, but he snagged her arm. "And, Mom...I'm glad you have Cole. Not just because he keeps you safe, but because you're happier than I've ever seen you. You deserve to be happy."

Yep, more water in her eyes. "Thank you, baby."

~

COLE SHOT a dubious look at the eggs. "They're green."

Anthony didn't even look his way. He just kept stirring. "Yeah, they are. Because I mixed kale pesto in with them."

"So these are kale pesto eggs?"

"Yep. Michele showed me how to make them. They taste awesome." Anthony looked at him over his shoulder. "You got a problem with kale pesto in your scrambled eggs?"

"Nope. I'm impressed." Really impressed, and not just because Anthony had made breakfast for everyone before school. "Michele's teaching you a lot."

A smile stretched Anthony's lips before he turned back to the stove. "She's awesome. She's been good for Zac too. Gives us hours around school. Shows us how to make her recipes and gives me jobs I can do while sitting when my leg gets sore. It's been great."

He wasn't surprised. Michele *was* pretty awesome. He'd always liked the woman. "If they're any good, I'll be needing you to make them a lot more."

Anthony chuckled.

"Seriously though, thanks for making breakfast." The kid

must have woken up super early. The damn table was even set, with juice and toast already in the center.

Anthony spooned the huge pan of finished eggs into a bowl. "I just hope Aria and Zac are okay."

God, he was such a good kid. Anthony set the bowl onto the table before Cole tugged him into a hug. "Thank you."

He'd had a lot of good chats with the boy since he'd moved in with them, and even more lately. Anthony was finally at a point where he'd openly talk about his sister and about what losing her had done to him, and Cole talked more about his father. They'd bonded over their losses, but also over their fondest memories. And it felt good.

When he pulled back, Anthony frowned. "You're not going to cry or anything, are you?"

He shoved him gently in the shoulder. "Watch it or I might."

Anthony chuckled, but before he could turn back, Cole touched his shoulder. "I have a question for you. Something I've been meaning to ask."

His brow creased. "Okay."

He pulled out a chair, and Anthony sat beside him. "Your grandmother technically still has guardianship over you. I was wondering how you'd feel if I asked her to transfer it over to me?"

His grandmother didn't give a shit about Anthony. He deserved better than that.

Anthony's frown deepened, and a beat of silence passed before he spoke. "Are you serious?"

"I don't joke." Well, not often.

"You'd want that? To be my guardian?"

"Yes." There was no hesitation there. He wanted this kid to know he had someone who *wanted* to be his family. "Would *you* want that? If I moved out, into a place with Aria and Zac, would you want to come?"

It was something he fully intended to do. It was crazy that a month ago, this kind of commitment would have scared the hell out of him. Now, it was all he wanted.

"Yes. I'd like that," Anthony said quietly. A grin spread across his face. "Of course, you'll have to fight Ryker for me."

Cole laughed and pulled the kid into another hug. He had no doubt Ryker would very willingly be the kid's guardian if he wasn't fighting his own demons.

They were just parting when Aria and Zac walked in.

Zac slid into a chair at the table and frowned at the eggs. "Why are they green?"

Cole rose and moved over to Aria before kissing her. It would never be enough with this woman.

"Guys," Zac groaned. "Can you save that for later?"

"I'm with Zac on this one," Anthony said.

Aria smiled as she pecked his lips one more time, then moved over to Anthony. "Everything smells amazing, sweetie."

The smile he gave her was wide. Yeah, the kid loved her already.

"Thanks. It's Michele's recipe."

"Aren't they all?" Ryker asked as he entered the room. "Now, where's this breakfast you texted me about?" He scuffed Anthony's hair as he sat at the table.

The eggs turned out to be the best damn eggs Cole had ever tasted. Not only that, but the juice Anthony had provided was freshly squeezed. Hell yeah, he was taking the kid with him when he moved out.

They kept the conversation light, and no one brought up the day before. Good. Aria didn't need reminding.

When Zac pulled out his phone, Anthony shoved his shoulder. "Hey. No phones at the table."

Cole had to hold in a chuckle.

"It's school," Zac said, eyes not leaving the screen. "Mr. Walker said he was posting the assignment pairs this morning."

"Shit, you're right." Anthony looked over his shoulder.

A few seconds later, Zac groaned.

"Don't like your partner?" Aria asked.

Zac scrubbed a hand over his face. "He put me with Benny. I can't stand that kid, and he knows it. I swear this teacher hates me."

A worried look came over Aria's face.

"Yeah, he *must* hate you. I like my partner. I got Gianni." Anthony rose from the table. "Benny probably won't even be at school after…"

He didn't finish his sentence, but they all knew he was talking about Ezra.

"Just be nice to each other and I'm sure it'll be okay," Aria said gently, squeezing her son's arm.

"Easier said than done," Zac muttered. He blew out a long breath. "I just started a TikTok account, Mom," he said, changing the subject. "I was on it a bit last night but couldn't find anything."

Her brows rose, but there was still worry on her face. Worry over Benny and Zac being partnered, or because he might just find a video with her in it? Cole couldn't be sure.

They started cleaning up the table. Zac carried his plate while flicking through TikToks.

"The eggs were awesome, Anthony," Ryker said. "I expect them more often, thanks."

"How about I give you the recipe?" Anthony offered.

Ryker scoffed. "Yeah, because I'm going to cook kale pesto eggs."

Cole laughed. Not a damn chance.

They were almost done cleaning up when Zac gasped from the table. Everyone stopped, and Aria ran to his side. She looked at his phone screen—and her face went completely white.

Cole walked over and stood behind Zac to see what he was watching. And when he saw the clip of Aria through her bedroom window, wearing nothing but a towel, anger ripped through his body. It was the night of the storm. The night he'd gone over and checked her house.

Someone *had* been there. They'd filmed her, then put it up for the world to see.

Zac clicked into the poster's account...and everything inside Cole went cold at what he saw.

# CHAPTER 28

*a*ria paced the living room. She needed to move. Hell, she needed to go for a ten-mile run and then keep going. But even that probably wouldn't calm the turmoil inside her.

Officer Hanon sat at Cole's table and watched a few of the videos from the account. They'd called him the second Zac found it. The boys had left for school and Ryker went to work, so it was just her, Cole and Hanon. She'd been disappointed to see the cop arrive alone. After everything that had happened, and now finding this account, she wanted him to bring in every damn officer in Lindeman. Okay, maybe not every officer, but a few.

Hanon ran a hand through his hair, finally leaning back in his chair. He looked tired and stressed. "I'm sorry this has happened, guys."

"I'm not." Both men looked at her. "I mean, I'm sorry there's some sick creep out there who does this, but not that he made an account. Because you guys can find him now, right? Trace back whoever made the account? Contact TikTok and ask for his information?"

The account name was Tander. The bio didn't tell them much,

and she had no idea how TikTok or tracing worked, but surely they'd be able to find this guy.

Hanon sighed. "I'll do my best."

His best? That didn't sound promising. "Hanon, there's a video of me being filmed through my bedroom window. He also filmed a car almost hitting me on the street." God, that day Cole had pulled her out the way... It was orchestrated. It had to be. Were they actually trying to hit her for *views*? "There's even a video of me almost leaving the bar with Rufus Maddon."

Yes. Someone had actually filmed that. Which meant whoever created this account may have also put Maddon up to drugging her drink that night. Had he then *killed* Maddon to keep it quiet?

What the hell was going on?

"I know what you're thinking right now," Hanon said, rising to his feet. "But going from filming and posting content straight to murder is a big leap. There's content of a lot of other citizens from Lindeman on this account, and no one else has died."

It was true. There were a lot of videos from many other locals. She wasn't the only woman who'd been filmed through her bedroom window. There were also videos of stolen cars doing burnouts on the street, vandalism and graffiti on people's homes and businesses... How this account hadn't been shut down or reported yet, she had no idea.

But it still didn't answer the question—why so many of *her*? Whoever owned this account posted daily, sometimes twice a day, and they had a big following. Hundreds of thousands of followers, and some of the clips had over a million views.

Cole moved over to her and swept an arm around her waist. "This guy clearly has a fascination with Aria. No one else even seems to feature more than once. He could be responsible for breaking into her house."

Her heart thumped. Exactly what she'd been thinking. That this person could have taken the Black Dust. They could have Marcus's drugs in their possession right now.

Hanon dipped his head. "It's possible. But let's wait and see whether we can track this guy down first. I'll go back to the station and get the tech guys working on it."

Aria lifted her phone from the table. She'd downloaded the app and found the account the second Zac had left. She was just about to click out when another video popped up. "Oh my God, they just uploaded *another* video." She clicked into it. And gasped.

"Black Dust," she whispered.

Cole slid the phone from her fingers, and Hanon moved beside him. It was a video with black powder being poured from a clear plastic bag. In the caption was a black heart emoji followed by the word dust.

It was them. Whoever created this account definitely broke into her home.

If Marcus saw this, he'd go nuts trying to locate this person. And he obviously knew about the account, because he'd *told her* about it.

Hanon shook his head, looking angry and more than a bit frustrated. "I'm going to handle this. Leave it with me. Text or call me if anything else comes up."

"Let me know if you need help from my team," Cole said through gritted teeth.

Hanon nodded. The second he was out the door, Cole wrapped his arms around her waist. "We're going to find the person who created the account." There was an underlying threat of danger in his voice. It had been there all morning. Hell, it had been there for a lot longer than that.

"We just keep getting hit by new things. It feels like the world is conspiring against us."

He touched his forehead to hers. "I know. I'm sorry."

"You don't need to say sorry. Whoever the asshole is, they're unbelievably stupid. Who does this shit, then films and posts it for the world to see?"

Idiots. That was who.

His jaw clenched. "I agree. It wasn't smart."

She shook her head. "Even though I hated finding that account, I was hoping Hanon would say this is it. This would tell him exactly who'd done everything. Especially after that last upload. They should be able to find out who broke into my house too. Search his home, find the drugs. Then find and arrest Marcus and this would all be over."

That, of course, was dream-level best-case scenario.

One side of Cole's mouth lifted. "Could still happen."

Could. But not likely. "I mean, one positive is that I can join you at work today and not look like some crazy, obsessed girlfriend."

"Hm. Girlfriend. I like it."

She felt too old to be a girlfriend, but she'd take it. She threaded her fingers through her hair. "Yep. And you're my boyfriend."

His voice lowered. "I've never had that title before."

"How does it feel?"

His mouth dropped to hers. "Good. Really good." He kissed her. "And we'll find this person. I swear to you."

"I JUST CAN'T BELIEVE IT," Michele said from the stove. "Someone posted all that. It incriminates them for…"

"Everything," Aria finished from the table. She'd gone over and over it in her head all day. The creator of this account had to have had something to do with Maddon's death. He'd died on the same damn night that he'd drugged her at the bar.

She was in her friend's shop after spending the morning at Mercy Ring. Michele had texted to check in and let her know she had a plate of comfort food for her. Seeing how the sound of fists hitting bags had started to grate on Aria's nerves, Cole had walked her over before returning to work.

"Well, I'm glad Hanon's looking into it for you. It sounds like he really listens to you guys. I could have used him when I was dealing with all the Tim stuff."

Aria frowned. "*Could* have used him?"

"Hanon's new in Lindeman." Michele crossed to the fridge and took out some vegetables. "You didn't know?"

"No."

"Yeah. The story, according to Mrs. Albuquerque, the town gossip, is that his ex was having trouble with their son, so she asked him to come here to help her."

That was news to her. "I didn't know he had a son. Although maybe I should thank the ex *and* the son, because he's been great. Anytime I call, he comes right away. And you're right. I feel very...heard." Yeah, that was the word.

Michele sliced some onions. "That's exactly what I *didn't* feel when I went to the police. I reported Tim several times." She shook her head. "That psychopath came into my shop, basically assaulted me, and *still* the police wouldn't do anything."

"Why not?"

She lifted a shoulder. "Didn't want the paperwork, I guess? Who knows. I was lucky I had Declan."

That was exactly how she felt about Cole.

She checked the time on her watch. Just after two thirty. Zac was going to pop into the shop when he finished school in twenty minutes. He wasn't working, but he and Anthony needed to sort out their shifts with Michele.

She closed her laptop and pulled out her phone to open TikTok again. She hadn't opened it since this morning, but right now, she couldn't stop herself.

She immediately frowned. "It's gone."

Michele's head popped up. "What's gone?"

"The entire TikTok account. Tander. Someone must have deleted it."

"Oh. Well, surely the police tech guys can still recover it. Isn't there a saying? Something about things online never really being deleted?"

She hoped that was true. She had no clue how difficult it would be to contact TikTok itself. "It's just strange that it's deleted now. I mean, wouldn't the time to delete it be after Maddon's body was found?"

"Even posting that video of you and him at Lenny's was incriminating," Michele said quietly. "This person obviously isn't very smart."

"True." She nibbled on her lip. She was just about to put her phone down when a notification from the school's app popped up. She clicked into it, and her heart gave a sad thump. It was a notice about a memorial for Ezra. It was scheduled for the following Wednesday.

Her gaze brushed over the photo at the bottom. It was an image of Ezra and Benny.

She was staring at the photo when a text came in from Zac.

*Hey, Mom. The teacher's put Benny and me up as the first to present our assignment. Told you he hated me. So we're going to stay at school for a bit and work on it. Anthony will go to the shop and work on the schedule with Chele.*

She frowned, quickly typing out a response.

*With everything going on, I'd really prefer you come home. Not just because of stuff with Marcus, but you don't get along with Benny at the best of times. Maybe you should bring him to our house.*

Zac's response was instant.

*He's been quiet today, and weirdly nice. I think the news about Ezra rocked him. I told him he should just go home but he said he's fine. And I don't really want him at our house. We won't be long.*

The poor kid. She didn't like Benny, but losing his best friend would be tough. Before she could respond, Zac sent another text.

*My phone's almost dead. Just wanted to let you know there's a rumor that Ezra overdosed.*

Overdosed?

She frowned, something niggling at the back of her mind. She flicked back to the school app and studied the photo at the bottom again. She was still frowning when she suddenly saw it.

"Oh my God."

Michele stopped what she was doing and looked at her. "What?"

"Ezra's missing a button."

Michele frowned. "So?"

God, she'd forgotten all about the button! Quickly, Aria closed the app and searched for Hanon's number.

"Hi, Aria, we're still working on—"

"I think I know who's responsible for the account."

There was the sound of a car engine in the background. "Are you at Mercy Ring?"

"Meals Made Easy."

"Okay. Hang on, I'm just down the street. Come out front and we'll head to the station."

She shot a nervous glance out the window. "I think I should call Cole."

"We can pick up him and Zac on the way."

The police car stopped out front. Wow, he *had* been close.

The second he hung up, she watched him through the window as he got out of his car and moved toward the door to Michele's shop.

Michele moved around the counter. "Is there anything I can do?"

Aria packed up her stuff and walked over to her friend. She pulled her into a hug. "No, that's okay. We're picking up Cole and Zac on the way to the station."

"Okay." Michele pulled back. "I hope you get this sorted out."

"Me too."

She grabbed her stuff and opened the door. Hanon offered a brief smile and led her to the car, where he opened the front passenger door and she slipped in.

"What did you find?" Hanon asked the second he was behind the wheel.

"The night that video was recorded through my window, I thought I saw a light in my yard. The next morning, I went around the back of the house. There was a button beneath my window." She spoke so fast her words were slurring into each other. "I meant to mention all of that to you, and give you the button, but when everything else started happening, I just forgot. And then I saw that photo the school posted of Ezra and Benny. Ezra was missing a button on his jacket—and the rest of the buttons were the same as the one I found in my yard."

It was him. The kid outside her window had been Ezra.

Hanon cursed and pulled the police car away from the curb. "Do you still have the button?"

"It's in a kitchen drawer. I think his friend Benny was likely involved too. Those two were really close."

Hanon gave a quick nod. "I'm really glad you called me. Have you told anyone else? Michele? Cole?"

"No. I told Michele I knew who it was, but I didn't give her a name."

"Good."

She frowned when Mercy Ring neared and he didn't slow. "Are we picking up Cole?"

He passed the gym and took a right turn at the end of the road.

Unease knotted in her belly. "The school's a left turn."

"I know."

She was still frowning when her gaze snagged on a small box in the middle console.

Klonopin.

Her heart thumped. "Hanon. What's going on?"

"I take it when I need it. I didn't know Benny took some until it was too late."

"Benny...?"

"He kept getting into trouble, so his mom asked me to transfer here." He blew out a long breath. "I didn't realize how deep he was getting."

The world seemed to tilt around her. "Benny's your *son*?"

"Yeah. His mother never set enough rules, and because I lived in another state, I couldn't be the father he needed. The kid was raised without boundaries. Dammit, all kids need boundaries!"

Her gaze caught on the Klonopin again. "Hanon...did Benny and Ezra kill Maddon?"

There was a long beat of silence. His next words were quiet. "His mother called me that night. Benny wasn't home, and she couldn't get in contact with him. I'd already put a tracking device on his phone, so I followed it to the Atlas Woods. When I lost the signal, I had to trek the damn woods in the dark until I found him. I came up behind Maddon, heard him threatening Benny. Ezra had already gone home, thank God.

"Maddon was asking for more money. I heard everything. What Benny and Ezra had paid him to do. Drug a woman at the bar. Bring her to them. He was demanding a shitload of cash, otherwise he was going to the police. I was so *angry*. And I knew we had to get rid of the guy. The information wasn't safe with him. So I hit him."

Her heart didn't just thump this time, it stopped completely.

Hanon killed Maddon. *Oh shit.*

He turned left. "I had a serious talk with Benny that night. I thought he understood this needed to stop." Hanon cursed under his breath. "But he just kept being a little shit! And that TikTok account..."

She swallowed hard. Her phone felt heavy in her hand. Carefully, moving just her fingers, she unlocked it.

"I had no fucking idea about the account until you showed me this morning. I went straight to the school. He said he did it for views. He posted incriminating shit for fucking *views!*" Hanon slammed his hand on the wheel. Aria jumped.

She'd shot a quick look down to make sure she clicked on the call button when he held out his hand. "Give it to me."

"Hanon—"

"Give it to me, Aria."

Slowly, she handed him the phone and watched as he switched it off.

"You and your son should run," she said quietly. "Marcus will find out who took his drugs, and he'll kill Benny. Probably you too."

"I'll shoot the man on sight," Hanon growled.

Her breaths grew shallow as she scanned the streets. "What are you planning to do with me?" She was pretty sure she knew, but she had to ask.

"I didn't want you to get tangled up in this, but the second you connected my son to Maddon, you sealed your fate. I can't let the truth about what I did get out."

He was going to kill her to save himself.

"Michele knows I left with you," she said quickly. "And even if she didn't, people saw me get into the car. If you do anything, people will already know it was you."

He frowned, his eyes flicking from her to the street, as if he was scrambling for ideas.

"I'll crash the car," he said quickly. "I'll say Marcus was behind us, and he caused me to crash. Then Marcus took you. I couldn't stop him. Everyone knows he's been after you. The police reports are already there. No one will question it."

Jesus, she had to get away from this man!

Her gaze caught on the baton on his hip.

Hanon slowed to take another left, and she didn't pause to think about what she was doing.

She yanked up the baton and bashed him in the head as hard as she could.

He cried out and grabbed at his head as he slammed his foot on the brake. Aria was already unbuckling her seat belt. The second the car careened to a halt, she opened her door and ran.

# CHAPTER 29

Cole carried three coffees across the street. He'd only brought Aria over to Michele's shop a couple of hours ago, but he already wanted her back in his sights. With any luck, once she'd seen the boys after school, he could drag her away again.

He hadn't been able to get that TikTok account out of his head all day. Fuck, it made him angry. She'd been targeted. There was no doubt. But why? And how had that account survived as long as it had? Shouldn't people have seen it and reported it? It had thousands of damn viewers!

All afternoon, the more he thought about it, the more he realized it had to be a kid. Who else would commit crimes, then be stupid enough to post about them and incriminate themselves?

Cole stopped in front of Meals Made Easy. When he looked into the shop window and only saw Michele, unease immediately coiled in his gut. No Aria.

He hit the buzzer, and when Michele looked up at him from behind the counter, she paused, her brows tugging together. Another sign something wasn't fucking right.

She hit a button by the register and Cole pushed inside.

"What you doing here?" Michele asked before he could get a word in.

"I'm here to see Aria. Where is she?"

Her mouth opened and closed. "She's with Hanon. They were supposed to pick you up."

His heart hammered. He set the coffees onto the table and lifted his phone to call her. When she didn't answer, he cursed under his breath, dread thick in his gut. "Tell me what happened."

"Aria was looking at the notification from the school about Ezra's memorial, when she suddenly said she knew who started the TikTok account. She called Officer Hanon, and he was just down the street, so he came and picked her up. He said he was going to pick up you and Zac on their way to the station."

The air in the room suddenly felt heavy. He lifted his phone to call Zac, but it went straight to voicemail. He called Hanon and the guy didn't answer. Dammit! He couldn't get through to anyone! God…was this Marcus's doing? Had he found Aria and Hanon?

"What do we do?" Michele asked, her eyes wide with fear.

"I'll call the station and try to get a location on his police car. You call the guys."

He was trying to remain calm, even though every part of him was alive with fear. Something was very wrong.

ARIA TURNED a corner and pumped her legs, forcing them to move as fast as they'd take her down the street. There were shops everywhere, but she didn't know any of the owners. If she entered a store and Hanon followed, all they'd see was a woman running from law enforcement. They'd believe him first.

She moved faster, ignoring the panic swirling in her chest.

She took another right, and that's when she saw the bar.

Lenny's. It was the best shot she had at hiding and getting in touch with Cole. Lenny would believe her...wouldn't he?

"Aria!"

Hanon's voice boomed from somewhere back around the corner. Her heart catapulted into her throat, and she forced her legs to move faster.

When she reached the door to the bar, she almost cried in relief when she found it unlocked. She fell inside, closing it behind her.

Shit. It was a key lock.

"Lenny?" She shouted the owner's name as she rushed through the bar. The big room was dark and quiet. Was he here? All the lights were off, but the door had been unlocked.

She ran into the back office. The lights were on and the computer screen alight, but no Lenny...

She'd just stepped back into the hall when the click of the bar door opening sounded. Her breath stopped.

"Hanon, you just caught me. I grabbed a coffee from Rise and Shine. What happened to your head?"

Her stomach dropped and a chill swept over her skin. Silently, she slipped back into the office. With shaking fingers, she swiped an empty beer bottle from the desk, then hid behind the open door. She gripped the bottle so tightly her knuckles went white.

If someone walked inside as far as the desk and turned, they'd be able to see her. She just had to hope that if Lenny and Hanon searched the place, they only stuck their heads into the office, saw it was empty, and left. It wasn't a great plan, but it was all she had.

Hanon cleared his throat. "Aria and I were driving to the station when we ran into some trouble with an ex of hers. He caused me to stop suddenly, and I hit my head pretty hard. She ran from him, and I haven't been able to find them. I need to make sure she's okay and safe." *Lying asshole!* "Could I check your cameras out front? See if they show me whether either of them went by here?"

*No...* They'd need to come into the office for that.

"Shit, that doesn't sound good," Lenny grumbled. "Come on back to my office."

*No, no, no!*

The thud of their footsteps echoed around the bar. Her heart beat so fast, she was almost scared they'd hear it.

"She's probably terrified by now," Hanon said. "The asshole had a gun and looked like he was ready to shoot."

The lies really just flowed right out of his mouth, didn't they?

"Shit. I didn't even know she had a dangerous ex on the loose. Does Cole know what happened?"

The footsteps grew closer as they moved down the hall. She bit the inside of her mouth to stop her teeth from chattering in fear.

"No, we were going to call from the station."

"Gotcha."

Someone stepped into the office. A second later, she caught sight of the back of Lenny as he walked in. He turned as he rounded the desk.

Their gazes caught briefly. Her heart stopped and she quickly shook her head. She knew her eyes were wide with fear, and holding an empty beer bottle up as a weapon, she probably looked as terrified as she felt.

Lenny had already looked away, back toward the entrance of the room. "You said her ex stopped you guys?"

"Yeah. The guy pulled out in front of the car, forcing me to stop, and just pulled a gun on us."

Lenny seemed to consider Hanon's words. "So, backup's on the way?"

There was a small pause. It took everything in her to remain silent.

"Of course."

Lenny gave a small nod and lifted his laptop. "Well, let's head into the bar and watch the footage."

The tightness in her chest eased. She closed her eyes. *Thank you, Lenny.*

The words had no sooner whispered in her head when the sound of a gunshot had her eyes flying open. Lenny dropped to the ground, blood instantly soaking his shirt. Before she could scream, the door swung away from her. Hanon stood there.

"I knew I saw him glance at something." He reached for her.

She swung the bottle at his head as hard as she could. It smashed, and he stumbled to the side, shouting in pain. She'd probably gotten him in the same spot as she had with the baton.

Before he could react, she ran. The back exit was closer than the entrance, so she beelined for the back door.

God, poor Lenny! She needed to find a way to call an ambulance. There'd been so much blood...

She threw herself at the back door and ran into the alley. She made it several steps before she slammed to the ground, a hard body on top of her. An arm wrapped around her throat and squeezed.

Her air cut off. She grabbed at his hand and dug her nails into his skin. She tried to scream. Say his name. Yell for help. Anything. But no sounds made it out.

"Fuck! This isn't how this was supposed to go," he growled quietly, tightening his hold on her neck. "I didn't want to kill anyone else. Fucking Benny and that goddamn TikTok account..."

Was he trying to justify his actions while he was *killing* her?

She tried to twist her body, elbow him, but his weight was too heavy and his hold too strong.

Black dots danced in her vision, and the ground in front of her started to blur. She was losing consciousness.

No, dammit, she had to fight!

She tried to headbutt him, but there wasn't enough force, and she barely grazed his chin. She was too weak.

Her body screamed at her to breathe, but it was impossible. There was no air.

Her eyes were closing even as a muted popping noise sounded.

Hanon cried out and dropped to the side. Aria sucked in a huge gasp of air.

She rolled onto her back and took a moment to breathe. That's when she heard his voice.

"Hey, babe. Guess you owe me for this one."

She forced her eyes open. "Marcus?"

His mouth stretched into a smile, but it wasn't kind. "Yep. I've been following you. Staying in the shadows. With that TikTokker so focused on you, I knew it was only a matter of time before you led me right to him." He glanced at Hanon. "This little episode with the dirty cop has sure piqued my interest. As did his mention of the TikTok account. I'm assuming he's talking about the one with my fucking drugs."

The air was still wheezing in and out of her lungs. She turned her head to look at Hanon beside her. He was holding his shoulder, blood oozing through his fingers, his eyes scrunched closed in pain.

"I only know who owns the account, not where the drugs are," she rasped. Words were painful through her abused throat.

Marcus snatched the pistol from Hanon's holster, quickly dismantling the gun and throwing the pieces to the side. "Who?"

She opened and closed her mouth. She didn't like Benny, but he was only a kid. If she mentioned his name, he'd be dead by morning. She didn't want a teenager's death on her hands.

When she remained silent, Marcus lifted his own gun and pointed it at her head. "I don't care if you live or die, Aria. You mean nothing to me. Tell me or I shoot. And you know Zac will be next."

Her jaw clenched. "His name's Benny," she said through gritted teeth. "I don't know his last name, but he's in Zac's grade."

At least Benny was at school with Zac. He shouldn't be home, if that's where the drugs were.

"And what's *this* guy to Benny?" Marcus asked, viciously kicking Hanon in the leg.

"He's his father."

"Ah. So *you'll* be the one to take us to collect my drugs." Marcus grabbed Hanon's arm and hauled him to his feet.

"Fuck you," the cop spat.

Marcus almost looked amused. "Call your kid. Find out where the drugs are, and I might just let your son live."

Yeah, right. Marcus needed little reason to hurt another person. Even kill them. And stealing his drugs… That definitely warranted death in Marcus's eyes.

When Hanon didn't respond, Marcus pushed his gun to the man's head. "Or, I kill you now, find your son on my own, and kill him next. After he returns my drugs, that is."

Hanon breathed heavily through his nose. "Fine." He pulled his phone from his pocket and called his son.

"Put it on speaker."

Hanon pressed the button.

"Dad?" Benny answered. "What is it? I'm still at school. I deleted the stupid account like you told me to."

Aria's breaths quickened. Was Zac still with him?

"I need to know where the Black Dust is, son."

There was a small pause. Then a whisper. "Some of it's in my locker, and some of it's in my bag."

Her stomach dropped. It was at school? *Please, God, tell me Zac has gone home.*

Hanon's eyes closed. "Okay. I'm going to come and grab it from you."

"Now?"

"Yes. Text me which classroom you're in. It's very important that you have it."

"Um…okay."

The second they hung up, Marcus took a step down the alley. "Let's go. *Everyone*."

Aria hurried to follow. If Zac was with Benny, she needed to be there. Needed to make sure he was safe. She'd do any and everything to ensure her son's safety.

# CHAPTER 30

$\mathcal{C}$ole slammed his foot on the brake behind Hanon's squad car. It was parked at an angle on the side of the road. Two other police cars were arriving at the same time, and he could also see Declan's vehicle stopping behind him.

He jumped out and checked Hanon's car. Empty. What the fuck was going on?

The door to one of the police cars opened, and he recognized Mandy Jenkins. She'd been the other officer on the callout that day at Lenny's Bar.

"He's not there?" she asked, running over.

He shook his head, scanning the street. His gaze stopped on a woman standing in the doorway of a clothing store, watching them with curiosity.

He raced across the road, toward her. Declan and Jenkins followed, stopping beside him. "Did you see a woman and an officer leave that car?" Cole asked.

Her eyes widened, and she nodded. "I was dressing the mannequins in the window when I saw the woman jump out of the passenger side and run. A police officer chased her."

Aria ran from *Hanon*...and he ran after her? What the fuck?

He was about to ask the woman which way they went when his phone rang from his pocket. He pulled it out, frowning when he saw the name on the screen. "Lenny?"

"Cole!" The man gasped his name. He sounded like he was in pain.

"Are you okay?" He quickly put the phone on speaker.

"The fucker shot me," Lenny gasped out. "They're gone now."

Every muscle in his body vibrated. "Who shot you?"

"Hanon. Aria was hiding from him in the bar, and the asshole shot me! I don't know where they went."

He turned to Declan. "Call the paramedics."

Jenkins was already barking into her shoulder mic. Cole ran back to his car, jumped in and raced off. He could have run the distance, but driving was faster, and he might need to leave the bar again in a rush.

When he reached the bar, he ran through the main area straight back to the office. A curse fell from his mouth when he saw Lenny. The bar owner was sitting on the floor, propped up against the wall, holding his stomach.

Cole grabbed a sweatshirt from the back of the desk chair and dropped in front of him. He used the top to apply pressure, but Lenny pushed him away.

"I'm fine. Find her."

Footsteps pounded through the bar. Officers stepped into the office, and he let them take over the pressure as he rose and went into the hall. Declan was already there. "We need to search the place. Look for clues." Every part of him vibrated with the need to find her and work out what the hell was going on.

Jenkins stepped out of the office. "I'm gonna check the last few minutes of Lenny's security footage. Let me know if you find something, but *don't* touch anything." She disappeared back into the room.

The bar door opened, and Jackson and Ryker both ran inside. They quickly filled the guys in on what had happened, then split up, Jackson and Ryker dashing out front to see if any other nearby business owners had seen Aria, while Cole and Declan moved out the back.

The second he stepped into the alley, he saw blood.

His heart crashed into his ribs. Fuck! Was that hers? He bent down for a closer look.

Still wet.

"What the hell happened?" Declan growled.

It was a good fucking question.

The back door opened, and Jenkins rushed out, closely followed by Ryker and Jackson. By the grim look on the officer's face, he knew he wasn't going to like what she had to say.

"What is it?" he asked.

She swallowed. "Lenny's camera on the alley shows Aria running out here. Hanon followed. He tackled her to the ground and tried to choke her."

Red-hot fury heated Cole's breath.

"Tried?" Declan asked.

"Looked like she was almost out when Marcus Allen entered the alley and shot Hanon."

Marcus. Goddammit! "What happened next?"

"He dragged Hanon down the alley, and Aria followed."

Marcus had her. Cole wanted to punch his fist through a wall.

"Why the hell did Hanon attack her?" Ryker growled.

A look of frustrated confusion crossed the officer's face. "I don't know. He hasn't been acting like himself for the last couple weeks, and today he was especially off. I thought it was because his son's best friend died, but—"

"He has a *son*?" Cole didn't know the guy had a kid, but then, he knew hardly anything about the officer.

"Yeah. Benny. The kid spends most of his time with his mother."

*Benny?* Cole's mind reeled.

"Benny's friend Ezra overdosed yesterday," Jenkins continued.

"I just found out before leaving the station that it was Black Dust, but we have no idea where he got it."

Cole met the gazes of his friends, things piecing together fast in his head. "The TikTok account has to belong to a kid. And Aria was looking at a picture of Benny and Ezra when she told Michele she knew who'd started the account. She must've figured out it was them."

Jenkins frowned. "TikTok account?"

That fucking asshole Hanon hadn't even reported the account. But of course he hadn't. The account had to belong to his son. He scrubbed a hand over his face as he quickly summed it up for Jenkins. "That drug Ezra died from belonged to Marcus —Aria's ex. He broke into her home and stashed it there, then someone else raided the place to find it. And either Benny or Ezra—or both—created a TikTok account documenting the nasty stuff they've been doing to people here in Lindeman. We reported the account to Hanon. He *had* to know those videos incriminated his son for a lot of shit, probably even Rufus Maddon's death. Now he's trying to protect his son by shutting up Aria."

"Except Marcus followed them," Ryker said quietly. "Somehow found out they knew where his drugs were."

"And the second the guy has his drugs, he'll get rid of all those loose ends." Cole turned to Jenkins. "We need addresses for both Hanon and Benny's mother."

ARIA DROVE Marcus's BMW while he sat in the back, one gun to Hanon's head beside her and another to her own.

"You get your drugs, and you leave," Hanon said tightly, his breathing labored. "You don't hurt my kid."

He was pale. Probably losing a lot of blood from the bullet wound.

"This isn't a fucking negotiation," Marcus said, the threat of violence coating his voice. "That little shit stole my drugs. They'd better all still be there."

She swallowed. At the back of her mind, she knew it couldn't *all* still be there, not if Ezra, and maybe even Benny himself, had been using the stuff. What would Marcus do if there was a noticeable amount missing? Kill him? Kill all of them?

"Remember, Aria," Marcus said quietly. "Drive to the wrong place and I kill you, then Zac. Then that asshole Cole and all his little soldier friends are next."

She gritted her teeth, trying hard to control her anger as she turned onto the street with the high school. "I remember from the last ten times you told me," she growled. Her gaze flashed to him in the rearview mirror. "So this is really what you're choosing to do with your life now, Marcus? Selling dangerous drugs that kill people? Kill *kids*?"

"I haven't been boxing professionally for a long time. Have to do something to bring in money."

God, the man had no ethics or morals. Had he been like that when they were kids, and she'd just been too young and naïve to see it? Or had he changed over time?

"Zac deserves so much better than you," she whispered before she could stop herself.

He actually laughed at that. "You're not wrong. I'm not father material. Never have been, never will be. Guess we'll put knocking you up at sixteen down to a big fucking mistake."

She flinched. Getting pregnant so young hadn't been planned, and her life would have been easier if she hadn't, but then she wouldn't have Zac. She wouldn't take that away for a second.

"If it was such a big mistake, why don't you leave us the hell alone?" she seethed.

"For the most part, I do," he said conversationally. "Until I need something."

He was such an asshole. She'd never hated anyone in her life as much as she hated him.

She was about to park in front of the school when Marcus pushed the muzzle of the gun into her head. "Park at the side of the building."

With a frustrated huff, she turned the corner and parked on a side street. The second she climbed out of the car, Marcus yanked the keys from her fingers. She and Hanon walked in front of him, both with guns pressed into their backs. There was no one else around, but he still walked close enough so that any onlookers likely wouldn't see the weapons.

The hall was eerily quiet and dark when they stepped inside. As they passed several classrooms, she noticed a couple of teachers working at their desks. All the doors were closed, and no one looked up.

They'd have phones. If she could get away, she could call for help. Hope fluttered in her chest.

They moved up a flight of stairs, then down another hall. When Hanon stopped in front of a classroom, the nausea that had been brewing in her gut began to crawl up her throat.

*Please, God, by some miracle, let Zac have left already.*

Hanon opened the door, and they stepped inside.

Her stomach dropped.

Benny sat at a desk with Zac in another beside him. There was a laptop in front of Benny and pen and paper in front of Zac. Both boys shot to their feet.

Benny frowned, his gaze dropping to his father's blood-soaked shoulder. "Dad?"

Zac flicked his gaze from Marcus to her, then back to Marcus. Dark rage filled his features.

*Calm, Zac.* She tried to silently plead with her son.

Marcus kept his guns trained on them as he closed the classroom door with his foot. Then he focused on Benny. "You the kid who stole my Black Dust?"

Benny opened and closed his mouth a couple times. "W-we

were watching her house to tag it when you showed up. We saw you go through a window, then hide something in the attic. We wanted to know what it was."

*Oh, Jesus.* And the silly kids had decided to take what wasn't theirs and...what? Trash her home for fun?

Marcus's voice went deadly quiet. "You stole from the wrong fucking guy. Give 'em to me."

Benny shifted his gaze from Marcus to his father.

Hanon gave him a small nod. "Give them to him, son."

Benny was still for another beat, then he lifted a black backpack from the floor. The same one Marcus had hidden at her house?

"Take out everything inside and show me," Marcus said.

Benny threw another nervous look his father's way before taking out small plastic bags of black powder and setting them onto the desk.

As Benny did that, she met Zac's gaze. He looked like he was a beat away from attacking.

Benny dropped the empty backpack. "That's all of it. The stuff from my bag and the locker." He looked again at his dad. "I grabbed the rest after you called."

Five bags of drugs sat on the table.

"There were *twelve*," Marcus growled. "Where's the rest?"

Benny started to shake. "Ezra took half. I-I don't know what he did with his. I used some and sold some."

Her heart thumped when she saw the rage transform Marcus's face. "Each bag had five hundred grams of Black Dust. That's over a hundred thousand dollars of street value *per fucking bag.*"

She gasped. Marcus had stored over a million dollars' worth of drugs in her house?

Fear crawled up her throat when the gun swung from Hanon to Benny. What happened next transpired so fast, it was almost a blur.

Hanon lunged at Marcus even as Zac threw himself at Benny, and the gun went off with a pop. Her world ground to a stop. She raced forward and dropped beside Zac. With trembling fingers, she ran her hands across his chest, his arms, his head. The air whooshed from her lungs. No bullet wound.

Benny sat up. He was breathing fast, his eyes wide with fear. He seemed physically okay too.

The sound of fists colliding with flesh pounded through the room, but she ignored it. She tugged Zac to his feet. Benny stood with them. She pushed both of them toward the door. "Let's go!"

Benny hesitated. "My dad—"

"We'll call for help when we're safe!"

He hesitated for another second, then rushed behind Zac. There was a loud thud behind them. Zac and Benny had just reached the hall when strong hands grabbed at her waist and threw her back into the room.

She hit the floor hard but barely acknowledged the pain, instead looking up to see Marcus heading after the boys. *No...*

She scanned the floor frantically, spotting the pen that had fallen from Zac's desk. Quickly, she grabbed it and ran out of the room. Marcus was just lifting his gun to shoot the boys when she plunged the pen into the flesh between his shoulder and neck.

His back arched violently, his arm dropping to his side. There was a terrifying pause. A heavy stillness.

Then he turned and channeled all his fury toward her.

Aria took a step back.

Her gaze flew to Zac. She mouthed the word *run*. He needed to get out. Get to safety and call for help.

As Marcus reached for her, she stumbled backward, but she already knew there was no getting away. When Zac didn't move, she screamed, "Go! Call the police! Please, Zac!"

It was Benny who tugged Zac away this time.

Thank God. He was safe. Now she just needed to focus on surviving.

# CHAPTER 31

Zac made it halfway down the stairs when he stopped.
What the hell was he doing, letting Benny pull him
away from his mother?

"I can't leave her!" he growled, tugging his arm out of Benny's
hold. "I don't need to run. I need a phone and a weapon." His
damn phone had died. He had to call Cole. The guy was his
mother's best shot at survival. He'd do anything and everything
to save her.

He hated himself for leaving. It felt so damn wrong. The kind
of wrong that boiled in his gut and crawled up his throat. But
that desperate look in his mother's eyes... He'd just let Benny pull
him away.

*Fuck.* He needed to go back.

Benny shoved his cell into Zac's hands. "I have a gun in my
locker."

Zac gave him an incredulous look. "You have a *gun?*"

"I stole it from Dad's stash. Call for help while I'm gone."

He disappeared down the stairs, and Zac dialed a number he'd
memorized. Cole answered on the first ring.

"Hello?"

"It's Zac. I'm at school. Marcus has Mom!"

Cole cursed. "They're at the high school," he said, speaking to someone else.

There was the roar of an engine.

"Get somewhere safe," Cole said quickly. "We're five minutes away."

Five minutes? That was too long. Marcus could kill her in that time. "I'm not waiting."

"Zac—"

"I need to go."

He hung up the cell, and a second later Benny returned, gun in hand. He handed it to Zac. "Are the police coming?"

"I called Cole." He was better than the police.

He took the safety off the gun just as he heard Marcus shouting.

"Get the fuck back here, or I shoot her on the spot!"

He'd suspected the asshole wouldn't kill his mom outright. His father liked to have an audience when he hurt people. It was why he'd loved boxing. He liked people to applaud his fucking inhumanity.

Today, it ended. Today, people would be applauding something else entirely. That his asshole father was going to breathe his last breath.

ARIA EXPECTED Marcus to just shoot her. Instead, he struck so quickly, she barely saw him move. The gun flew toward her face. She jerked her head back, narrowly missing the hit. But before she could run away, his left fist smashed into her ribs.

The pain was an explosion through her abdomen that had her vision blurring. When she inhaled, a sharp pain stabbed at her chest. Something was broken.

A groan sounded from the classroom. She shot a look over

and could barely see Hanon. He was lying on the floor, his face bruised and bleeding. She had no clue why Marcus hadn't just shot him, either. She didn't have time to wonder because fingers tangled in her hair and yanked.

She cried out as her hair tore at the roots. As pain stabbed at her ribs.

"You're going to fucking pay for that, bitch. And that kid who stole my drugs? He's next." Blood flowed from Marcus's wound but he barely seemed to notice.

"Get the hell off me!" She kicked at his legs. Sank her nails into his hand, trying to loosen his hold. "Haven't you destroyed my life enough?"

He ignored her struggles and pulled her down the hall. She was whipped in front of Marcus, the pain in her ribs excruciating, and he pressed a gun to her head. "Get the fuck back here, or I shoot her on the spot!"

When Zac stepped out of the stairwell, her blood froze. *No.* Why didn't he run?

Her gaze dropped to the gun in his hands.

For a moment, the chaos and danger of the situation faded, and she felt like she was looking at a younger Marcus. Even the rage in Zac's eyes matched his father's.

"Put the gun down, Zac," Marcus said quietly from behind her.

"You first."

The muzzle of the gun pressed harder to her skull. "I still don't believe you'll shoot me."

Benny poked his head out from the stairwell, then hid again.

"Believe it." Zac took a step forward. There was no fear or hesitation on his face. No uncertainty. Just focus. "I'd shoot you and not lose a second of sleep over it."

There was a moment of pause before Marcus spoke again. Like he was considering Zac's words. "Maybe you're more like me than I thought." Did he sound *proud*? That his son was holding a gun on him?

"I'm *nothing* like you," Zac sneered, emotion filling his voice. "I don't even consider you my father. That's how low my opinion is of you. You're a coward and a loser. Unable to be the man you should have been."

Marcus stiffened behind her. Jesus. Zac knew how to hit all the right buttons. Knew that, above all else, Marcus wanted people to see him as strong. He wanted people to fear his very existence.

"Let. Her. Go," Zac growled.

"No." This time there was anger in Marcus's voice. "She fucking stabbed me in the neck, and she's been a pain in my ass for years. Time to say goodbye to Mommy, kid. Then I'm going to kill that fucker Benny."

Her breath stopped. He was actually going to kill her—

A piercing alarm sounded through the building.

Both Zac and Marcus froze at the loud noise.

Aria ducked her head, swung a hand down to grab him between the legs, and twisted as hard as she could.

He howled and keeled over.

She tried to run, but he grabbed her arm and threw her into the row of lockers. She fell to the floor. Agonizing pain rippled through her ribs. She ignored it, pushing to her feet—

A gun went off.

Not Marcus's. He looked down at his left arm in surprise. Red bloomed on his shirt.

Rage like she'd never seen exploded over his face. He whipped up his gun—but he didn't point it at her.

Her entire body iced. *"Run, Zac!"*

Her son took off toward the stairs while she ran in the other direction. Bullets popped but she didn't hear a body hit the floor, so she ran until she reached the stairs at the other end of the hall. Then she turned. "Hey, asshole! Come and get me!"

Marcus's attention switched to her.

"You know you want to. This is all my fault. It was *my* house the drugs were stolen from. You've lost all your money because of *me*."

The gun swung her way. She dodged into the stairway and ran up a flight of stairs. Pain rippled from her ribs, but she pushed through it. She couldn't focus on that. He'd follow. She knew him too well for him not to.

She made it to the third floor and ran into the hall. Heavy footsteps sounded on the stairs. Relief swamped her. As long as he wasn't chasing Zac…

She reached the second classroom and pushed inside, cringing at the round of pain from her ribs. She closed the door quietly behind her just as she heard Marcus's footsteps hit the hall.

She worked to silence her breaths as she took in the room around her. A science lab. There were a dozen tall, double-seated tables, all with front wooden panels. Perfect to hide behind.

She moved to the back row, pulled out a stool and quickly slid down. Then, she pulled the stool in after her.

Marcus entered the classroom next door, his movements muffled through the shared wall. He spent a few minutes in there before moving back into the hall. When the door to the science lab opened, she gritted her teeth and forced her body to remain still.

"You in here, babe?"

*Silent breaths, Aria.*

"You can't hide from me forever."

She'd been hiding from the man for eleven years. Another few minutes was nothing.

"You know, if you hadn't gotten fucking pregnant, I probably wouldn't have entered the ring to make us money, and I wouldn't have been introduced to the world of drugs and gambling."

Really? He was blaming *her* for his poor life choices? The man was such a coward, he couldn't even take responsibility for his own life.

Every step he took drew him closer to her.

"I'm gonna tell you what's about to happen, Aria. I'm going to find you. I'm going to kill you. Then I'm going to kill that fucking kid *and* his father. I'll let Zac live…for now. On the off chance he becomes useful to me."

Zac would kill him. If Marcus killed *her*, her son would kill his father the first chance he got. She couldn't let that happen.

His voice lowered. "Let's just save each other the time and get this over with."

He took a step toward her hiding spot. Her heart slammed into her ribs.

Then she heard footsteps somewhere outside the classroom.

# CHAPTER 32

*T*he car wasn't fast enough, dammit!

Aria was with one, possibly *two* damn predators, and Cole wasn't there to protect her. The thought made him want to lose his mind.

Ryker rounded the corner. Before Zac's call, the group had split in two, Jackson and Declan going to the mother's house, and he and Ryker heading to Hanon's. He'd called Jackson, then Jenkins, the second he hung up with Zac. Thank God he hadn't been far from the school.

They couldn't be too late. God, please tell him they wouldn't be too late.

When Ryker turned onto the road with the school, Cole opened the center console and took out a Glock. Then he switched off his emotions, letting his training take over. The second Ryker stopped the car, Cole jumped out and ran toward the school.

He'd just stepped inside the building when he collided with Zac. There was a gun in the kid's hands, and his eyes were wide and frantic. "Cole!"

"Where are they?"

"She ran up to the third floor and Marcus followed."

*Fuck.* "Go to Ryker. Police are just arriving."

He didn't wait for Zac's answer. He flew up the stairs to the third floor. Then he stopped and listened. Silence.

The silence made dread pulse through his limbs. He wanted noise. He wanted to hear that she was alive and fighting.

He kept his steps soundless as he moved down the hall. He crept into the first room, keeping his weapon drawn and his eyes alert. He checked around the desks and inside every closet.

Nothing.

It wasn't until he entered a science lab that he felt it. It was a feeling he often got on missions when danger was close. The prickling of his neck. The thickening of the air.

With his back to the wall and his gun at the ready, he moved further into the room, scanning behind every desk. If Aria had been looking for somewhere to hide, this would be the best place. The tall tables were such that if you hid behind one, you couldn't be seen from the front.

He checked each row.

It wasn't until he reached the last one that he saw her. The air soared out of him. She was alive. He took a step toward her—but she shook her head. Instead of looking happy to see him, she looked terrified.

She nodded toward something at the back of the room. Marcus was here. There was no one beneath the other desks... but there was a tall cabinet against the wall.

His eyes had just fallen on it when the door flew open and a gun went off.

Cole dove behind a table, the shots narrowly missing him.

More bullets fired. Marcus was aiming at the desks, trying to shoot him through the obstructions. Cole moved, shifting from one desk to another.

"Get out here and face me like a fucking man, Turner!"

Bullets continued to pepper the desks as he moved again.

"Not just me, Marcus. Police too. They're all here. Your time is limited."

On the next shot, the gun clicked. He was out of rounds.

Loud footsteps pounded toward him.

Cole rolled away from the table, shooting the asshole's leg moments before he lunged and landed on top of him.

Marcus growled in pain, but he didn't pause. He grabbed Cole's wrist and slammed it to the floor hard enough for the Glock to fly out of his grasp.

A punch flew toward his face, but Cole dodged and Marcus's fist hit the tiled floor hard. Another growl. Marcus swung. He ducked again but the asshole was ready, quickly following up with a hook that caught Cole in the jaw.

He vaguely registered the gasp from Aria as he threw a punch into the guy's gut. Marcus groaned, and his return punch got Cole in the ribs.

He absorbed it and rolled. When he was on top, he threw a fast punch straight at the asshole's cheek.

FEAR SLOWED Aria's world so that the fight in front of her was almost in slow motion. The powerful men on the ground stole her entire attention. Every hit had her stomach turning. Not all of them landed. The men were each as good defensively as they were at throwing punches.

Marcus had a bullet wound in the leg and a puncture to his shoulder, but neither seemed to slow him down.

When Marcus rolled them back over and threw another punch, it landed right in Cole's face. Her heart leaped into her throat. She had to do something!

She shot her gaze around the room, spotting one of the fallen weapons.

Cole's gun.

She lunged forward, lifted the gun and aimed—then she paused. Could a bullet go through Marcus's body and hit Cole? She had no idea. Oh God, she couldn't take that chance!

Aria was still trying to figure out what to do when Cole wrestled Marcus onto his stomach and wrapped an arm around his neck. Marcus growled and sputtered, his elbows hitting Cole in the ribs. Cole barely seemed to register the hit. His hold on Marcus looked tight, and slowly, Marcus's struggles weakened.

The air whooshed from her chest. She lowered the gun in her shaky hand as Cole eventually dropped an unconscious Marcus to the floor. He stood and rushed over to her, tugging her against his chest.

"Are you okay?" she breathed.

"I'm fine." He pulled back, his hand cupping her cheek. "You?"

"I'm alive." After the afternoon from absolute hell, she was alive. "Benny's behind the TikTok account and Hanon's his dad. Hanon killed Maddon! He was going to kill me to keep me quiet."

Cole closed his eyes and breathed out a long breath. "I'm going to fucking murder him."

He'd have to be alive for that. Marcus had beaten him pretty badly.

She touched Cole's chest. "You saved me. Again. Thank you!" She was about to drop her head to his chest when movement flashed in her peripheral. "Cole!"

Before she even finished his name, Cole lifted the gun in her hand, slid his fingers over hers, and shot Marcus between the eyes.

He dropped.

Her mouth gaped. Marcus had been mid-reach for a weapon on his ankle.

Now he was dead.

The man was *dead*.

Finally.

Cole slowly slid the gun from her fingers, set it on a desk, then cupped her cheek once more. "Still okay?"

She gave a quick nod. He pulled her back into his embrace and she leaned into him, needing his warmth. They took a step toward the door and she immediately winced, once more feeling the pain in her body. She definitely had broken ribs.

Cole growled. He probably had a broken rib or two as well, after the beating he'd taken. He didn't give any indication of pain. Instead, he gently lifted her into his arms and carried her out of the room.

The adrenaline that had spiked inside her began to ebb, and suddenly she felt drained. She rested her head on his chest, over his heart. They'd just reached the stairs when she whispered the words she should have said days ago. Words she'd been afraid he'd never hear. "I love you, Cole."

He paused and looked down. His eyes shifted between hers. Then his mouth moved to her ear, his breath brushing her skin. "I love you, Aria."

She closed her eyes and sighed. She was okay. Zac was okay. And the man she loved...loved her back.

"If I'd lost you today..." he said quietly.

She pressed a hand to his chest. "You didn't. I'm not going anywhere."

His next words were whispered. "Thank God."

Footsteps echoed on the stairs, then Ryker and several uniformed officers appeared. Cole pointed them toward the room, then they continued down the stairs with Ryker at their side.

"You both okay?" Ryker asked.

Cole nodded. "We're alive and Marcus is dead."

"Good," Ryker said firmly. He didn't put his gun away, though.

She kept her head resting on Cole's chest until they stepped outside and she saw Zac.

Carefully, Cole set her on her feet as Zac rushed toward her.

She ignored the pain to her ribs when he pulled her into his arms. She needed to hold her son. She needed him as close as he could get.

"Is Marcus…?"

"Gone," she finished for him as she pulled away and studied his face. "He's dead."

Only relief filled her son's face. "We can finally live."

Tears flooded her eyes, and she touched his cheek. "I'm so sorry he was such a burden on our lives for so long."

"Don't apologize, Mom. I owe you everything. You've spent your entire life sacrificing and protecting me. Thank you."

She pulled him back into her arms. From over his shoulder, she saw Cole talking to the female officer she recognized from Lenny's Bar all those weeks ago.

She stepped out of Zac's embrace just as Hanon was wheeled past them on a stretcher. Jenkins hurried over to him and cuffed his wrist to the gurney.

Aria looked away, meeting Cole's gaze. In his eyes, she saw everything. Relief. Protectiveness. And love. So much love.

# CHAPTER 33

*A*ria folded another shirt into her suitcase. For the first time in her adult life, she wasn't packing in a mad rush to protect herself and her son. A smile was firmly in place on her lips, as it had been for the last two weeks.

She still couldn't believe so much time had passed since everything had happened. Even her fractured ribs hurt just a little less.

Cole and Zac had barely left her side, and Anthony had never been far either. Not to mention River and Michele. Even with all those beautiful people surrounding her, she'd never felt as free as she had these last couple weeks. Marcus was dead. And for the first time in years, she didn't need to worry about running. About the chaos and danger he'd always brought to their door.

She paused and closed her eyes, taking a moment to just appreciate her new reality. Zac could stay in one place, graduate school with friends and just be a kid. While she could set down roots with Cole.

Hanon had suffered a concussion and needed stitches in a few places, he'd also lost blood from the bullet wound, but he'd survived. And the second he'd been released from the hospital, the police took him away.

Benny had confessed that he and Ezra created the TikTok account. Apparently, it had started as a joke. They'd posted some stupid stuff where people got into fights or were injured doing stunts. When a couple of those videos went viral, the boys started posting content frequently, making each video more extreme.

Benny had even admitted to paying Maddon to drug a random woman in Lenny's that night. Ezra had snuck into the bar and filmed it. Benny had no clue at the time that Aria was Zac's mother.

She shuddered at the thought of what they might have filmed if Maddon had actually delivered her. Benny claimed he'd just wanted footage of her being drugged for his account, that they hadn't decided what they'd do with her if Maddon had actually gotten her out of the bar, but who knew if that was true. She hated even thinking about it.

And, after some intense questioning by the police, Benny had finally admitted to watching his father kill Maddon to keep him quiet.

She grabbed the last shirt from her drawer and had just folded it into her suitcase when thick, familiar arms slipped around her waist. The smile returned to her lips, and she leaned back into Cole's warm body. "I'm almost packed."

His lips went to her shoulder, and he trailed a line of kisses up the column of her neck. "Good. I was missing you over there."

She chuckled. Cole had been home, packing his own stuff, and both boys were packing as well. They'd found a house only a couple streets away that was big enough for all of them, and tomorrow was move-in day.

When Cole had told her he was becoming Anthony's guardian, and he wanted the four of them to find a place together, she hadn't been able to say yes quick enough. It was the fresh start they all needed.

She turned and wrapped her arms around his waist.

"How are your ribs?" he asked, one of his hands sliding up her back.

She hadn't known fractured ribs could be so painful. But it could have been worse. So much worse. "They're fine."

A small growl vibrated from his throat, and he bent his head and kissed her. It was a slow kiss that made her heart beat faster and her skin tingle all over.

"I can't wait to live with you and kiss you whenever I want," she said when they eventually separated.

"Me too," he whispered. More neck kisses. She tilted her head to give him better access. "Thank you for accepting Anthony into our family."

Her heart skipped a beat at the word "family." That was all she wanted. All she'd ever wanted. Safety. Family. Stability.

"He's a great kid and you're his guardian." Her voice softened. "So he *is* family."

And the fact that Cole didn't blink an eye at them being a family together... It was huge. The man who'd been scared of commitment and loving a woman was gone. And in his place, someone who was able to give his whole self to others.

His lips stretched into a smile. "Perfect. It's all damn perfect."

Her heart softened. "God, I love you."

COLE WANTED to close his eyes and replay those words in his head again and again. Fuck, he loved hearing them. They were everything. *She* was everything.

There had been moments over the last two weeks where her words of love were all that kept him going. Memories of Aria being out of his reach, knowing he couldn't protect her from Hanon or Marcus, had plagued him.

"I love you too," he whispered, kissing her again. He hadn't been able to stop kissing her lately.

He felt her smile against his lips. "Is Anthony finished packing?"

Cole chuckled. "I think it took the boys all of two minutes to pack up their things, and they've been playing video games across the road for the last hour."

She frowned suspiciously. Yeah, he didn't trust them either. They'd better not have left half their stuff out of boxes for him and Aria to pack.

"I think everyone's over there," Cole said, adding another kiss to her lips.

"Everyone as in..."

"Everyone. All the guys. The boys. River and Michele."

Aria's smile broadened.

His fingers slid down her arm, then he grasped her hand before leading them out of the house and across the street. Jackson's and Declan's cars sat out front. He was pretty sure he'd seen pizza delivery arriving before he entered Aria's house.

He stepped inside to find the boys exactly as he'd left them. On the couch, playing *Grand Theft Auto*, while everyone else sat around the dining table. Anthony's grandmother had signed the guardianship forms the second they'd been put in front of her. She obviously had no idea what she was losing. But as far as he was concerned, the woman didn't deserve him. And Anthony deserved to be with people who wanted him and cared about him.

"Hey, look who it is," River said, popping a Whopper into her mouth.

"All packed?" Michele asked.

Aria nodded. "Just about." She moved over to the boys, squeezing Anthony's shoulder before pressing a kiss to Zac's head.

His heart thumped as he watched them. Family. They were a

family. *His* family. How the hell he'd feared this only a short month ago when now, every part of him needed it desperately, he wasn't sure.

"You're gonna be all alone," Declan said to Ryker.

"Good. Less mess and fewer people annoying me," he said. But a smile played at his lips.

"Well, you'll just have to find a woman to move in with you," Jackson retorted, lifting a beer to his lips.

Ryker scoffed. "No, thanks."

Aria walked back over to Cole. She was about to sit on the chair beside him, but he pulled her onto his lap and whispered once again, "I love you."

Her eyes softened. "I love you more."

Not possible. And right here, with his woman on his lap, surrounded by his closest friends, he knew this was about as close to perfect as it got.

# CHAPTER 34

"So...Chele, Aria and I have come up with an idea."

Ryker just held in a groan at his sister's words. When River had an "idea," it almost always ended with him doing something he didn't want to do. The last idea was his "resurrection party," as she'd dubbed it. He wasn't a party guy, which she knew full well.

Then there was the time when they were kids and she'd made him dress up as yellow mustard on Halloween because she'd wanted to be red ketchup. She'd thought it would be fun.

Nope. Wasn't fun. And there'd been countless ideas between then and now.

"You've all decided to dedicate the rest of your lives to catering to your men's every whim and desire?" Declan said, humor in his voice.

River thumped his shoulder playfully. "You wish. No, Aria was talking about how lucky she was to have an online business while she was running from her ex. It meant she could afford to stay mobile. Most women don't have that. They have to stay in the same place, making them easy targets for their abusive exes."

"I was very lucky," Aria said quietly.

Ryker swung his gaze to Aria and Cole. Cole's eyes were a shade darker, no doubt at the mention of her ex. Ryker was pissed too. They all were. He and his friends hated men who abused their strength or position to take advantage of people more vulnerable, especially a partner who'd put their trust in them.

"There are some great charities that support women who have become victims of domestic assault," Michele said.

River nodded—and met his gaze.

Another internal groan, because this definitely involved him.

"We want to do a bachelor auction to raise money for a charity," River said.

He scowled. "A bachelor auction?"

"Mm-hmm." She tried to sound innocent. Didn't come off so well.

"I'm literally the only bachelor at this table."

"We're going to ask Erik too," River said. "And we'll find plenty of other bachelors for the auction."

Michele wet her lips. "We were hoping to leave you or Erik for last, though, because I think you guys will be in highest demand."

He scrubbed a hand over his face. "I don't—"

"You don't need to give us an answer right now," River interrupted. "We're still in the planning stage. We'll let you know when we need an answer."

"I'm single," Anthony shouted from the living area.

"Me too," Zac added.

The group chuckled.

"This is an adults-only event, kids," Aria said.

"Boo," Zac shouted back. Neither boy took his gaze off the TV screen.

"I'll think about it," Ryker said, even though it was the last goddamn thing he wanted to do.

"That's all I ask." River reached across the table and squeezed his arm.

He sighed. He loved his sister, even if the woman was a giant pain in his ass sometimes.

Michele lifted her glass of juice. "All right, should we toast to Cole finding his woman and everyone being safe?"

Ryker raised his glass. He was glad his friend had found someone, but he knew exactly what would happen now. His sister would be all over him with the pressure to find love too. Hell, she already was.

His friends remained for another couple of hours, then he helped Anthony and Cole move all their boxes downstairs. They were sleeping across the street tonight, and tomorrow the entire team was helping them move.

Once everyone was gone, the place was silent. He'd offered to let Cole, Aria and the boys take this place, because it was huge, but they'd insisted they wanted to move into a new house together for a fresh start. Which was fine. Ryker didn't mind being alone. In fact, he welcomed the quiet.

He went to his bedroom and changed into workout clothes. He'd just lifted his phone to leave his bedroom when it rang in his hand. His gut twisted when he saw the name on the screen.

Blakely.

Her calls were becoming more frequent, though he hadn't answered in a long time. She'd been an aid worker to some families in the Middle East. The very families who'd been killed by Ryker's enemies.

What was he supposed to say to her? Sorry I got everyone you were working with killed? Sorry they're all dead—the parents, the damn kids—because I got close to one of the families, then pissed off the wrong person?

The familiar rage began to sweep through his limbs. He ground his teeth and waited for his phone to stop ringing. When it did, he let the disappointment sit heavy in his gut. He hated *that* even more than the rage. Disappointment that he couldn't hear her voice. Couldn't allow her words to soothe some of the anger that had taken root inside him.

With a deep exhale, he stepped into the small gym next door to his bedroom.

The phone rang again.

God, the woman didn't give up. But he knew that about her already.

For a moment he felt weak, and he almost answered it. She had always done something to him that no one else could. And their one night together...

*Fuck.* It had been everything.

He shook his head and forced the memories away. He couldn't think about that right now. Hell, he couldn't think about that *ever*.

The ringing stopped.

He told himself it was better this way. He damn well shouted it in his head. That this was the way it had to be. The only way he could ignore the tug at his heart every time the woman entered his thoughts.

He pulled training gloves onto his hands and started pounding the heavy bag. He hit it so hard, the entire thing flew back with the power of his hits. He'd only been going for twenty minutes when his phone rang again.

He looked down and paused. Not Blakely.

The fast-moving breaths in his chest slowed, and he pulled off a glove and snatched up the phone. "What do you have?"

"He left." The guy's heavily accented voice was low. Like he didn't want others to hear him.

"What do you mean, he left?" Ryker growled.

"I mean, he boarded his family plane and left the country."

Ryker took three deep breaths as he let that information sink in. "And I'm guessing you don't know where he's flying?"

There was a small pause and a rush of wind through the line. "There's a whisper that he's heading to the States."

Every muscle in Ryker's body tensed and rippled. The asshole was coming to *him*? He couldn't be making it that easy, could he? "Keep watch and let me know if he returns."

He hung up. And for a moment, he didn't move. This was the fucking asshole who was responsible for the deaths of all those families. The parents. The tiny kids.

The day he found out, Ryker had vowed with everything he was that he was going to locate the guy and end him. And now, he just might be able to make that happen.

Order RYKER today!

# ALSO BY NYSSA KATHRYN

*PROJECT ARMA SERIES*

Uncovering Project Arma

Luca

Eden

Asher

Mason

Wyatt

Bodie

Oliver

Kye

*BLUE HALO SERIES*

*(series ongoing)*

Logan

Jason

Blake

Flynn

Aidan

Tyler

*MERCY RING*

Jackson

Declan

Cole

Ryker

JOIN my newsletter and be the first to find out about sales and new
releases!

~https://www.nyssakathryn.com/vip-newsletter~

# ABOUT THE AUTHOR

Nyssa Kathryn is a romantic suspense author. She lives in South Australia with her daughter and hubby and takes every chance she can to be plotting and writing. Always an avid reader of romance novels, she considers alpha males and happily-ever-afters to be her jam.

Don't forget to follow Nyssa and never miss another release.

Facebook | Instagram | Amazon | Goodreads

Lightning Source UK Ltd.
Milton Keynes UK
UKHW011614070223
416598UK00007B/1132